THE GUARDIANS
DEATH

AMELIA WADDELL

TW

Published by Twisted Words Publishing, LLC

twistedwordspublishing.com

Copyright © 2025 by Amelia Waddell

Paperback ISBN # 979-8-9934106-3-0

Ebook ISBN # 979-8-9934106-5-4

Book Design by Lyndsey_Graphics

lyndseygraphics.wixsite.com/bookcoverdesign

Map Design by Alec M

Illustrations by Twisted Words Publishing, LLC

First edition October 2025

Contents

To those who fear, turn that into your power

THE GUARDIANS

DEATH

AMELIA WADDELL

Twisted Words

Chapter 1

Who's Knocking?

I was in big trouble. This thought consumed my mind as I ran down the crowded hallway as fast as I could. This was probably the millionth time I've been late to Training and a small part of me still cared. The halls were swarmed with faces I recognized and they parted as I rushed by like I had some sort of disease. I accidentally bumped into someone, their textbooks flew across the hallway and landed on the marble floor with a loud thud. I quickly muttered my apologies and with a wave of my hand sent them flying back to their hands.

"Um, thank you, I'm sorry!" The guy's voice called down to me. I stopped telling the other kids at DEATH not to be afraid of me years ago because no matter what I did they still avoided me at all costs. Not that I blamed them. I was a part of the Prodigy unit and a daughter of one of The Five. If I was them, I'd probably do everything to avoid me too.

As I approached the large ornate grey Training Room double doors, I heard Luke and Daniel wrestling. I took a peak in and debated just going back to sleep. Luke had Daniel pinned to the multi-colored mat with his foot. Daniel tapped the mat twice and Luke stepped back with a chuckle.

"'Ow, Luke that hurt!"

"That's because you're a wimp, Danny," Luke teased.

"Alright! I think he's had enough," I heard Harrison call out, as Daniel rolled on his side and stood up. Luke winked at me. I smiled, but didn't enter the room yet. The last thing I wanted was to be scolded...again.

Luke glanced my way, sauntering away from Daniel, but Harrison must have signaled for them to go again because Daniel got back into his clumsy fighting stance.

"Scared?" Luke's voice came into my mind, as he took a drink of water. I slammed my magic into his presence trying my best to block him out. He winced, but not enough for anyone to notice. Luke and Daniel returned to fighting. Daniel evaded Luke's first attack pretty well, but then took a nasty hit to the stomach. I always tell Daniel he should really try to-

"He's already in a mood. Just get in here. Also stop giving Danny advice he's got to do it on his own. Although, yes he should block and drop his weight at the same time," Luke's voice sounded again.

"Jerk, you're just afraid that he's getting closer to beating you," I replied, as Luke hurled Daniel across the air. I hated when he was right. My feet were cemented to the floor. I took a deep breath and tied up my hair, gritting my teeth as I stepped into the training room. Harrsion's intense glare was on me in an instant, but I refused to look at him.

"Heyyy Dawn, want to help me knock out Mr. Grayson?" Luke finally spoke out loud to me, his sparklingly blue eyes ignited with his mischievous power. I fought the urge to stick my tongue out at him. He reminded me the other day we are almost "adults" in the Elder's eyes and we had to start acting like it, another thing he was right about. If I kept coming to Training late, I wouldn't make it to my sixteenth birthday.

Daniel ignored me and stomped towards Luke with a fierce look in his eyes. Daniel was strong for his age but small in comparison to Luke. An out of control fight would result in Daniel being a poor loser, sending him into a pout that would last the rest of the day. Before I could say just that, the angry voice I knew all too well barked at me. Daniel stopped snapping his head to Harrison, afraid of his tone.

"You're late!" Harrison shouted down at me from atop of the winding staircase where he liked to watch his training class, interrupting my thoughts. I finally met his cold eyes and decided to not cause a scene with him today.

"I'm sorry I overslept," I hurriedly said.

I heard a snort come from the left corner by the punching bags. Hailey regarded me with a disappointed look. I balled my fists and gritted my teeth. Hailey has been my frenemy since we were five. She was Little Miss Perfect. A straight A student and did whatever she was told. The only thing she has not been able to do is beat me in a fight. Harrison put her in the Prodigy unit to "challenge" me to do better. It hasn't really worked.

Harrison muttered something under his breath, probably cursing at me. I stayed silent as he fumed. When he calmed down slightly, he pointed at me with a strong finger.

"You know the "sorry" will not cut it when you're outside of the Boundary," Harrison's face turned red and his eyes ignited a bright white. Harrison rarely used his magic and when he did it was always for emergencies, so I nodded, pretending to be upset.

Harrison was our instructor, really more like an uncle. He was one of the original founders of DEATH. The top school for training Guardians in the world or so they say. I've known Harrison for as long as I can remember, my mom said he was one of her best friends. One of the only things I remember her telling me before she disappeared when I was four. My sister, Lila, was only a couple months old. I spotted her with her legs hanging over the rusty monkey bars that lined the hall doing crunches. I'd have to talk to her about not waking me up later.

"Are you even listening, Dawn?"

He had been lecturing, but I decided not to listen. Harrison has basically become judge, jury, and executioner around here. I've heard rumours that he was the happiest guy anyone could ever meet before my mom and the other founders disappeared, Harrison being the one left behind. I'm not going to lie, I did feel sorry for him.

Harrison straightened out his fancy dark blue suit, heaving an exasperated sigh.

"The Elders are coming here in less than a week, Shadows. You have to start getting up on time, or I'll send you out to live like a stray. Do you hear me?" Harrison leaned over the metal railing giving me a look that used to make me cower. I almost smirked at that ridiculous threat. Harrison may be tough, but he would not make me homeless. If he wanted to punish me, all he had to do was make me sit through one of his lectures on the First War. The Elders have never scared me, although I could feel Luke's fear radiating off of him. I wanted to reach out and hold his hand.

Harrison cleared his throat waiting for an answer.

"Got it, sir," I saluted him. He shook his head and released me with a dismissive wave.

Luke's voice came into my head *"Nightmare again?"*

"Yeah, same one," I answered.

"Do you want to talk about it?"

"Please stop asking about my dreams. It's creepy," I said as Harrison gave a whistle for us to line up. Luke chuckled as we made our way to our assigned spots. Lila flipped off the bars, straightening out her black tank top, Daniel was rubbing his shoulder still recovering from his fight with Luke, and Hailey threw her boxing gloves to the ground giving me a glare for the ages.

"You'd rather I ask out loud?" Luke pressed.

Luke and I have always been able to talk in each other's minds. As of right now, we are the only two Guardians in all of history who have a constant mind connection. It makes Luke and I close, but I've never been good at telling him or anyone how I feel. He nudged my shoulder pulling me out of my thoughts. Luke can get extremely annoying but he's my best friend.

Harrison yelled, "Grab a partner now that we have everyone!"

I rolled my eyes at the sass in his voice.

Everyone stood like bricks. No one likes to be the first and say, "Hey, I wanna punch your guts out". We are more than capable of hurting each other. Once when I was about ten Luke and I were sparring and I accidentally hit him too hard in the chest which caused his lung to collapse. I never was careless again, luckily we were able to heal around that age so it took Luke's lung only a minute to heal. The only thing we can't heal from is decapitation. Demon venom also slows down the process making a normally non-fatal wound, a Guardian six feet under. It was the one and only time I've ever welcomed a grounding from Harrison.

"Oh for goodness sake do I really have to do this again I feel like a broken record," Harrison raised his voice in frustration.

Our response was a canon of nodding heads.

Harrison huffed, "Daniel and Lila partner up."

"You always put me with Lila. Why can't I fight Luke? She's mean," Daniel whined, probably because Lila beat him every time. My eye roll was almost audible. Daniel and Lila are our youngest ones. They have never gotten along.

Lila shoved him to the ground, "Say that again and I'll burn you to pieces," her hand ignited with fire. It took everything in me not to laugh.

"Hey! Whoa Lila, no burn victims today please," Harrison said without looking at her and picked up a tablet, probably reading the news. I wondered if there was something going on that would finally give me a mission. Harrison might keep me here forever.

"Hailey, switch with Daniel after he taps out...," Harrison barked out orders.

"Luke and Dawn pair up!" I finished his sentence putting on my best Harrison voice. "We know!" Luke and I said in chorus together. Luke began to chuckle and immediately tried to cover it up as Harrison started to glare at us. I kept a smug smile on my face. Harrison thought it was fascinating the way neither of us could really beat each other. Would Harrision make all the students in DEATH do this? We rarely spend time outside our assigned units.

"*So what was it about?*" Luke inquired in my head.

"*Like I said I don't want to talk about it,*" I readied myself into position and rolled my neck out.

"On your mark!" Harrison shouted.

"*Not even a little detail?*" Luke asked again, getting to his stance. He was trying to distract me.

"Get set, Go!" Harrison shouted again in his corny race voice. I launched for Luke, but he saw it coming and rolled under my arm. He came up behind me and started to swing. I quickly turned and grabbed his fist, shoving him backwards. He landed on his butt, but quickly recovered. I didn't like hand to hand as much as I liked small handheld weapons imbued with gelical magic, but I was still pretty good with my own two fists. We launched into a series of combinations. A two, two, three-which I easily evaded. I can sense Luke's movements before he makes them and I knew he could sense mine. It used to frustrate him, but now he sees it as a game. We have a running tally of ties, we're up to about five-hundred. There have been times where there's been a clear cut winner, but that hasn't happened since we were ten years old.

Luke and I fell into our usual rhythm, our breath synced. My mind found peace in the familiar movement and the way my body created a dance out of it. The feeling was always thrilling. Finally, I managed to get a lucky shot to the jaw causing him to stumble backwards with a chuckle. Luke recovered and tackled me, I landed on my back with a hard thud. He didn't have me pinned though so with a standard headbutt I was able to stun him. He chuckled and his leg slipped. It allowed me to use that slip to force him on to his back. Luke quickly pushed me to the side where we proceeded to try and choke the other. We stared at each other waiting for the other to let go or tap out. I coughed and gave a little whimper. He immediately let me go then shook his head getting to his feet. I smiled. He falls for that every time.

"I got you again! I won!" I laughed triumphantly.

"Oh please, no you didn't. I let you," Luke heaved me up and spun me around. I giggled because I knew it was true he wasn't even trying that time.

Two big loud bangs coming from the front door made us all jump. Harrison went to check the monitors giving a heavy sigh.

"Those damn birds banging into my Boundary again. I swear I'm going to-," Harrison broke off suddenly. There was something out there that made him do a double take with thinly pressed lips. Then he teleported down the stairs.

"You know Uncle, I don't see why you get to do that. I thought you said no Flashing inside the Training Room, cafeteria, or hallways," Lila grumbled. Harrison didn't stop to answer her as he ran for the Training Room doors. Then he let out a sigh like he was forgetting something.

"This once just please listen to me and stay put," Harrison pointed at me. I rolled my eyes as I watched him Flash out of the room. We waited and waited. The door never opened and whoever or whatever it was didn't try to break down the door. He just left us here, which if we were in any real danger he'd never do. Why would he do that?

"Alrighty then, so who's going to answer the door?" I clapped my hands together, everyone stared at me like I was some kind of demon. Of course, they weren't going to be brave. I pivoted on my heel toward the front door.

"Hey, hey no you don't, not this time. You are not getting in trouble so we all get detention. Last time you just sat there while *we* had to clean the cafeteria," Luke grabbed my hand and wrenched me back.

"Luke, c'mon as much as I would love to blame it all on her, it was me too," Lila said, flipping her small gelical pocket knife in her hand. I smiled at her and she gave me a wink. Luke came at me and I could read he wanted to restrain me. I shoved him aside. He grunted as he stumbled back a little bit and decided not to try again.

The truth is I felt bad for that particular incident that caused everyone to get detention. My intentions were pure. Harrison did not appreciate Lila and I accidentally putting a hole through the cafeteria wall. I tried to help Lila control some of her fire powers by getting her angry then working on calming it. It was working until I called her Little Lila Hottie Head.

"Thank you Lila, and I did apologize," I threw my hands up in the air and started to walk away from my unit. I wanted to Flash, but that would just get me in more trouble. Hailey came up behind me.

"Yes, you said and I quote, 'It was the right thing to do, sorry not sorry,'" Hailey said, making air quotes with her perfectly painted royal blue fingernails. I turned balling my fists and Hailey stepped away slightly. That was satisfying. Luke stepped between us.

"Okay, but listen. We don't know who it could be," Luke followed close behind.

"No demon, human, other Guardians, or even gelicals can get past the Boundary without Harrison's permission. You should know that you're the smart one," I huffed. Hailey gave a sigh. I was always causing trouble for them. If I was lucky, they wouldn't have to deal with me here much longer. The Elders would send me away. I walked out of the Training Room right towards the front door half expecting Harrison to be there blocking my path. Luke grumbled something in my head, but I ignored it. I punched in the code I'm "not supposed to know" that opened up the door and scanned my eye. The door started to tick like a bomb, a sense of dread went up my spine, I could feel my pulse beginning to race. My breathing quickened as the ticking sped up. I shook my head to try and get rid of the feeling. My power vibrated at my fingertips. This wasn't my brightest idea. The ticking stopped. The door burst open and a golden ray of sunlight peeked through. I could feel its warmth on my skin beckoning me to step outside where there was always this force pulling on me. Luke sucked in a sharp breath his power enveloped me, trying to shield me. My power reached out to him, but I reigned it in. I could shield myself. The door swung all the way open, and a breeze swept through my hair.

As if my day wasn't already ruined, someone covered in blood from head to toe came stumbling in.

Chapter 2

Secrets

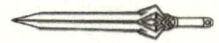

The body collapsed in my arms. I tried my best to support them, but I fell to my knees. I started to check vital signs, but Luke started to run. There were a few kids in the hall, it wouldn't be long before a crowd started to form.

"*GONNA GET HELP,*" Luke screamed in my head.

"Wait, don't leave me!" I yelled back, not even bothering to talk in my head. He didn't even look back as he turned the corner. I wondered why he didn't just use his Flashing ability. Harrison wouldn't be mad at him for that right now.

I look back at the person lying in my arms. An enchanting woman looked up at me, her eyes fluttered open. She had a pulse and was still breathing. I could tell she was beautiful even with all the blood. The strangest thing was she looked very familiar, but I couldn't place it. I looked at her eyes wide. My breath came out in shallow pants. She opened her eyes barely and a wheezing sound escaped her mouth.

"I- I-," She croaked out then swallowed hard.

"What?" I asked and leaned closer. This was too much. I didn't know what to say. My voice was weak when I finally thought of words. I looked around, no one was in the hall, everyone was in class. No doubt Harrison was trying to figure out how to deal with this.

"Help is coming," I said. I put my hands on her to start to use the little healing power I had. Overwhelmed with a sudden regret for not thinking of it sooner.

"You are the key," She said, lower than a whisper. I flinched back and my power recoiled. When I opened my mouth to ask, Luke's voice rang in my head.

"Harrison's coming, hang in there."

"Dawn!" Harrison urgently yelled to me as he ran down the hall. He came and knelt beside me and a look of recognition crossed his face as he looked at the woman.

"Jada," He whispered, then picked her up and Flashed away.

***

I stared into the mirror for a long time before I washed my hands. It had been a few hours now since I held the woman in my arms, but I feel like even after a shower I still had blood on me. Then I splashed water onto my face and took a deep breath. Things are getting weirder and weirder around here. Lila was already asleep in the bed beside me, snoring softly. I tiptoed to my bed and picked up a book titled *The Real History: What Humans Should and Can Never Know*. I have to read it for class, but I'll probably never actually read it. As I was about to open it, Luke's voice echoed in my mind.

"You ok?" He asked in a concerned tone. I could try to avoid him, but I know he would just persist.

"Perfectly fine," I lied. I could never tell if he could sense my lies from our connection or if it was just Luke. When I was able to lie, I always tried to push a sense that I believed my words were true, but it has never truly worked. He always caught on.

"I've been trying to sleep and your thoughts have been slamming into my head. Explain how that's fine," Luke said, a little annoyed.

I sat up straight and threw my book. It landed with a perfect thud on my dresser, the sounds making me cringe and look at my sister. Lila didn't even stir. Pressure built in my head as Luke was trying to get me to answer. I normally don't get bothered by it, but this felt intrusive. I clenched my fists as I tried to respond calmly.

"We agreed. No more mind speak after curfew."

If he was in front of me right now, he'd be giving me that guilty look I know all too well. I tried to block him out of my mind and winced at the force it took.

"Hey, don't do that. The agreement was after midnight," Luke hissed in my head. I could tell something else was bothering him. A pulse of annoyance came from him. There was something he wanted to say.

"If you have something to say just say it," I crossed my arms just like I would if he was standing in front of me.

"What you did today could've put the entire school in danger," He said in my head.

I went dead silent. Wow, he was actually mad at me. I tried to force the urge to cry down. It was stupid and irrational. Luke would stop his tantrum soon and I'd be waiting for his apology. He's just being Mr. Perfect, doing what everyone else wants him to do.

"I protect my unit as I have protected you your entire life. Leave me alone," I angrily get under the covers.

The woman's face was still at the front of my mind. She said I was the key. What does that mean? I sat there silent and thought the only way to get answers was to confront her.

"Dawn don't, wait to see her until Harrsion says it's okay," Luke sighed. There was no way I was answering him. What was the name Harrison said?

"He said Jada," Luke said with a tint of regret in his voice, trying to be helpful and to make up for his hurtful words. Although he did have a point, I was extremely tired and thanks to my dreams I haven't been sleeping.

Luke was purposely thinking how sorry he was and how'd he make up for it. He knew me too well. The worst part was I knew he was right.

"Thank you," I said unwillingly, my eyes grew heavy as I was pulled into darkness.

***

Night after night the dreams came. If only I knew what they meant, maybe I could control them. This one was different. I could feel it in my bones.

The trees swayed like I was looking at my reflection in the water and the wind whispered dark secrets in my ears, as I watched the woman run while I was paralyzed. She was covered in blood running away from...something. No. Someone. The woman's hair looked like it was red with black streaks, but with the blood coating her body I couldn't tell. I wanted to help her, but I couldn't get to her, my body was weightless.

The woman was running like her life depended on it. When she staggered falling to her hands, letting out a grunt of pain, my stomach dropped. I felt my jaw clench in frustration as I tried to reach for her and remembered I wasn't really there. There was a strong connection to this stranger that survived deep in my chest.

She got off her knees and kept running, her clothes were torn and deep wounds bled beneath. The sight of them sent anger through me. My body felt like it was being compelled to follow after her, to try to help her in some way. Although I knew it was impossible, because this wasn't real, at least I hope it wasn't.

She stopped abruptly behind a tree and I heard male voices taunting her in the distance. I couldn't make out what they were saying, but they wanted this woman and they weren't asking nicely.

I hissed. My natural instincts were screaming at me to defend her, to send those males running back to whatever hole they crawled out of, but I was frozen in place.

The woman waited till the voices got closer and came out from her hiding place. The men were blurry and hard to make out. No matter how hard I squinted, all I could see were outlines of them. On the other hand, the woman started to have a faint glow. She held out her hands towards the blurry boys and purple light burst out. It swirled around her finger tips, as she gave the males a satisfying smirk. That look was all it took to make me instantly like this mystery woman. The males were paralyzed as the purple magic froze them into place, dissolving into their skin.

My eyes widened. The air around the woman was electric as it pulsed with this foreign power. I felt it then as goosebumps bubbled on my skin: the power. It sent my nerves into a sweet overdrive that I had only ever experienced when using my own magic, but more than anything I was startled. The call of that power was something I had never felt. It was dangerous, yet I needed that danger. I realized that feeling scared me.

The woman broke through the forest's edge and made it onto a street. I sucked in a breath as I got a good look at her face. She had violet, all-seeing eyes that sent a chill down my spine. I knew her and she knew me.

"Wake up, Dawn. I'll see you soon," She said in a melodic voice.

The wind was knocked out of me as that power surged toward me. Just like that, the world around me shattered into a million purple pieces.

***

My heartbeat rang in my ears, pounding against my rib cage. Dawn Shadows. My name came back to me as shudders rocked my body. My room was dimly lit with an old bumblebee night light, Lila insisted on keeping. Fear shot through me as I snapped my head to my right. I scrambled for a weapon that I realized wasn't on my dresser. In the panic of today, I forgot to grab it from Harrison's office after he confiscated it yesterday.

My sister was laying on her side, her face slightly obscured by her plush grey comforter. I let out a slow breath calming myself down. If I stretched up just a little bit, I could see her clutching to her gelical stuffed animal. That would normally make me laugh, but not tonight. My sister's mere presence was calming me down. There were some nights she would come to sleep in my bed. The nights where the dreams were more like nightmares. My breath hitched deep in my chest.

She was fine. I was fine... maybe.

I threw my covers off of me and sat on the edge of my bed, placing my head in my hands.

When I closed my eyes the dream flashed in distorted images. The blood that coated the woman's body, the haunting male voices, and the way those violet eyes that looked straight through me. Fighting back tears, I took a deep breath and started to list things I knew were real.

I was born into the world of demons, gelicals (angels if you're a human), and Guardians. I'm fifteen years old. I attend the school of DEATH. My sister and my room is the seventh door from the start of the hallway. I'm training to be a Guardian.

Lila snored, making me jump a little. I looked to the old wood floor and my copy of, *American History: What Humans Should and Can Never Know,* lay open, from when I threw it the corner of the pages bent. I groaned, picked it up and smoothed out its pages. It was for my History of Guardians class, and opened to Michael the Warrior Gelical chapter, but if I have to learn about Michael again I'm going to rip my eyes out.

I glanced at the clock, it was three in the morning. I bit my thumb nail. I needed to sleep, if I didn't I would most likely sleep in...again. I laid back down in my bed and stared at the ceiling. Then rolled on my side, flopping my hand against the headboard. DEATH's logo was carved into it. I began to trace it with my finger lingering on the capital D. The name DEATH is an inside joke the last generation of Guardians made up; it stands for Darcy, Elianna, Amidra, Thomas, and Harrison. Decades later the name sort of stuck. It was rumored they could defeat thousands of demons and come out unscathed,

Then four of them disappeared, leaving their children to take their place. My mother, Darcy, was one of those Guardians. Lila and I were left here at DEATH. The "authorities" have pronounced them dead, but I know she's alive. The magic in my blood has called out to her and sometimes I think I've heard her call back.

No, no I hate when my mind goes there. It's sometimes worse than the night-mares. My mind would not calm down. I curled up into a ball trying to think of anything that wasn't the dream or my mother.

Then the woman's face came back to me. I bolted straight up and launched for the door. These past few weeks I've been dreaming of Jada.

***

By the time I turned into the infirmary, I was breathless. I've never really been in this room because there was no reason to since my healing powers came when I was five. Well, once when Lila got her fire powers at eight months old and she burned me. My ability to heal came the day I turned five, when I cut myself on a knife and it went away in five seconds. I'm not the most careful kid and certainly not the most careful teen Guardian.

I rounded the corner and that's when I saw her. She was just as gorgeous as I thought. A woman with red and black streaked hair. She was covered with a fluffy white blanket and had bandages on her face and arms. That means she's not a Guardian or she wouldn't need those. I could faintly feel Luke in the back of my mind, thinking things incoherently. I pushed him away which is very hard to do. I could tell he was mad that I wouldn't involve him in this. I felt him flinch, but then his presence was muted. She was awake and I opened my mouth to say something, but she turned her head towards me.

I gasped. Jada's eyes were a stunning purple and in those eyes purple eyes it's as if she knew everything about the world. The ones that had looked right into my soul in the dream.

She all of a sudden flinched and looked away and said, "I told you."

"I don't understand," I managed to get out. What was she talking about?

"Come on my girl you're the daughter of the Warrior you must know what I am," She said, still not looking at me as if I was not even there. Was she referring to my mom? I knew that my mom was recognized by the Elders for her heroic deeds and deemed the Warrior. It was the only story Harrison would willingly tell me.

I had no idea what she was talking about and that's when I saw an odd thing on her arm. It was an eye with a swirly black curl making up the pupil and a line that led to a letter J beneath the eye. It also had lightning bolts on either side in place of the veins that are on a normal eye.
I jumped back in shock, "You're a Seer!"

"Correct my girl, correct," She whispered. I think I caught a glimpse of a smirk. She was impressed I figured it out, but of course she knew I would. She *Saw* that I would.

"But they're supposed to be extinct!" I squeaked in surprise.

"Yes, I am the last of my kind," Jada said in a grim voice, still looking at the ceiling.

I needed to ask her what she meant earlier.

"What did you mean by, I'm the key? How have I been dreaming about you?" I asked, stepping closer.

Jada looked at me with amusement in her eyes, "Now if I told you, it wouldn't be a surprise now would it."

A playful smile danced across and almost made her eyes look less sad. She was gorgeous, but in a very different way. Otherworldly. My fist balled involuntarily. That was cryptic. I didn't have the patience for this. I tried asking more questions, but she just stared silently looking at the ceiling.

I then lost my temper, I felt my power explode out into the room, "I don't care just tell me-!"

"Dawn!" Harrison's voice came from behind me and made me jump. I turned around slowly, Harrison was glowering down at me, his dark brown eyes scorching into my bright gold ones, it was as if he melted me.

"What. Are. You. Doing?" He said through clenched teeth. I looked around and saw I had accidentally broken glass and put cracks in the walls. Jada had a shield of purple wrapped around her, just like in my dream.

"I was- I was just-," I choked out. My mouth couldn't form the words.

"It doesn't matter now. Get out," he pointed in the direction of the door.

I held my ground and looked at Jada. She frowned at Harrison.

"Harry she has to be told at some point. It's not her fault," Jada said, trying to sit up. Harrison's face softened a little and I thought maybe he'd explain what she was talking about.

"Uncle Harrison-," I tried one more time using the familial title I never used with him. It was the wrong choice. He gave me an icy look.

"Out now," Harrison commanded, his voice becoming deadly. I could feel the tears building behind my eyes.

This time I listened and Flashed to my room launching myself onto the bed. Lila got up and came to lay beside me, but refrained from asking what happened. Harrison has never spoken to me like that before. I felt like crying, but the tears wouldn't come. If Harrison or Jada wouldn't help me get answers, I'd just have to get them on my own.

Chapter 3

Research

"**D**, this is bad come on, you're gonna get in a lot of trouble for this," Luke anxiously rambled, fidgeting with his hands.

I rolled my eyes. I still don't understand why he keeps trying to persuade me. Did I listen to his fifteen other attempts?

It has been twenty four hours since Jada entered my life. I broke into Harrison's office and grabbed the key to the restricted records section. This is why Luke is acting like I might die. I never understood why we had keys. We are a high tech society of gifted people yet a simple key can still unlock a door. There was nothing special protecting it, just pure simple doors that are very easily broken into.

"This is bad. I mean really bad, you have broken every other rule. What makes you think he won't kick you out to the streets this time? Then you'll become a stray-," Luke continued but was stopped by my glare at that stupid word. He stopped for a second trying to figure out how to word it correctly. It was uncalled for to refer to fellow Guardians that are not at DEATH a word that belittles them when they are just kids they don't want to take responsibility for.

Still he went on with his speech, "You'll have nowhere else to go. What if trying to find out about this Jada woman is a bad idea? What if Harrison is just trying to protect us? What if this is all just a misunderstanding? What if Jada is a demon or something? What if she's lying? What if-."

"Seriously, Luke, I don't care. They're hiding something from us and I have every intention to find out what that something is. Please, enough. You're going to make your hair fall out with all the stress you're letting *my* actions cause you," I said, trying to sound like I knew what I was doing. I looked back at the papers.

"Look, I can't tell you how sorry I am for what I said last night," He said. Luke looked at me with teary pleading eyes. I quickly looked away.

He thought that would make me feel better, after what he said to me. "Doesn't matter, now can you guard the door like a good little doggy," I knew that was harsh and I looked up ready to apologize and take it back, but the words didn't come out. I couldn't even say them in my head.

Luke flinched, but did as I asked of him. He was too good for me.

***

I was stuck in endless piles of records with history books, textbooks, and profiles. The piles made a maze that had me at the center. It was ten o'clock, an hour before curfew. I was about to give up on finding anything on Jada when I found Harrison's profile.

> Name: Harrison Grove Scott
> Gender identity: Male
> Species: Guardian
> Parents: John Louis Scott and Clare Elizabeth Benson
> Protecti: Jada Anne Moon
> Gender: ~~Female~~ *Whatever the hell I want it to be* -JM

I smiled at Jada's handwritten comment because I'd do the same thing. My eyes started to feel like sandpaper as I kept reading.

> Species: Seer
> Mission: Find Amidra Fera Carson, Elianna Beatrice Marce, and Darcy Hanna Russel-Shadows
> Mission report: Failed
> Information verified by: **HGS and JAM**

Jada was Harrison's protecti and he still taught us that all Seers were extinct? I knew there was something he was hiding.

This led me to my mom's profile. Attached was a picture of her with a big red X on it. The X, made my eyes water. I knew it was unlikely she was alive, but this was the first time there was proof that the Elders had given up. I had always been told they were still looking for her. The Elders didn't even give her a funeral. A small part of me hoped that was still the case, but that glaring X said differently. I forced myself to look at the picture.

My mom's enchanting eyes looked like they were filled with genuine happiness. I shut my eyes to keep the tears from coming.

Suddenly, a shiver went up my spine. I felt a weird presence in the room, something powerful but when I whipped my head around, no one was there. Great, all I needed was to be going crazy, too.

"*You're not crazy. I felt it, too,*" Luke said quietly, but still remained in the hall. I sighed. He's always trying to make me feel better.

"*About what I said-*," I started, but Luke cut me off.

"*It's forgotten. Is there anything else about your mom?*"

I bit my lip and went onto the next page. It barely had anything on it and a lot was redacted.

It read:

> Name: Darcy Hanna Russel- Shadows
> Husband: ----- Shadows
> Gender: Female
> Species: Guardian
> Parents: Richard Michael Russel and Cortina Mary Brince
> Protecti: ----- ----- Cassie
> Mission: Find his protector along with Amidra Fera Carson and
> Elianna Beatrice Marce
> Mission report: Failed he went missing in the process
> Information Verified By: HGS and JAM

I slammed the profile down on the table. There was no information to help me here. This file was the same as the files I could access everyday. It was also weird that my father was mentioned at all. From what I gather, something happened to him before I was born.

When I asked Harrison, he got this look as if it pained him in some way then said, "No one really knew him."

My mind raced around itself looking for anything about my mom. When I was younger, I used to pretend my parents became gelicals and were always watching over me. There are some conspiracy theories that when a Guardian dies they become gelicals and join Michael in the Divine Realm. Did I believe them? I don't know, not so much now. Why was my dad's name crossed out? Why? Unfortunately, I could not find an answer to any of my questions. I came looking for answers, but got more questions in return. One question stood out among all: Who were my parents?

Luke's voice blared into my head. It made me jump, "*HARRISON ALERT!!*"

With a wave of my hand I sent things flying through the library, ducking and crashing into tables, when things were finally back to where they were supposed to be I sat farthest from the restricted library. Then I saw the key. That golden key with the crimson ribbon attached to its back. Harrison's office key. I concentrated hard and saw Harrison down the hall. I made the key reflective so that it looked invisible and sent it to Harrison's right pocket. Luke Flashed to my side pretending to study just as Harrison burst in.

"Alright, which one of you did it? Why am I even asking that? Dawn, what did you do?" Harrison pointed at me with a stern finger.

"Did what?" Luke and I both said at the same time our heads snapped up. Harrison shook his head, and his face turned red.

"My key- the key you took it you- you!" He yelled as his face grew a darker red.

"Which key? You have a lot of keys?" Luke asked, playing dumb. I snickered. He knew how to play Harrison even if he was a goody-two-shoes.

"The key to the restricted library!" Harrison waved his hands around, his face now turning purple.

"Oh, that one, well did you check your pocket you tend to leave things in there?" I laughed and pointed to his pocket. He huffed and shoved his hand into his left pocket, then his right pocket. Then he pulled out the key.

He gave a big sigh of relief. "Nice try, girl. You still have detention from your stunt this morning," Harrison said bluntly and stormed back into the hall.

Luke and I let out a snicker, increasing to a full out laugh as we both high fived. The files weren't very helpful, but at least I knew my last name was real. Luke had become immersed in a book by my side and a few other students trickled in. They passed us giving us a little side eye. I tried to smile, but that made them walk faster. I slammed my head on the table, trying to think.

"What's your last name?" I asked, turning my head towards Luke, realizing in all these years he's never told me. I knew Luke didn't know his parents. Harrison said he was left outside of DEATH'S Boundary.

He shrugged, "I don't know, I guess I was never given one." He started to read the book again, but something else came to mind

"Luke?"

"Hmmm?" He said, his mind on school work and soon I would lose him to his very important education.

I knew he paid more attention in History of Guardians (H.O.G.S) class then I did.

"Is there anyone in the H.O.G.S book with the last name of Shadows?"

He seemed to think about it for a few seconds, then it was as if a light bulb went on in his head. He snapped his fingers, "As in related to you? Lillian Shadows, your great-great grandmother. She made Flashing a lot easier by creating a way to do it through your mind instead of using the contraption um... I forgot what it was called, I'll remember eventually," Luke laughed and went back to reading his book.

I shook my head. I was definitely losing his attention, "Did it talk about her children's children having a son," I prodded.

"Um.... No," he said, still not fully paying attention to what I was asking. I got up and Luke murmured goodbye. I waved at him. Class tomorrow felt irrelevant. I had to go though or Harrison might actually kick me out. Sleep evaded me the rest of the night.

The next day I went through feeling numb, not sure what to make of anything. My detention was just cleaning up the mess in the infirmary. Jada was now out and into her own room. She is a Seer. My mom was officially declared dead without my knowledge, and my dad was erased. This was shaping up to be a wonderful week.

Chapter 4

Sameness

I t was dark. I was sitting in a chair with my hands tied behind my back. Then a light flickered over my head and a hooded figure appeared.

"Miss Shadows," the figure said. "Would you like to see your mother ever again?" The mysterious voice said menacingly.

I didn't respond. I fought against my restraints. Why couldn't I break them?

The figure put its face close to mine. I could only see black eyes, with specs of light in them.

"Where is she?!" the figure roared.

I did not respond. The figure started to laugh hysterically. I tried to scream, but the scene shifted.

All of a sudden I stood over corpses. My sister's, my mom's, Luke's, Hailey's, and Dan's.

I snapped awake drenched in sweat gasping for air. That was a new one. A completely terrifying nightmare I'd rather not think about on a day like today. Lila had already left the room, probably went to get breakfast.

Getting out of bed to get dressed. Today is supposed to be a happy day, I kept telling myself. It was just a dream. No matter how real it felt.

As I was getting dressed, I looked at the symbol on my arm that shows I'm a Guardian. Every Guardian is born with this symbol on their left arm. It's a capital G with two swords crossing over it with an X representing I have killed demons. When I first killed a demon, I was ten years old. Each Guardian is put in front of the Elders and they release a demon and pray and hope you don't get killed. A little barbaric, but Guardians aren't meant to be coddled. We're raised as trained soldiers. Other creatures have symbols too such as; Seers, Changers, Demons, Deceased (Vampires), etc.

A gasp escaped my throat. Looking at my arm again. My symbol changed. It no longer had a G, it was now replaced with an eye like Jada's. I groaned because I knew I'd have to show it to Harrison. I inspected the rest of my symbol to make sure nothing else had changed. The moon and stars representing I came in contact with a Changer that turns into a wolf. I was still waiting to come in contact with a Deceased. The Deceased symbol which was a sun with six rays representing their six clans was a design I always admired on Harrison's arm.

After I pulled myself somewhat together, I went to my door and pulled it open.

"Surprise!" Everyone yelled in excitement. Lila, Luke, Hailey, Dan, and Harrison stood outside my door with cake and party hats. Yes, today is my sixteenth birthday. The day I become an adult. Yay, I guess.

"*Why didn't you tell me?*" I looked at Luke accusingly.

"*Well, it wouldn't have been a surprise if I had, now would it?*" He said in my head, rolling his eyes. I tried not to give him a smile, but failed epically. Luke smiled back. It was a triumphant smile. Luke had celebrated his 16th birthday a month ago. Although we are unsure of his real birthday, we have always celebrated it a month before mine. He loved to hold that he was older over my head, but we both knew it wouldn't matter how much older he was, I would always win.

"Happy birthday sis!" Lila gave me a forceful hug. I hugged her back and closed my eyes, breathing her in, relieved she was still alive. Opening my eyes, Luke was staring at me with a confused expression. Sticking my tongue out at him, "*Get out of my head.*"

"*Whatever,*" He rolled his eyes. Luke backed off ever so slightly, but did not leave completely. It is impossible to leave each other's minds completely; we can only try to block the other. It's exhausting to block each other out.

I hugged her tighter to me, lost in my thoughts. Lila started to loosen her grip on me and I let her go. She too looked concerned, but I squeezed her hand.

Jada came around the corner, no bandages, all clean and bright. Her purple eyes still looked sad and all knowing. She gave me a tiny smile and glided over to Harrison then whispered something in his ear.

"Sixteen, is that the year you get assigned missions and stuff?" Daniel asked excitedly. Lila punched him in the gut which led to Daniel wincing in response, "Yes! You idiot, it's when you get assigned a protecti and missions."

A protecti is a magical creature The Elders deem valuable. We can protect species anywhere from humans to the Deceased. Then we go on missions with them and make sure they're safe like our pledge says, "We the Guardians were created to fight, protect, and keep the peace. Kill the demons and protect the Creators. I pledge to die for what is right and never for what is wrong. I pledge to follow the light and never the dark. Protect. Fight. Peace. Light. We are the Guardians!" In my opinion that pledge is really cheesy and pointless. We only said it when we were little. Luke chuckled out loud, amused by my thoughts.

Harrison cleared his throat to get my attention, "We will be finding out your protecti today. Jada just told me the Elders have arrived and I have some very exciting news for you, Luke," Harrison rubbed his hands together excitedly.

"You're acting weird," I said and Harrison gave me a quick glare.

Luke looked at everyone's confused faces.

Harrison continued, "The Elders have decided to have both you and Dawn be assigned a protecti at the same time!" Harrison said "at the same time" as if it was the most exciting thing in the world. I rolled my eyes pretending not to care, although I was somewhat intrigued by the idea, but also incredibly annoyed. I just wanted this one thing to be just mine.

Luke looked at me with a fake smile. I tried to push myself back into his mind. He let me in on the first try.

"*What if they find out?*" He was saying it over and over again. My body stiffened. I had almost forgotten why Luke was so afraid of the Elder's. I went over to him and poked him, pretending to be excited.

"*They won't, I'll make sure of it,*" I reassured him.

After some more discussion, Harrison began walking away from us giving us a lecture on being respectful in front of the Elders. Luke and I jumped into a mental discussion and tuned out Harrison.

"You two understand?" Harrison's voice sounded muffled as I was lost in Luke's terrified thoughts.

Harrison snapped his fingers in our faces, which caused us to look at him.

"Alright you two, get to the Training Room you're already late," Harrison shooed us away. I looked back to see everyone smiling. Lila gave me a thumbs up.

"They're here right now?" Luke squeaked pointing at the ground. Dan covered up a laugh.

"Good luck," Lila called after us and waved. Dan copied her and she gave him another punch to the gut. This led to Dan attempting to tackle her. Lila's hand sparked with flames. Harrison merely separated them both. I looked away shaking my head.

Luke was silent by my side all the way to the big Training Room doors. He had his fists balled at his sides. They were shaking slightly. Luke looked at the doors and panic swelled up in his eyes. I took his hand and squeezed, "Everything is going to be fine, they're never going to find out." He took another shaky breath and squeezed my hand back. I too breathed in deeply, steadying myself. I squeezed his hand a final time. It was all going to be fine. I turned to the door, but before I could even think about opening the door, it swung open with an eerie creak.

A long line of chairs stretched from one end of the room to the other and in them sat a variety of older women and men chattering amongst themselves. They had on T-shirts and jeans. This was surprising because I'm used to seeing them in long purple robes. In the center, was the head Elder chair. This was not the head Elder from when I was ten. First, this Elder was a man and the last Elder was a woman. Secondly, he carried a long black staff with a snake carved into the top of it. It gave me the creeps. I felt like it was actually real, as the red eyes watched me move.

"Ah... there they are," the man spoke in a light British accent. His hair was striking white and long, resting just past his shoulders. The other Elders grew quiet as he spoke, as if his words demanded attention. The man's eyes were a pale green and his lips stretched thin, the ends of them curled up into a tiny smirk. His walk was proud, swift and determined, as he came closer to us.

"It is so nice to meet the young Guardians of this generation! I personally am excited to see what you have to offer our small community. It's wonderful to see you two. I have been interested to see how you both grew and it looks like you both have blossomed into magnificent Guardians!" His voice echoed throughout the room with power and also lightness. The Head Elder spoke as if we were long time friends. It made me nervous that he seemed to know everything about Luke and I, but we knew next to nothing about him. He shook both of our hands, his hand swallowing mine in his firm grip and papery skin.

"Sioena, if you would, their symbols please," He spoke with joy, but also command as he gestured to a young woman with spiky brown hair. She gave him a swift nod then pulled a censor out of thin air, as she came closer I noticed her eyes were a startling black. She wore a black dress and sharp purple heels. She is either the Head Elder's assistant or an Elder in training. She glared as I examined her up and down.

"Arm please," Sioena grabbed my arm anyway, her voice unexpectedly high. I cringed as she held my arm with sharpened nails that could easily pierce my skin. I did not want to show this stranger my symbol. She put me on edge, but I knew if I resisted it would cause problems. Harrison would put me on clean up duty for a month. I gritted my teeth in frustration and clenched my fist so my symbol would be more prominent and held my breath. Sioena put the scanner on my arm and pressed hard into my skin. It was blazing hot, I thought it was going to burn me, but then after what seemed like forever even though it was like thirty seconds it beeped. Sioena looked at the scan then at me with questions lingering in her eyes. My brows furrowed as I looked at her. She swiftly moved on to Luke pulling her surprised face back into a glare. Then she went over to the man with the white hair and showed him the results.

"Interesting. I've never seen readings such as this in my life and it's been a long one, hahaha. Hmmm," he murmured under his breath, putting his hand to his temple. He was obviously perplexed by what the scanner had shown.

"Um... sir please excuse my interruption, but we don't know your name," Luke said politely, all traces of nervousness gone.

The Head Elder did not look up from the scanner as he answered, "Talahan, Elder Talahan."

Sioena held my gaze; she did not change her expression from her menacing glare. I shifted eagerly, wanting to wipe that look off her face.

"*Easy, D,*" Luke's voice whispered in my head. I tried to calm myself down. I didn't want a fight to break out.

"Incredible," Elder Talahan crooned, then passed the scanner back to the other Elders. They started to nod and whisper in agreement, some of them even gasped.

I couldn't resist not asking, "What's so interesting?"

Luke shot a look at me.

"*Dawn, he literally has the power to destroy our futures.*"

I sent him an image of me sticking out my tongue. They couldn't sit there and discuss us like we're not even here.

Elder Talahan seemed eager to answer my query, not the slightest bit offended. I was hoping to get some kind of reaction out of him.

"Well my dear you must know," he said, perplexed. When he saw my facial expression, he knew I had no idea what he was referring to.

"Both of your symbols are completely the same and the energy in them is at 100%!" He laughed as Luke gasped in shock, apparently 100% is a rare thing.

"What do you mean our symbols are the same?" Luke asked fast as though he was being timed.

"They fluctuate, position, and appear at the same time and the same way. I've never heard of such a thing. Guardian's symbols are always unique, no two have ever been the same. You two might just be the most powerful Guardians I've ever met!" Talahan said, utterly amazed. There was something in his eyes that made me uneasy. The intense stare he had, like he found something he's been looking for his entire life. He was excited about us, while the other Elders seemed scared. They shifted uneasily in their chairs, whispering to each other in nervous tones.

"Well, I already knew that," I said confidently. Luke visibly cringed. There were nervous chuckles from a couple of the Elders.

"I wouldn't say they're that unique, sir," Sioena said, bitterness seeping into her voice and her eyes almost in silts. I shifted again, really having an urge to punch this woman. Talahan gave her a sideways glance that meant, "shut up". She then bowed her head in resignation.

"Enough," Talahan ordered. The chattering of the other Elders stopped. "On with the ceremony!" He gestured to Sioena.

All the Elders then took their seats like dominos falling, one after the other. Sioena on the other hand did not sit, she walked over to us, her face no longer in a fierce glare, instead she had no expression at all, a complete and perfect poker face.

Luke and I exchanged a glance. Harrison had told us what to expect during the protecti assignment, but it was very different now that it was actually happening. Sioena waved her hand, podiums with each species symbol on them appeared. They made popping sounds as they came into existence, out of interdimensional pockets.

"Follow my instructions exactly," Sioena said coldly, still expressionless. As Luke and I approached the podiums, two gold strips of light appeared on the floor, leading to two different sets of podiums. I took the left strip and Luke took the right.

"Stick out your hand out like this," She demonstrated her long arm ascending gracefully into the air. Her fingernails were long claws that sent shivers down my spine. She had put her left arm up which made her Guardian symbol more prominent. It started to glow slightly as her power flowed through it. I did what I was told, although I so badly wanted to run out of the room.

"Now close your eyes and let your power surge through your body, feel it, see it, let it take control," Sioena's voice started to become muffled and slowly her voice disappeared. I have done this many times before, but this time I was completely out of control and my power was in the driver's seat. I could almost see what it looked like, blinding, but a beautiful white color that slowly turned to grey the longer I focused on it. It was growing and pulsating as I tried to get a better look at it. I felt my legs carry me forward. I felt beckoned to move, but I wasn't consciously moving my feet. I started to panic, but the more I fought it the more it took over. As I came closer to a podium, images swirled in front of me. A burning campfire with kids dancing around it, a pair of green intense eyes, paws crunching through a forest.

I gasped as the connection to my power broke.

My eyes fluttered open. When did I close them? I found myself staring at a bright blue swirl. It turned into an image of a moon with stars, the wolf Changer symbol. My fingers brushed one of the stars. It felt good, like water washing over my sweaty hand. The star then floated down into my palm, the moment I closed my hand around the blue silvery star it turned into letters. The letters swarmed and grouped into words then fell back into my hand. I looked down and saw a piece of paper with a name. Hunter Louis Loves, written in bright iridescent blue

I let out a sigh. Then it was like nothing happened. I felt like myself again. My power was back where it was meant to be, I could no longer see the grey light inside me. I sensed the presence of someone next to me. I looked over to my right and there stood Luke, his expression back to terrified. Luke didn't travel through his strip of light; he went down mine with me. He was looking down at his piece of paper, Jordan Cassie. I know that last name. Then I realized that we went for the same symbol. It was the Changer symbol of a wolf. Oh, no this was very bad. Luke wouldn't be able to hide anything for much longer. I promised him the Elders would never find out. I needed to do something fast.

The Elders went in outbursts of confusion, excitement, and anger. Elder Talahan banged his staff on the ground and shouted, "SILENCE!" All the Elders immediately stopped everything with no hesitation.

Talahan turned to Luke and I, "I think I speak for all of us when I say we are all astounded! We have never seen two Guardians in training pick the same symbol! This could mean something very big!" Talahan shouted excitedly.

He turned to a stoic Sioena, "I think the wise choice would be to take them up to Galrich with us and-"

"Wait, wait," I cut him off, "You mean the capitol? So you can, what?" I said, my voice growing more angry with every word. This wasn't what I meant by wanting the Elders to send me away. Would they experiment on us? The thought set my teeth on edge.

Talahan put his hand up in defense, "My dear, my dear please, you must understand that both of you are very unique. We need more information. It's your duty, " He put on a crooked smile, avoiding my question. I glared back. I looked at Luke and saw he was visibly shaking.

"*Get me out of here,*" Luke pleaded with me.

I looked back at Talahan, he was discussing with Sioena in hushed whispers. She nodded as her face remained expressionless. Sioena strode over to us with two packets in her hands, "Here is all the information on your protecti's that you could possibly know," Sioena didn't even look at us. Talahan whispered something to the Elder on his left. They were obviously planning on how to take us away from our home. I wasn't going to let that happen. Harrison couldn't let this happen. There was no doubt in my mind that he wouldn't even try to stop it though. It was up to me.

"May we leave now, please?" I asked as politely as I could.

Talahan smiled but it did not touch his eyes. They narrowed on me like I was a target. "Well my dear, we have to explain the information in your packets and there's more to discuss about your...visit to Galrich," he calmly responded. The way he said visit made my stomach flip.

"As Spiky Hair here clearly stated," I held up the papers and cleared my throat.

"This has all the information we could possibly know," I mimicked almost perfectly the coldness of Sioena's voice, "Harrison should be having this discussion with you, not us."

Sioena let out a little squeak, "You are not permitted to leave!" She had finally let some expression come into her face. It was not just a glare, there was venom behind her eyes. Talahan put a hand on her shoulder restraining her back. She did not relax even a tiny bit. Talahan's little Guard dog.

"*Dawn please,*" Luke sounded as if he was on the verge of crying, although he was keeping it together on the outside. It was hard to say how much longer he could keep it up for. If he shifted...I didn't even want to think about the consequences.

Sioena started to yell random things about manners and disrespect, while Elder Talahan repeatedly said her name trying to get control of her. Then a light bulb went on in my head. I remembered the time when I made my homework disappear. Once a couple years ago it went up in black smoke and it ended up in Harrison's office. It wasn't where I wanted it to be though, sending Luke off somewhere could be dangerous, but maybe if I really focused he'd be alright. I wonder...

I put on the most apologetic face ever, "I'm sorry, so so sorry please, I didn't mean any disrespect," I whined like a little four year old on the brink of tears. I glanced at Luke and he looked terrible. I really hoped this worked. I just had to picture somewhere outside of DEATH then Luke could take care of the rest.

"Oh my dear, no need to apologize," Talahan's eyes softened.

"Okay," I responded in a small voice. Concentrating on Luke and prayed he didn't get hurt from this. My power released from me, engulfing Luke in black smoke that swirled around him.

"Get somewhere safe," I said.

"What the heck are you doing?"

When it cleared, he was no longer there. Everyone gasped. I actually made Luke disappear. I smiled wildly then started to laugh. I did it! *"Luckily I'm in one piece, Shadows. I'm going to analyze how you did that when I get back. Thank you,"* Luke's voice sounded muffled in my head, but he was okay.

"Take that sucker!" I screamed at Sioena who was visibly shaking with anger. I was in big trouble now, but Luke was safe. The Elder's facial expression made it worth it. I turned around to leave when someone's power dragged me back. I was fighting it until something sharp hit my head. My vision turned black.

Chapter 5

Anger

My eyes fluttered open.

"You didn't have to hit her," Harrison's voice muttered.

"She's fine, Harry," Sioena's ear piercing voice snapped back. I groaned and rolled over. I was in Harrison's office on his green battered couch. "Where is he?!" Sioena's face was three inches away from mine and her eyes blazed with anger. I smiled and sat up, my head aching. Sioena must have hit me pretty hard that it knocked me out.

"You do realize there will be consequences" Sioena hissed. She looked like she was going to attack me. I prepared myself for it. I wanted her to come to me, beckoning her forward with my hand. She shrieked as she took a step towards me.

Harrison held her back and said in his parent voice, "Let's deal with this maturely." Sioena backed off slowly, scratching her nails against Harrison's large oak desk along the way.

"Dawn you humiliated yourself and this school in front of the Elders. You're grounded for a month," Harrison said and crossed his arms. I was expecting more yelling from him. I got up with a sigh and headed down to my room.

I wasn't even mad about getting grounded. I tried to contact Luke, but he was blocking me out of his head. I huffed. The nerve he had! I just saved him and he was keeping me from knowing what he was up to. I tried for almost an hour to get him to take down the block, but no luck. At least I knew he was alive, I'd hit him later. I laid on my bed and went to sleep.

***

Harrison gave me the punishment of studying in the library, which of course was very convenient for me to do research on my family. I got the key from Harrison's office and broke into the restricted library again. When I came across my mom's profile, I closed it. My hands shook every time I saw the red X over her face. I sighed and opened it again. I scanned it again and found a familiar name.

Protecti: ----- Cassie

I know that name! Cassie is the last name of Luke's wolf changer protecti.

"Luke, you need to get back here now!" I screamed in his head. He had dropped the block as soon as I was awake, but I had been ignoring his presence.

"Okay, you don't have to scream," Luke answered my call, *"So do you have a story made up for my disappearance?"*

"Ummm... No," I said, confused. He could've just read what happened in my brain. He was always butting in. Why would this be any different?

"Wait, they know it was you who did it?" He asked.

"Duh! I'm grounded for a month, but for my punishment I get to study in the library," I said with pride.

He laughed, *"Don't get kicked out."*

I still couldn't see where he was. The image around him was clouded like he was purposely hiding it from me. I decided to move past it for now.

"I called you because I found something," I said.

"Well... what is this something? It could be a dog, a clue... oh, I know Harrison's lizard!"

That made me laugh. Harrison's lizard, Frizzo, disappeared a year ago. Lila was chasing him in the yard near the Boundary. The lizard just went right through the Boundary and never came back. I hated Frizzo to be honest, he scared the heck out of me. I was ecstatic when he was no longer in my presence, Lila on the other hand sobbed for the whole night. Luke was trying to distract me. It worked for a little bit there.

"Very funny. What's your protecti's name?"

He sighed. It hurt that he didn't want me to know.

"Jordan Cassie," He took a long pause considering a thought I couldn't make out, *"I'm actually staying with her and her fellow changers,"* Luke responded, with admiration in his voice.

"Wow sounds amazing, but listen," I started to talk really fast, moving past my shock. *"That was the last name of my mom's protecti, and he's missing. What if Jordan is related to him and knows where he is, then he could lead me to my mom and tell me if she died or missing or alive or -"*

"D stop, you're giving me a headache," Luke interrupted my rambling. Luke was pushing me out of his head again. I winced. He was trying to hide something from me. I pushed back, forcing myself in. He was fighting me with everything he had, but I found a hole in his block, slipping in. I gasped at what I found. He knows Cassie. The image of him was still clouded in his mind, but he has known him for a long time. I pulled back and Luke immediately put his block back up.

"Hey, listen please I'm sorry, but you have no idea why he's hiding. I think we should just leave them alone. There are reasons-" He started to defend himself, but then I cut him off.

"Fine," I snapped. *"You want to choose some girl you just met over your best friend? Don't bother even coming back if you want to protect them so much! We have never kept secrets, ever! I have protected your secrets your whole life. Oh wait, what about the biggest one ever! Luke is a wolf and oh no one can know because that would result in punishment from the Elders. You think you would at least have some respect!"*

I could feel his anger and frustration almost like it was my own. As he shredded into his wolf form, it felt like I was standing right next to him just like when he first transformed in front of me when we were five.

***

Luke has been gone for almost three weeks. I was frustrated with him after he repeatedly ignored my pleas to come home. Harrison was so angry with me. I've been banned from classes and basically quarantined in my room. Although, I did manage to convince Harrison that it was an accident. We at least agreed that we didn't want the Elders involved. He seemed to not trust Talahan either. He also seemed to be scared of Sioena. I decided there was something I had to do before I went and dragged Luke back by his ears. I snuck out of my room past the Boundary, which was surprisingly easy to do. I don't know why I haven't tried it before. When I snuck out, I passed a sleeping Harrison this morning. He had taken it upon himself to sleep outside my room. It was funny that he couldn't even keep me there. I read the paper in my hands as the wind whipped my hair.

Name: Hunter Louis Loves
Gender: Male
Age: 17
Species: Changer (Wolf)
Parents: unidentified
Classified: Rulebreaker. He manipulated and broke a lot of laws such as fighting with other changers, stealing, illegal trade

The list continued onto the next page. I laughed. This was my kind of guy. I stood outside his house reading his profile. We weren't technically allowed to meet our protecti until the graduation ceremony, but I could seriously care less. Luke had met his protecti, I found it only fair that I met mine too. Harrison wanted Luke back, but didn't want me looking for him. I need access to a changer who could.

I took a deep breath and knocked on the door. No answer. Then suddenly I heard a crash, break, and shattering sounds coming from inside. I busted down the door and there stood a wolf in front of me with chestnut fur, and sea green eyes.

Chapter 6

Breaking the Ice

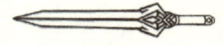

"I w-wouldn't d-do t-that if-if I w-were y-you," The boy said growling and shivering.

Basic wolf changer 101, get an out of control wolf in some freezing water and it will bring them back to human form. You could do what I did and actually freeze the poor guy. I panicked and lost control of my powers and froze him, literally. I was currently defrosting him. Ice chips were falling at my feet, turning into water.

"I'm just trying to get you warmed up," I said, but backed away as he glared.

"S-So wh-o–o a-r are you a-a-again?" He asked, still glaring.

"Dawn Shadows," I said, "I'm a Guardian, I'm here to protect you or– whatever," I rolled my eyes.

"So y-y- you wh- what? P-p-p- planned too sca- scare m-m- me to death?!" He yelled, still shivering.

"No, of course not!" I yelled right back, "Why did I scare you?" I asked calming myself.

"I-I do-don't g-get m-m-many vi-visitors," he whispered.

"Is it just you living here?" I asked politely. It was a quaint little home. It looked like he had been trying to eat. The plate was shattered on the floor, its contents spewed over the rug. There were a lot of toys in various places around the floor.

"Mos- Most o-of th-the ti-time," His teeth still chattered and his eyes were sad. I could tell he didn't want to trust me, I couldn't blame him.

"What does that mean?" I was curious to say the least.

"You're nosy, has anybody ever told y-you th-that? I guess that's typical for Guardians though" He shivered at the end of his sentence.

I laughed, "Oh, yeah loads of times. I just thought it would be easier if we break the ice now since well, pun intended. We'll be spending a lot of time together in the near future."

"Yippee," He said with no enthusiasm.

"Do you have something against Guardians?" I asked, crossing my arms. He grabbed the towel he had around him tighter.

"Nnn-ope. Just you," He tried to smile, but his teeth were chattering. I laughed.

Then awkward silence. He was interesting, but I didn't know what to say. It was hard not to feel awkward after I froze him, since he changed back from his wolf form and wasn't fully clothed.

"Okay I'll start," I said and took a deep breath, "My full name is Dawn Gabriel Shadows. My favorite color is black and yes I know it's not technically a color. My birthday was just a few weeks ago. My best friend is a Changer like you, his name is Luke, but as you know you can't be a Guardian and another species, so no one knows except for me. We're in a fight right now. He's keeping secrets from me and I hate that. I'm currently sixteen years old. I was four when my mom went missing, dead, or...worse. I've never met my father. All I know is that his last name was Shadows and my only father figure I have ever known pretty much hates me now," I took a deep breath, "Did I forget anything?" I asked, a little acid to my voice.

"You have a temper and over sharing with a complete stranger," He laughed, his teeth no longer chattering, but still shivering.

"Thanks so much for the compliment," I said sarcastically.

"You're welcome," He laughed again.

"Your turn," I said and gestured with my hand to him. The ice was almost gone.

He looked at me for a second then nodded, "Okay, my name is Hunter Louis Loves. My favorite color is green and yeah I know I'm not very creative. My birthday was a week ago. I'm currently seventeen. I live here with my brother Tyler, but he's five so I try to keep my...condition a secret from him, but I have a feeling he'll be changing soon. He's my best friend. My mom was, well, let's say I know what it's like for parents to not be around, four years ago on this very day, she disappeared. There was a knock on the door... that's why you scared me. My dad walked out when I was four, I barely remember the guy. The first time I changed I was five years old. I've never had a girlfriend and I don't know how to ride a bike," Hunter was sad as he told me about himself, but still kept his sense of humor. I could tell he was the type of person you could trust. I decided that I wasn't going to use him to find Luke. He would come back on his own.

"Can I warm you up now?" I asked. He was still soaked and shivering, at least the ice was gone.

"Sure," Hunter said, scooting closer to me, "But don't you dare burn me, Shadows."

"Oh, I wouldn't even think about it, Loves," I smiled, placing my hands on his shoulder.

Chapter 7

Past and the Future

After I left Hunter's house, I Flashed to DEATH. Harrison was standing at the Boundary, his hair disheveled and his eyes glowing a bright white.

"Are you serious? Don't you care about anything?" He asked, throwing his hands up in frustration. I went through the Boundary and felt a jolt of energy as I passed Harrison.

"I'm the only one who cares around here," I said calmly. Harrison Flashed in front of me, towering over me.

He clenched his hands into fists looking like he might actually hit me. I kept walking forward with a roll of my eyes. Harrison kept pace at my side until we reached the entrance stairs.

"I would kick you out if it weren't for your mother-,"

I whirled around, "Yes, let's talk about *my* mother. You act like she doesn't exist when it's convenient, but the second I take my life into my own hands she's what you use to make me feel guilty. Kick me out Harrison. I dare you," I said, as anger burned through my veins. Harrison's entire body was shaking as the sky started to darken. He was normally composed. I'd never seen him lose control of his power. The air grew colder and lighting streaked the sky. I felt someone touch my shoulder. Jada came up behind me walking towards Harrison. She placed her hand on his shoulder and he relaxed immediately. The sky cleared and Harrison's eyes became more focused. He looked at Jada with a vulnerability that I have never seen from him before. There was something between them. It might have been romantic, but I'm not sure.

"Let me talk to her," Jada whispered to him, "She deserves some answers," She stated in an airy voice. Harrison's shoulders slumped in defeat, shuffling away huffing and puffing. I watched him go, then turned my focus to Jada.

"What do you want?" I snapped at her, giving her my best glare one that makes even Luke shy away.

"Your understanding," She said in a calm and careful way, while staring at me. Her expression was soft, but then her eyes went out of focus. The purple color in her eyes clouded over and drained out, turning to grey then to a light gold. Jada's body went stiff and rigid, then her eyes turned blood red and she made a choking sound. She must be having a vision.

"Jada?" I asked, concerned. Stepping toward her, I almost went to get help after two minutes of standing there with her, making weird choking noises. When Jada snapped out of it her eyes changed from red, gold, grey, and back to her purple. She grabbed my wrist and then gave me a sweet smile. "Follow me," Jada looked completely normal and relaxed again. I let out a big sigh. This woman was getting on my nerves. I followed her through the door, down the hall, past the Training Room, past the bedrooms, and the lunch room. We finally came to a big silver door.

"I've seen this before," I gasped, "But it disappeared when I tried to open it." I couldn't have been more than eight or nine years old at the time. I thought I was seeing things.

"Good, that means I did my job. Only people who are Seers or people with a spark of Seer magic can see this door. I hid it when I left, no one could see it in case DEATH was attacked," Jada said this like it was the most obvious thing in the world. She opened the door and a shimmering light danced across my feet. Jada stepped in, pulling my hand with her. I tried to get my eyes to focus and get used to that annoying bright light. Everything started to become clear. It was a garden with flowers all over the place. There were birds of all different species flying around with what looked like scrolls in their beaks. The flowers weren't just flowers, they were making images of people. Pictures made up of all different kinds of flowers of all shapes and sizes. It was magical and astounding.

"What is this place?" I inquired in wonderment. Jada smiled. She seemed more alive here. Her skin started to show more color and her all-knowing eyes lit up. Jada stepped in front of me, giggling with excitement. She spun around in a circle, her arms stretched wide looking like a kid. The sun glistened on her skin and she took a deep breath giggling again. She couldn't help herself. I smiled at this amazing creature before me. She looked so happy and so exuberant that I laughed along with her.

"It's called a Seer's Domain; it's where the past and future are seen, collected, shown, and recorded. There are only two of these in the world, one here at DEATH and one in Galrich. There used to be three, but it was destroyed when the Seers were wiped out in the third Djinn and Creator war," Jada stayed in her outstretched position as she answered my question. The way she talked about it sounded as if she was there for the destruction. I would have to ask about that later.

"Why did you bring me here?" There were thousands of questions speeding through my mind.

Jada suddenly lost her smile, "I'm trying to help as best as I can. I can't tell you everything, I am *unable* to tell you everything. As I said before, I want you to understand where you came from and you deserve some answers, no matter what Harrison thinks," Her eyes became glassy as she finished talking. The way she said Harrison's name, I've never heard someone say his name without some form of annoyance, there was only love in her voice. I didn't say anything, but I was starting to like Jada. She was odd, but caring. I would have to ask her about Harrison eventually.

"Follow me," As she continued to walk on. We passed by many pictures of faces I knew, faces I've seen in history books. I even saw one of-what's his face- George Washington? I stopped to look at it. Jada laughed, "Oh yes George, he could've been a Guardian if he wanted to. He turned it down, just like he turned down being king at the end of the American Revolution."

I had no idea what she was talking about. We barely covered human history, maybe once or twice, but I never paid attention in class anyway. We started walking again. Suddenly, my stomach knotted within itself causing an uneasy feeling. I turned and saw a very dark part of the garden; all the flowers were wilted and blackened. Jada saw me looking at them.

"Those are fallen choices," Jada explained, "They're choices people could have taken. A path they could have walked, but chose not to, after a while the flowers start to wither and die." I couldn't keep my eyes off them.

My feet seemed to carry me forward. A voice beckoned me, "Dawn, Dawn!" it yelled in distress. I burst through the blackened bushes. I realized they were roses, black roses. I ran faster as more voices called to me. Coming to an abrupt halt. My mom's picture made up of flowers was above a thick black bush. I reached for a black rose, a gasp escaped my lips as my fingers contracted around it, like an invisible person was forcing them closed. The rose started to change to a deep red as colors swirled before my eyes. I no longer saw the rose. My body was nailed to the ground and something inside of me was yanked back.

***

I saw my mom with two boys on either side of her. They were standing in the rain outside a mansion. I tried to shout her name, but couldn't speak.

"Don't do this, please, for me?" A boy with curly black hair and striking dark golden eyes pleaded. His voice sounded distant and muffled. He squeezed her hand and my mom slowly looked at him.

"I'm so sorry, this is my choice and my only escape," She said mechanically. The boy yanked her arm back, his grip tightened. "Let me go!" she growled at him. He released her reluctantly, dropping his head in defeat. My mom then turned to the boy on her left. He had light caramel hair and green eyes. He gave her a warm smile, but it didn't touch his eyes. He then hugged her and she hugged him back. "They'll be here in two minutes and I won't stop them," the one with the dark golden eyes said. My mom glared at him.

"Go, go!" The guy with the green eyes said and pushed my mom away. She looked at both of them panicking, her eyes welling into tears. They both gave her a sharp nod. She closed her eyes, the boy with the dark golden eyes waved his hand and the rain surrounded her...It was like someone tore the image up in front of my eyes. I could only see colors and I was pulled back.

"Dawn?" Jada appeared through the bushes. She had a worried look on her face. I bolted upright from the darkened grass. I looked down at the rose in my hand. It was back to its mysterious black color. What just happened? I put my hand to my head, it throbbed a little and looked at Jada.

"We'll talk about this later," As she hurried me out of the patch of Fallen Choices. My mom left or she had thought about leaving, maybe she left us instead of disappearing. What was she trying to escape from? What was her "only escape" as she had said to the boy with the weird eyes? I looked around. We were coming up on two very long grey pillars. In the middle of them was a circular brown table with a letter on top.

"Before we start with the future, we must know the past," Jada's voice sent a chill down my spine. "Every memory clings to an object or animal. In your mother's case she wrote a lot or she spent most of her time reading. I am almost certain that a few important things of the past have clung to these letters. It's letters written to me from when we were younger, when I was away becoming a Seer. Well, more like learning how to be a Seer. Seers are always Guardians first. Pick up the papers and we'll start from there," Jada explained further as she leaned against one of the pillars.

I took steps towards the letters, my feet clunking loudly against the ground. I stood in front of the circular table and hesitated, my hand hovering over the letters. My eyes closed when I picked up the letters. The same feeling as picking up the rose raced through my body, ripping me from the present into the past. The bright swirling colors were all I could see before my vision suddenly cleared.

My mother stood before the Elders with the boy with dark golden eyes. They looked around my age. The Elders were wearing long purple robes, they used to wear them before they changed the rules. The Elders sat down one by one. The boy and my mom raised their hands. The symbols of each species appeared. My mom went directly to the Wolf Changer symbol and the boy... things got blurry. I was pushed forward just a little bit.

"Hi, I'm Jackson Cassie," The boy with light caramel hair said to my mom, grinning. "Darcy Russels," She said with a small smile. The scene changed again.

I saw my mom pulling a knife out of a demon, soaked with black blood. She was holding an ornate Guardian knife with a purple jeweled handle. She chucked it toward the wolf that was in the middle of changing back to human; he caught it in midair, stabbing the demon about to be on top of him. He stood up, brushing the dirt off his legs. I recognized him, this was Jackson Cassie.

"Thanks Darcy, that was a close one," He laughed, looking back at the dead demon lying on the ground.

"Yup, close one," Darcy gave a weak laugh, stumbling to her feet.
"Darcy, are you okay?" Jackson asked, concern lacing his voice, as he went over to her.

"Fine," She took a step forward, swaying.

"You're bleeding!" He said in shock, pointing to her right arm.

"He bit me. That son of a gun bit me," As she crumpled to the ground. I wanted to help her, but all I could do was watch.
Ow!

I was pulled back to the present. I blinked and saw Jada's face in front of me. My breathing was fast and hard. My body felt like it had been through rigorous training, like when Harrison doesn't let us leave until we've gotten a move just as easy as breathing.

"How is this even possible if I'm not a Seer?" I asked.

"You have a spark of Seer magic in you, which allows you to see the past if given a guide and an object from the past," Jada answered, her voice always sounded like it held a thousand secrets that I couldn't possibly understand. Before I could tell her how annoying that is, she spoke.

"Now, I can show you a snippet of one of my visions," She continued, placing her hands on either side of my face and closing her eyes.

A swirly purple light spun faster and faster in front of my eyes until it burst into the image in front of me. I saw a blurry Hunter running toward me screaming my name.

I screamed back, but I couldn't make out my own words. Then he was holding on to me, but arms were banded around my waist. The arms contracted tighter as I tried to twist to see who was carrying me. I couldn't get a good look at their face. I took a knife out, a feeling of resignation sweeping through me. "I'm sorry," I whispered to Hunter and cut his hand. He let go rolling away. "Dawn!" he screamed for me.

"Take care of them," I screamed back and then everything went black.

I gasped awake. Tears were streaming down my face.

"Dawn," Jada was shaking me hard. She sounded worried. Somehow I ended up on the grassy ground.

"Urgh," I responded in a whisper. My head was pounding now like someone was constantly hitting my head. The knife handle in the back of Jada's pocket touched my arm and my whole body stiffened, I was wrenched back in time once again.

***

"Stop!" Darcy yelled at a younger Jada who was sitting at the kitchen sink with glass in her hand, her arm held out.

"You can't make me," Jada whispered. She took the glass, slitting her arm. Blood dripped down into the sink. Darcy stepped toward her, but Jada took one look at my mom and she stopped. Jada used her abilities, freezing Darcy to her spot. Darcy struggled, trying to get out of it.

"Why do you keep doing that?" Darcy said, holding back tears, "There are people who care about you, people who need you. Please stop! You're freaking twelve years old!" She was furiously screaming by the end of the sentence.

"I have to stop Seeing, Darcy!" Jada yelled. I was crying as I fell forward through time.

The sound of a monitor came to my ears. Jada was on a hospital bed, it felt similar to when I saw her just a few days ago. However, her hair did not have the black stripes it had today and she was much younger. This was not too long after the scene I had just witnessed. Harrison was in the corner curled up in a ball crying his eyes out. Darcy was leaning over Jada crying too, but not as hard as Harrison. Darcy's tears were dripping off onto Jada's face. Jada's eyes slowly fluttered open and she rasped in a small voice, "Why am I all wet?" Darcy burst into hysterical laughter, relieved her friend was okay.

Harrison launched himself out of his ball, his place of comfort, and fell onto Jada. He cried, hyperventilating. Jada, in pain from Harrison's weight, winced, "I'm okay, I'm okay." She hugged him.

"Don't- don't ever-ever d-d-do that t-to me a-a-a-again," Harrison said, still hyperventilating. Jada slowly wrapped her arms around him. "I'm sorry," she said. Harrison kept crying. Jada's arms had scars all the way up. She looked between my mom and Harrison. Darcy pried Harrison off Jada. Harrison tried to collect himself. Darcy smiled at her and she smiled back.

***

Snapping back to the present. I felt different emotions as I looked at Jada. This was too much. I needed to get out of here. Jada kept trying to talk to me as I left the Seer's Domain. My ears were ringing, so even if I wanted to I couldn't hear anything she was saying. There is only one person I can talk to about this.

Chapter 8

Connected

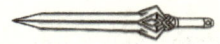

"I'm sooo confused," I said to Luke who was lying on my bed reading a book. I was throwing my Guardian knife up and down, for the last thirty minutes I told him everything about Jada. He came back today and so far has been no help to me. He seems so distant. He was in my room as soon as I returned from the Seer Domain. He said he got worried after he felt everything I had gone through and Flashed back to DEATH.

I immediately wanted to question him on everything he has been doing while he was gone, but he pulled me into a hug instead. I lost all the anger I was holding in and ended up hugging him back. Jada had tried to talk to me about what I saw, but I ran. I couldn't take it anymore. Luke was afraid of what I was able to do. He was also suspicious of Jada which was weird. I liked her. She obviously didn't mean to show me everything I saw. Luke can usually sort out my problems, but all he's done is read that stupid book. "Luke, I think I might jump off a cliff tomorrow. Does that sound good?" I crossed my arms.

Luke nodded, "Yup, maybe later."

I clenched my teeth. He was asking for this. I threw my knife, it skimmed his hair, finding its mark in the bed above his head. He looked up at the knife, not noticing it grazed his hair. I started to laugh. The spike on top of his head was no longer there and a patch of hair was gone. "That was funny." He said sarcastically. "You could've killed me!" He growled as he yanked the knife out.

I tried to scowl at him, but his hair...I cracked up and I couldn't stand it anymore, I fell on the floor laughing until my stomach hurt.

"What?!" Luke shouted as he started to laugh too. "What- are- you – laughing about?" He said between chuckles.

"Go- Go," I tried to say but couldn't stop laughing. I took a deep breath. "Go check your hair," I managed to get out and pointed to the bathroom. He went into the bathroom very confused. I started to laugh again in anticipation of what he was about to see. I counted in my head.

5..

4..

3..

2..

1..

"OH MY GOD MY HAIR!" Luke screamed in a shocked girlie voice. I launched myself onto the bed. I was in hysterics looking at Luke as he came out of the bathroom, his face red. I was laughing to the point I was in tears. After him cussing and screaming at me until his face was blue, he sat down on the bed.

"Do you even know what I was reading about?" He asked.

"Here we go," Rolling my eyes.

"I was reading about a Bound," He said, like I would know what that was. I knew he was going to continue so I didn't respond. "Bounding was created when Guardians wanted to be able to communicate better. It was very rare and only some Guardians were born with it. It was a great tool, but it died out because Sway demons started to hunt people with the Bound. It made Guardians stronger and harder to kill when they were together. The Sway demons would feed off the Bound's power and keep the Guardians as slaves. The Bound allowed the Guardians to read each other's minds, their symbols would change at exactly the same time too," Luke raised his eyebrows seeing if that got my attention, which it did.

"Sameness," I whispered. Did Elder Talahan know about Bounds? This must be why he wants us at Galrich. We could be of great use to him. Could Harrison know about this?.

"Exactly, it was like two people were one person," He said as he stood up starting to pace.

"So you think we have this Bound and that's why we are so valuable to the Elders?" I asked, even though I knew the answer. Luke and I are completely different people. Sure, we could talk in each other's minds and we've been attached at the hip, but being one person? That is just crazy.

"Yes, definitely, it's the only explanation to why the Elders want to take us to Galrich," He responded.

They probably want to do a test on us, lock us up for safe keeping, then use us as their own personal soldiers. I obviously wasn't going to let that happen. The Elders need to be taken down a peg anyway.

"Why would the Elders want us? I mean aren't there others out there with Bounds?" I asked as he handed me the book. I flipped through it. The words were making my head spin.

"No, according to that book there are no more Bounds left in the entire world. The Elders even banned receiving any Bounds. The Elders realized they made a mistake, that those were the Guardians that were the strongest. It doesn't explain how you receive a Bound," Luke explained. He was in deep thought, I could feel how hard he was thinking. This could be a huge problem for us, especially if there's nothing Harrison could do about it. Not that he would do anything in the first place. I'd have to get us out of this mess. I kept looking through the book, searching for answers to our questions.

"Do you think they want us badly enough that they'll go as far as using force or decreeing a law to get us to Galrich?" I inquired. As I flipped through the book, I saw a picture of the Bound symbol. The Guardians with the Bound are supposed to have it on the opposite arm of their Guardian symbol.

"I wouldn't be surprised if they did," Luke laughed, plopping down onto my bed. I didn't even hear what he had said next, I was too focused reading about the Bound symbol. It was very eye-catching. As I looked closer at the illustration, it looked like it was pulsating before my eyes. My heart skipped a beat.

"I wouldn't jump to conclusions," I interrupted whatever Luke was saying, tossed him the book to look at the Bound symbol. "It says that if you have a Bound, then you will have that symbol on the right arm. One person has half the swirl and the other person has the other half. When put together, it looks like a heart," I pointed to the picture, stupidly blushing.

"So..." Luke waved his hand, telling me to go on.

"We don't have a Bound because we don't have that symbol," I pointed to the symbol again. I thought it was obvious. Luke nodded then started to read what I already read about the symbol. He murmured the words and nodded again. Luke gave me the book and started to pace. He had his thinking expression on again, his face was scrunched like he was forcing his thoughts to make sense and he bit his bottom lip to the point where I could see his front teeth stick out. Why did he care about this so much?

"*It's not that I care. It's just interesting,*" Luke said in my mind, defending himself.

"That was not a rhetorical question," I scolded him. Luke barely paid any attention to what I said. After a few minutes, he snapped his fingers.

"What if someone forcefully hid our symbol to protect us? It's a theory, yes, it would make sense. I bet Harrison would know about our Bound, if we had one. The question is why would someone hide this from us? Well, the Elders of course, but someone or something else other than the Elders might be a threat. Huh, I'll have to give it more thought," Luke said, talking to no one but himself. I was done with this conversation. Luke was going off of very little facts and more of what he wanted to hear.

"C'mon let's fix your hair," I gave a laugh.

"Oh, no you're not touching my baby!" Shielding his hair with his hands.

"Don't act like a baby, if you want your hair to look ugly that's your problem," I turned to walk out.

"Alright, but do not cut me or I swear you will regret it for the rest of your existence," He lightly threatened. I pulled scissors out of a drawer. Slowly, I turned around opening and closing the scissors. Luke put his hands up, eyes widening and took a step back. I stalked over with the scissors in hand.

"I would never!" His blond hair fell to the floor after each snip I made to his hair. I watched in the mirror after every snip his eyes clenched tighter shut. He was thinking about five things at once; Bounding, what his last name was, homework, The Elders, and how I would not mess things up. Good luck with the last one Luke. The thought that worried me most was he wanted us to have a Bound, more than he wanted to know who his parents were.

Chapter 9

Frank Summers and Time

I walked out of the room with a bag of hair and a grin on my face. Skipping down the hall, not bothering to Flash passing Harrison's office.

"Dawn," Harrison's familiar voice called to me. I shut my eyes and cursed maybe I should've Flashed. "Can you come in here?" He phrased it as a question, but it was totally an order. I sighed and walked back. He probably wanted to talk about me breaking his rules or my visit with Jada. I wouldn't be surprised if she told him. I shoved the door open.

"Wha-, "I started to say but then I realized he wasn't alone. Someone was sitting in front of his desk.

"Hey," a boy looked up at me with dark brown eyes and a mischievous grin.

"Dawn, this is um-Frank-um," Harrison was trying to remember his last name.

"Summers," the boy finished Harrison's sentence.

"Oh, that's right. I am terribly sorry, I'm not very good with names," He smiled but it did not touch his eyes. Harrison was a different person than what I saw in the vision. He had no feelings anymore. I know that's mean, but I'm sure about that. I looked back at the boy and he smiled back. Frank Summers had a toothpick in his mouth and a black leather jacket on. His eyes were oval shaped and his hair was swooped to the right. He smiled back halfheartedly.

"You are to show him around," Harrison instructed me. I almost scoffed at Harrison's tone, but I looked at Frank. He looked uncomfortable with the tension between Harrison and I. I felt bad for him and I wouldn't mind showing him around. It wouldn't take long. Seeing the future, possible Bound, and Elders problems could wait.

"Fine," I snapped and pushed Frank out of the room. I slammed the door and started to walk with Frank by my side. Luke came down the hall with a bag of chips in his hand stuffing handfuls in his mouth, then he saw Frank and did a double take.

"Frank!" He said in a surprised voice, "Is that *the* Frank Summers standing before my eyes?" He asked. How does Luke know this guy? I started searching his mind for the answer. He was blocking me. Again. I crossed my arms and resisted the urge to punch him in the face.

"Hey buddy what's up?" They clapped hands and did the guy hug. I gave Luke an annoyed look while he averted my eyes.

"Nothing much where you've been?" Luke said and slapped him on the back.

"Oh you know, here and there," Frank shrugged. This guy gave off handsome without even trying vibes.

"I see you took me up on my advice of coming here," Luke said and gestured all around him. Wait, his advice? Why didn't Luke tell me about him? What other secrets was he keeping from me? The glare on my face had Luke avoiding my gaze.

Frank laughed and rubbed Luke's head, "Dude what happened to your hair?"

I looked at my beautiful hairstyle techniques again. His hair didn't look as good as it used to. It was very short now you could only see blond fuzz. His hair didn't need to be brushed now, Luke should thank me for that.

Luke laughed along with Frank. "Someone decided I needed a haircut," he said, finally looking at me. He indicated to Frank that the incident was my fault. Frank turned to me and I held up the bag of hair in my hands and shook it.

"Oh I'm sorry Dawn. This is Frank," Luke said matter of factly. I rolled my eyes. He was trying to annoy me now.

"Really, I had no idea," I said sarcastically.

"She was going to show me around," Frank said.

"That's okay. I can do that for you," Luke said, like I couldn't handle it.

"No, I can," I retorted. Then we glared at each other. Then we started to laugh. I was still mad at him, but it wouldn't last for long. I also couldn't keep a straight face with his hair.

"That's fine, I don't want to get in the way of your bromance," I said. Luke rolled his eyes.

"Are you two like a thing or something yet?" Frank asked, indicating with his finger what he meant connecting us like puzzle pieces.

"What?" I asked and blushed. He wasn't serious. Frank had to be joking. Luke is like my brother. He is my brother.

"You know, like dating," Frank explained, grinning. Luke stayed silent. Why wasn't he denying this?

"No!" I said, horrified.

"Well this guy right here has been in love with you for-," Frank was cut off by Luke. Luke smacked him in the back of the head and grabbed the collar of his jacket. Then he dragged him away. "I'm just saying you should give it a thought, he loves you!" Frank yelled as he was being hauled away. I just stood there shocked, my mouth wide open.

"Don't worry Dawn, he's just Franking around with you," Luke said and slapped Frank again and started to drag him by his arm. Frank started to go into another tangent. Then he was silenced by Luke. Frank made a heart with his hands and pointed to me mouthing loves you. Then they were around the corner. I took a step towards them, but then thought better of it. I'd let them sort this out. I had more important things to worry about.

"Ouch," I heard a voice say. Frank I'm guessing. I didn't know what to do. It's probably best for them to work this out. I started to walk away, spotting a trash can, and threw away Luke's bag of hair.

"What the heck man!" Luke yelled at him. I started down the empty hallway, my mouth wide open. My first impression of Frank Summers is that he is going to cause some trouble around here. That made me smile a little bit.

***

I sat in my room thinking a lot about Bounds. Was it possible that Luke and I had a Bound? What did that mean? I wasn't sure what to make of this possible discovery. I could ask Harrison. I laughed to myself, that wasn't going to be helpful, he would just lie. This would explain why Luke and I have an extreme connection to each other. Luke was a constant presence in my brain. Although I have some tactics to keep him out, they don't work for long. Tactics that he has also been frequently using, which irritated me. This wasn't the only thing I had on my mind either. I was worrying about the concept of time. Jada had made me question a lot of things. She said I had Seer magic in me. Did my mom have this ability or was it my father? The questions that were gnawing at my very soul were endless. I hopped off my bed and headed straight for Jada's room.

I'm not sure what more answers she could give me, but I was losing my mind. When I was in front of her door, I waited outside hesitating to knock. Jada was an interesting person that was the absolute wisest person I've ever met, probably more than I will ever meet. If all she could create was mystery, was I coming to the right person? I sighed and stepped back from the door.

"You may enter, Dawn," Jada's voice came from inside her room. She knew I was here. That's creepy. Going into her room, Jada was sitting on her floor surrounded by candles. It looked like she was performing some kind of ritual, it didn't look to be going well. She sat with her legs crossed leaning forward while rubbing her temples. Jada also appeared to be hovering just a few inches off the ground. I shifted uncomfortably. She knew I was there, but seemed to be ignoring my presence.

"Ahem," I grunted trying to get her attention. She continued to rub her temples, her red and black streaked hair falling over her face. Jada must have been in some sort of vision before I stood outside of her door contemplating if I was even going in. Finally, after some time she looked up at me. Then slowly lowered her body back to the ground.

"Are you ready to explain what you saw and why you ran out on me, Dawn?" Jada asked, arching a perfectly shaped red eyebrow. She looked healthier and more stable. The crazed and sad look in her eyes had all but vanished. I didn't want to talk about that which I had a feeling she already knew. I didn't know where to start. Jada motioned for me to sit. I sat and crossed my legs like how she was sitting.

"Suppressing your feelings is never the answer, trust me. I was the queen of it," She said, putting a hand on my knee. I moved it away. It's not like I didn't want to accept her touch. I was afraid of being sent to the future. Jada looked a little hurt by my resistance, but she recovered quickly.

"You know I usually find tea calms me. Would you like some?" She asked, reaching for a pot of it on a little table next to her. I didn't answer. She poured me a small cup and instead of handing it to me she put it in front of my crossed legs. I was grateful because I was still uncomfortable touching her. I took it in my hands and took a sip. It burnt my tongue, but tasted sweet. Jada smiled at me waiting patiently for me to say what was on my mind.

"You knew my mother well?" I asked, my voice cracked as I said mother. Jada's smile faded a little, as I mentioned her.

"She was my best friend. We lost touch after I went to train to be a Seer. I was very lost and in emotional turmoil back then. Darcy helped me through it," She said, her voice staying neutral. I remembered the vision I saw of Jada. I felt bad for making her talk about it. I decided to move on.

"You also know Harrison," I said just stating a fact, not asking because I already knew the answer. Jada's mouth twitched at the corner and her eyes looked at me as if she was seeing something from a distance.

"Ah yes, Harry and I's past is quite...complicated. We dated for a while. There was talk of marriage before your mother went missing. She was going to be my maid of honor. I liked human traditions. My father was fully human. Anyway...Harry...well... we grew apart after we failed to bring her and the others back. I moved to Galrich to teach more Seers, leaving him here," She said, reminiscing and struggling with what exactly to tell me. I held onto my tea and felt the heat on my hands trying to comprehend what Harrison was like back then. Jada and him were in love. I wonder if they'll ever be again.

"Why did you come back?" I asked her, looking deep into her purple eyes. She pursed her lips like she wanted to choose her next words very carefully.

"I came back because I thought I might have found a key to finding the four missing Guardians, but it ended up being another dead end," She said looking frustrated. I couldn't tell if she was telling the truth. She had given me what she thought was the key when she first got here. It was still sitting on my dresser in my room. I believed she told all of the truth she could about why she came back. I needed to ask her a question that was more pressing.

"Did my mother have a Bound with my father?" I asked. Jada looked taken aback by my question. She even looked a little bit shocked. I didn't think she was capable of not knowing something.

"Now, why are you asking about Bounds?" She asked me, her voice a little too high. There was the adult interaction I was used to. Harrison and her were hiding stuff from me, maybe Luke's theory about hiding our Bound was right. I didn't know if telling her about what Luke had discovered was a good idea or or not. I decided it couldn't do any harm. Jada wouldn't tell me anything she didn't want to.

"Luke thinks we have one. It's just magic he came across while reading. I wanted to know if it's genetic?" I said trying to sense if Jada knew anything.

"Bounds are tricky business. They used to be given to Guardians in arranged marriages. As for your first question, I do not know if your mother and father were Bounded. They were rare even back then because of how the Bounded were mistreated in the past. I will say that Luke's theory has some merit to it. That being said your parents would have had to perform the Bound themselves when you two were no more than babies. I'm not saying it's impossible, but with both of your situations it would be very unlikely," Jada said deep in thought. She really didn't know anymore than I did about this, or she was lying. It made me a little disappointed. Not that I wanted this Bound, but I would love an explanation as to why Luke and I have the connection we do. Jada seems to know about everything, but I guess her powers are limited.

"I'm sorry I couldn't be of more help, but you know you can tell me anything, right?" Jada said looking like she wanted to reach out to me again. I looked at her and suddenly felt like I needed to spill everything I was feeling to her. She had that weird effect on me.

"I feel like Luke is pulling away from me and I don't know how to get him back. There was a time when we never fought and never kept things from each other, now he has all these secrets. I sent him away to keep him safe and he keeps shutting me out!" I explained to Jada in a panicked voice. Jada nodded because of course she already knew.

She smiled and gave a little chuckle. I glared. This wasn't funny. "Oh no, I'm sorry. You misunderstand me. It's just, well, you remind me so much of your mother." Jada's smile grew bigger. I smiled too, but also felt very sad. That was the first time anyone has told me that. Harrison rarely talked about her and no one else I know knew her.

"She had the same passion, bravery, and dedication to her friends as you do. As I told her on her wedding day, if he's your best friend he'll come back. He won't have a choice. Just be patient and hold on for the right moment, it's coming," Jada said, giving me a little wink and added, "Sixteen year old boys never know what's good for them." She was saying Luke would explain everything in the future and my mom had also struggled with this. I sighed, feeling a little bit better.

She cleared her throat. "I believe there was another thing you wanted to talk to me about," She said. I looked at her and gave a big sigh. I guess she could help me understand what I saw in the visions and why I was able to do it. I explained everything that happened in as much detail as I could. I was surprised that her facial expressions became more worried as I continued. I hope I wasn't saying the wrong thing. I started with what I saw with the Fallen Choices rose, then moved on to what she showed me in the letters, then I told her how I saw a future vision with my protecti in it, and then I explained how when her knife touched me I was pulled back in time and saw her past. Jada listened intently, my worry increasing with every word I spoke.

"...And that was it. I was just so disoriented and scared of what had happened I had to get out of there. I'm sorry for running," I said as I saw her eyes darken. She acted like she didn't hear me. She stood up from her seated position urgently and I followed her.

"What? What's wrong?" I asked, but she didn't move, she just stared at me intensely.

"I can't believe it," She whispered.

"Can't believe what?" I asked, trying to get her attention. After a few moments of complete silence, Jada snapped out of it. It was like she returned to the room.

"You weren't supposed to see what you saw, Dawn. I thought I was controlling you to see completely different aspects of your mother's life. I had no idea that you were even capable of seeing what you did. You even saw Jackson Cassie, and I made him a secret to everyone in the Guardian community. I did everything he told me to do. I even erased his location from my own mind," She said, while clenching her fists. Jada was keeping Jackson a secret, but why? He never actually went missing. I knew she was keeping secrets. I can't believe I told her all this. I stood there not knowing what I was supposed to do now. I was paralyzed. Jackson Cassie was alive. The one who had the most information about my mother.

"Dawn, you might just be one of the most special people I know. I'm sorry for losing my cool-I just couldn't believe it," She said when she finally calmed down. I didn't know what to feel. I was surprisingly not angry with Jada. She gave me answers when I asked for them and she just revealed to me information she didn't have to say anything about. She could've kicked me out the moment I told her what I saw, but she didn't.

"Dawn, there are many things you have to try to understand. I am under oath to not reveal certain information. I can't tell you everything, but I promised to tell you as much as I could. Unfortunately, this is where I have to stop," She said, looking at me with those deep mysterious eyes. I nodded my head and looked at the floor. I figured as much. I was glad I got to get some information out of her though. She was very helpful. It just wasn't enough. I needed more. I could tell she wanted to approach me and give me a hug. I walked over to her, closing the space in between us and wrapped my arms around her waist. She was shocked at first, but slowly wrapped her arms around me. She too was afraid to trigger a vision. We hugged for a long time and had more tea until I finally said goodbye. Jada said she had to talk to Harrison about this as I was leaving and I immediately shut her down. She raised her hands up in defense.

"Dawn, he deserves more credit than you give him. He has done a fine job taking care of you," She said, patting the top of my head and I swiped it away. I trusted Jada and I knew Harrison had to be informed, but it didn't mean I liked it any more.

"Okay, how about this? I tell you embarrassing stories of Harrison every time he is stubbornly mean and you let me help him keep you safe," She smiled at me. I laughed. I liked the sound of that.

"You got a deal," I said and gave her another hug.

Chapter 10

Pranks and Frank

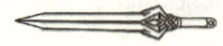

I was heading back to my room from Jada's when I heard a voice from behind me.

"Hey Dawn," someone called me. I turned around and it was Frank running toward me.

"Hi," I said and kept walking. He caught up to me, "I'm sorry about before," he leaned down to my level and continued in a whisper, "I mean I'm not, but Luke is watching so can you say something like I forgive you or it's okay please?"

I felt bad for the guy. A mad Luke is not a pretty sight. "Don't worry about it. I forgive you," I smiled.

Frank let out a sigh of relief. "Thank you, can we start over?" He stuck out his hand, "I am Frank Louis Summers."

I took his hand and shook it. "Dawn Shadows."

He smiled and said, "So do you want to show me around or should I go back to mister can't take a joke!" Frank said loudly so Luke could hear him.

"I heard that!" Luke yelled back.

"That's the point," Frank muttered softly so only I could hear.

"Luke didn't want to do it anymore?" I asked him.

"Oh no, he's sick of me already," He chuckled, "If you're still up for it, I would love a tour." Frank shoved his hands in his pockets giving me puppy dog eyes. He didn't know I was immune to that look.

I laughed and rolled my eyes, "Yeah come on," I took him to the weapons room first where he bumped into a lot of things and almost got himself impaled on a spear. I quickly rushed him out of there before he killed himself. Next, I took him to the lunch room.

"I never really had an actual place to eat before, I basically ate in our camp and with the other Guardians, but that was always outside. Sometimes we didn't have any food and were always in hiding because of the demons," Frank said.

"You're joking," I laughed. He stayed silent, eyes straight ahead. "Wait, you're serious?" I asked.

Frank nodded and looked to the floor. "Oh," I tried to get a better look at him. I was so insensitive. I decided to apologize, but his face brightened and he continued walking.

"Yeah," He laughed, "Just forget I said anything." He walked in front of me. I figured it was best not to push it. I didn't want him to think I was being nosy like Hunter did. I took him to the library next.

"I never liked reading much," Frank commented looking around. "You guys seriously have a restricted library? Harry Potter around here much?"

It took me a minute to understand the reference. I then remembered a piece from Human Literature class with Harrison. He told us about a life changing novel. I would never admit it, but I read them all.

"Yeah, I actually think that's where Harrison got the idea from, but it's a huge library not a section. It would be awesome if Harry Potter's world actually existed. A wizard would be way more interesting than a Guardian," I said.

"I actually like being a Guardian. I think it's plenty interesting," Frank said and tapped the door to the restricted library.

"It's not quite restricted as you might think, it's easily broken into," I said with a laugh, ignoring what he just said.

"Ooooooohhhhhhhh, can you show me?" Frank asked, jumping up and down. He realized what he was doing and quickly recovered.

"Sure, but we have to break into Harrison's office," I said and raised my eyebrows challenging him.

A mischievous smile spread across his face, "Even better."

***

I picked the lock and went right in. I could've used my abilities, but Harrison has defenses put in place for that. He doesn't think of a simple bobby pin. Frank skidded in behind me.

"See those keys, the one with the crimson piece attached to it is the one we need," I pointed to the key I have used so many times now. I reached up and yanked it off its hook. "Got it," I announced.

"That earns you a chip," Frank said and gave me a high five.

"Huh?" I said bewildered.

"Oh sorry, I forgot you wouldn't know. Chips are a game some of the younger Pa-I mean-Guardians a few years back made up. It's a game that's almost like truth or dare, but every time you do something against the rules or a prank, you earn a chip. A chip is like money where I'm from. The person with the most chips gets a prize like extra food, a pillow or even a house to stay in for a little while. We take this very seriously," He explained.

I stared at him in shock. He glanced at me and noticed my shock and bowed his head. I quickly got it together. "I bet I could get more chips than you in a day," I shoved him.

"Oh, you're on!" Frank shoved me right back. "Wait, but first I have to tell you because it's the one rule if a prank doesn't go to plan you lose all your chips and no "powers"," He said with a sly smile using his fingers as quotation marks.

"You think I'll fail without my powers?" I asked, mimicking his voice.

"Nope," He laughed and raised his hands up, backing off.

"Alright let's go," I walked on.

"Who's first?" He asked, rubbing his hands together.

"Hailey," I answered and walked to the H.O.G.S classroom. Hailey sat in her assigned chair 30 minutes early. This is an everyday thing.

"Hey," I said and sat down next to her.

"Hi?" She said, confused.

"Harrison's looking for you," I said.

She didn't even say anything, she just got up and left. Frank watched as she swiftly walked out. I went and searched through Hailey's desk and found what I was looking for; last night's homework. I took my crumpled piece of paper out of my pocket.

"What's that?" Frank asked.

"My homework," I answered. I wrote Hailey Green in her exact penmanship. Then on her paper I wrote Dawn Shadows in my messy handwriting. Finally, I straightened out the paper as best as I could and put it back on her desk.

Frank laughed, "This is not going to work. How do you know Harrison won't notice?"

I laughed and rolled my eyes. I pointed to the desk on the right of Hailey's, "That's your desk," I said. Then I pointed to the desk left of Hailey's, "This is mine," sitting down just as Harrison walked in with Hailey. She sat down and crossed her arms. She threw me a look that meant that was not funny. I kept myself from laughing. A few other students walked in giving Frank weird looks as they passed him.

"Turn in your assignments please," Harrison said and sat down at his desk. "Make sure your name is clearly written since it was a fill in the bubble paper," Harrison started to say just as Luke ran in. Luke took his seat embarrassed. I was surprised. Luke is never late. Harrison cleared his throat, "As I was saying then, work on page ninety-five in your work books and then read page one hundred and answer questions one through seven."

Everyone handed in their homework. I sat down and grinned at Frank. He gave me a look that said you're not done yet. I opened up my workbook and started to work. Then something hit my face. I looked up with careful precision. Frank threw another piece of crumpled paper at me. So that's how it's going to be, well two can play at this game. I took my eraser and chucked it at his head. It hit him straight in the middle of his forehead. He was caught off guard and shouted "Ouch!" I giggled and put my head down as Harrison spoke, raising an eyebrow, "Is there a problem Mr. Summers?"

"No, Sir," Frank answered and strangled a laugh. Harrison went back to work. As soon as Harrison's eyes were not on Frank, I picked up a crumpled piece of paper and sent it flying through the air with nothing but a look. He threw it back. We continued like this for two minutes.

"Stop," Hailey whispered to me. I stuck my tongue out at her like a two year old.

"Idiot," she whispered. She looked at Frank who was making weird faces at her.

"Correction idiots," Hailey said and raised her hand.

"Yes, Miss Green," Harrison called on her.

"Can I please move? I am very distracted," She pleaded. Then Frank's hand shot up.

"Mr. Summers, is there a piece of knowledge you'd want to share?" Harrison asked, turning his attention away from Hailey's question.

"I'd be happy to move," He said then quieted his voice so only Harrison couldn't hear, "If Miss Green is distracted by my beautiful face," Frank said. The class erupted in laughter.

"Shut up Frank!" Hailey shot up out of her seat.

"Chill, Hay," I said. She took a step towards me, her eyes were like daggers piercing me.

"Hailey I would be very careful since you failed last night's homework assignment and distracted my class! You are dismissed! Now!" Harrison yelled at Hailey. Hailey was in shock. She looked as if she might say something, but then saw Harrison's expression and stalked out of the room in a daze. I stared in shock. Hailey Elizabeth Green, Miss Goody Two Shoes, just walked out of class without a fight! I didn't know that was even possible. Frank smiled to himself then turned to me and gave me a thumbs up. I giggled quietly.

Luke's voice came into my head asking a question like always, *"What was that about?"* He shifted his eyes from me to Frank then back at me. Did I detect jealousy?

As usual I ignored him and stared at my workbook. I read the question: How many years was the Dijin and Creator War? How many years after were Guardians created?

Created? *"Yes, created if you paid more attention you would know the answer,"* Luke said annoyed. I did pay attention most of the time. I knew about the thirteen realms. The first realm is Galrich, the Guardian capitol and where our government is located, the humans call it the Eiffel Tower or something. The second is the Divine realm; the entrance is located at the Vatican. This is where most of the Gelicals live. It's also supposed to be the gateway to Heaven. The third realm is called Electi. The most powerful Guardians and the stuck up rich live there. The entrance is located somewhere in Washington D. C. I don't know enough about the human government to give its exact location. I'm sure Luke would know, but I'd never ask him. There are a few human representatives who know everything about the Guardians in Electi or so Harrison says.

The fourth realm is called Interium. This is where most middle class supernatural creatures are located. It's located at someplace called the Empire State Building. The fifth realm, Domum, is where I live and where the best Guardian school is located.

Galrich, Electi, and Interium residents send their children to DEATH because their schools for lack of a better word...suck. I don't know. I may be a little biased. We're located in what the humans call the French Quarter in New Orleans. There are a lot more humans that are aware of the Guardian presence here, but they'd never admit to knowing. I also have never left our realm to meet any of them. I will someday...hopef ully. The sixth realm is called Iaiunus. This is where a lot of "lower" creatures live. The Deceased, the aquatic shape shifters, large sea monsters, and peaceful Djinn live here. It's located at the Bermuda Triangle and surprisingly easy to get into. Humans end up there accidentally all the time. The seventh and eighth realms are called Carcereums also known as the Castaways. This is where the Guardian prisons are located. It has two interconnecting realms. One entrance is located in Antarctica and the other is located in Australia. There are only certain Guardians who know the exact locations. The ninth realm is known as Serepeo. I am not allowed to know what is located here. Harrison said only a few select members of the Guardian community know and they all work for the Elders. It's a place for the most ancient demons the Guardians haven't been able to kill. It's located at a human place called Area 51 or something. The tenth realm is called Astuto. This is where the smartest Guardians work to create new technology and magical advancements for society. Its entrance is located at a human college called Stanford. The eleventh realm is called Umbra. This is where you would find what you call ghosts and what Guardians call Whisks. It's essentially what humans understand as Purgatory. This is located at a place called Stonehenge in England. The twelfth realm is called Somniabut, but mostly known as Terra. It encompasses what we know today as Earth and where all humans live. It is the largest realm and has no permanent entrance. You can pretty much get there through any of the Thirteen realms. The thirteenth realm, Arcanum, is by far a place apparently no one wants to visit which means I want to go even more. It is said to be the entrance into Hell. There has never been a Guardian alive to travel there and make it back. I also know that Flashing is the best way to travel realm to realm, but there are a few portals scattered across the globe. There are a few ways, but most Guardians have the gift of Flashing. They can teleport themselves to places as long as they can envision it in their mind.

Then before I could tell Luke all this a piece of paper flew through the air and floated on to my desk, breaking my train of thought. I looked at Frank motioning with his hands for me to open it. I did, it said in handwriting I could barely read:

Dawn should team up with the guy to her right and take over the school.

I laughed, he was weird and sometimes stupid. I could hear Luke's disapproving thoughts in my head which I ignored. I wrote back in my neat handwriting:

Very funny. Maybe. What makes him think he can handle my awesomeness?

He was without question going to burn DEATH to the ground.

***

"Class dismissed," Harrison said.

Everyone slowly walked to the Training Room. I ran past them to catch up with Frank. Luke watched me go. I could feel his stare, as I caught up with Frank. I punched his arm, "You made Hailey walk out of class!"

"Yes, but you telling her to chill out was the last straw," He said with a laugh. I laughed.

"So who's next?"

"Hmm, Daniel has a fear of spiders," I said with a sly smile.

"I know where to get some," Frank said, as he Flashed out of sight.

***

The rest of the day was filled with mischief as expected. Frank put a spider on Daniel's head which made him scream like a baby and do a weird hoppy dance all around DEATH screaming, "They've found me. They're going to eat me!" I laughed so hard. I know I'm mean, but that's just me. He scared Ile Renrut, this really tough guy who's about two and a half years older than me, by making howling noises after shutting off the lights in the library. Ile actually screamed. He also made Mira Swodah, a girl who just graduated from DEATH and was here visiting, think that there had been an explosion in Harrison's office and she had to go to him. She ended up setting fireworks off in the office.

I managed to give Lila a cool down without freezing her. I dumped ice and water on her. I gotta admit I feel a little bad about that one because Lila had trouble making any sort of fire the whole rest of the day after that, not even a spark. This was an accident, but Frank doesn't need to know that. I also made Derhat Cacklemouth (yes, that is his real name) throw up by leaving some spoiled milk on the cafeteria counter, which he drank. Then I stole Luke's precious history book which he's been trying to find all day since class. I also stole the chips he was eating, now Frank and I are sitting on a high window sill in the Training Room eating them, celebrating our day of mischief.

"Are you ready to accept your defeat?" I asked Frank.

"I have to say it was a tie," Frank said, shoving more chips in his mouth. I nodded agreeing. To be honest he won, but I will never accept defeat. Then Frank blurted out, "What'd you fear the most?"

Confused, I answered, "I don't know what's yours?"

"You're gonna laugh, it's the dark. I'm not sure it's the dark itself just what could come out of it," Frank explained.

"I'm shocked, the big bad Frank Summers, afraid of the dark like Ile," I never promised not to laugh so I let out a little giggle.

After a moment of silence, I answered his question in a whisper, "I'm afraid of the future," I said and looked down.

"That's deep," Frank said and laughed. He knew I was serious, but he had to lighten up the mood.

"Yeah I suppose it is," I responded, thinking about what Jada had told me earlier.

We talked about our favorite games, memories, colors, and the not so awesome stuff like how he was abandoned by his family because he was a Guardian and they were humans. I told him about my situation. We talked for what felt like hours. Harrison came bursting in. He hustled straight to us looking mad; he didn't even look at us when he said, "You two, my office now."

We jumped down and slowly followed Harrison to his main office. Once we were in and the door was closed Harrison unleashed his anger yelling, "Irresponsible" and "Childish". After a few minutes I tuned him out and just stared at his red face. I closed my eyes, imagining Harrison actually smiling. I don't remember a time that he had a true genuine smile on his face. I opened my eyes.

"Dawn, I don't know what to do with you and Frank. If this continues like this, your days at DEATH will be very short, you understand?" He said, looking at Frank.

"Sorry sir," Frank muttered and nodded weakly. Harrison sat down then gave a huge sigh while waving us out.

We stared at the door as I started to giggle. Frank however remained silent. We walked around in silence after that. Passing by the library Frank came to an abrupt stop then called me over. Luke was sitting in the library staring off into space, a book laying under his arms. In his head he was conducting a plan to ask out Jordan. "Oh, he has a crush on someone," Frank said with a laugh.

"Yeah, I know," I said. Luke knows how to hide things I want to know, anything I'd rather not, then he's an open book. Apparently Frank also knew things I didn't know about my best friend since birth. I wonder how they became friends since we are on strict rules to always stay inside. I picked at Luke's brain looking for the exact memory of meeting Frank; his mind was sorted into what looked like files, whereas mine was scattered and unruly. All he had on his mind was Jordan. I groaned internally and kept looking. I've been trying to not think about him keeping the location of her father a secret from me. It only worsens the irrational jealousy this girl I've never met gives me. I finally find the memory. I'm happy he wasn't trying to block me. I wasn't even sure he was paying enough attention to even feel me snooping around.

***

The memory was a little fuzzy. Luke was running away from something, his clothes were ripped and torn. He ran fast and changed into wolf form uncontrollably. Luke looked young, about 6 or 7. He tripped and fell forwards. He tried to get up, but his leg got caught on something that he couldn't see and he was in pain. He pulled and yanked at it and it wouldn't come out.

"We got him, boys!" Someone screamed who wasn't in sight. Luke panicked and started to pull even harder. Then a shorter Frank with younger features came out of nowhere and without a word helped Luke with his leg. They both started to run, Luke with a little bit of a limp.

"Where'd he go? How could you lose him?! We had him trapped!" The same voice that earlier thought he had him, bellowed in rage.

Luke and Frank kept running and finally came to a stop in front of DEATH, both breathing heavy.

"Thanks," Luke said out of breath.

"No problem," Frank mumbled, "I'm Frank Summers by the way."

"Luke, just Luke," He whimpered as he stepped forward, putting weight on his leg.

"Well, just Luke, what were you doing running away from here?" Frank inquired and crossed his arms. The way Frank looked at the place made even me excited.

"I- I don't know. I thought I could handle it-them-and I don't know if I belong here," Luke mumbled and gestured to DEATH.

Frank snickered, "All you pampered Guardians think you've got it so hard, but you're wrong. At least you don't have to sleep with a weapon beside you waiting to be killed or captured!" Frank's voice grew angrier as he spoke, shouting in Luke's face.

"Is it really that bad for you?" Luke's voice rasped.

"Worse," Frank said quietly. There was a moment of silence exchanged between them. Luke was still out of breath, but Frank seemed recovered.

Luke finally coughed, "I didn't know, I'm sorry."

"I would give anything to be at DEATH," Frank rubbed the back of his head. "How about I get you into DEATH since I owe you for saving my life," Luke stepped on his bad leg again, this time almost crashing to the ground.

Frank caught him, "You don't have to-."

Luke interrupted him, "Frank, you saved me from the Packers when they had me in one of their traps! Please, just say okay, okay?"

"Okay, but in return I will find a way to keep the Packers off your trail that way I'll never owe you."

"Fine," Luke shrugged. Then he swayed and his leg started to bleed.

"I think you should go get that taken care of," Frank pointed to Luke's leg.

"Yup," Luke went through the Boundary stumbling. He lost consciousness after that and the memory fades away.

***

I remember that day. Luke never really told me what happened and I never asked either. They kept in touch all these years after and he never told me?

"Dawn, you okay?" Frank, annoyed obviously, asked me a few times already.

"Yeah, sorry I was looking through a memory of Luke's."

"You can actually do that?" He asked, astonished.

I didn't answer him. I walked into the library and shouted at Luke, "HEY WHAT'S UP?!" No answer from Luke he just stared off into space. Luke is always obvious about everything even if he thinks he's covering it up. He can never multi-task.

Frank went over to him, rubbing his head roughly, "Hey, little buddy!"

Luke didn't acknowledge his presence; he just stared off into space and said, "It's on the table." Frank and I chuckled.

"I think we'll just dye his hair green," I said to Frank tugging on what was left of Luke's hair.

Luke responded, "Okay, I'll do it later."

Frank then sighed and plopped down on Luke's lap and jokingly said in the best imitation of a girl's voice he could pull off, "Hey handsome." Then silence.

Frank sat there on Luke's lap and Luke's expression didn't even change a bit! I don't think I've ever seen Luke this out of it. I walked slowly over to a bookcase. Frank was laughing as I walked back over to them and slammed about ten giant books onto the table.

Luke snapped out of it and pushed Frank off his lap, "What the heck!" This of course made Frank and I laugh until we were rolling on the ground clutching our stomachs.

"Dude, I sat on your lap and you didn't even move. She slams books on the table-" Frank was cut off with another round of laughter. When Frank finally caught his breath he asked, "Who is she?"

"Who's who?" Luke asked innocently.

Frank then turned to me, knowing I already knew. "It's Jordan, his Protecti," I answered, slapping Luke on the shoulder.

"What no I mean n-'" Luke was caught off by Frank who slapped him on the back of the head.

"Alright yeah it's Jordan, but will you two please stop hitting me!" Luke finally admitted.

"Nope," Frank and I said in sync then slapped him again.

Then I discussed with Frank to Luke's embarrassment how we could get her to like him back. I really just wanted to tease him. It was bad enough that Jordan was stealing all the attention, but I was still his friend and would be supportive, especially because I could see how much he liked her.

"You guys are not going to do anything," Luke said with a warning in his voice.

"And what are you gonna do to me, big guy," Frank said with a laugh. Luke's face turned red with anger.

I started to search his brain. Dull whispers crowded my mind. He was trying to push me out and I winced. It felt like little shocks all throughout my brain. I didn't like that he was pushing me out more and more; I've only done that to him. If this is what it feels like, maybe I shouldn't do that anymore. He was definitely conflicted; it was easy to see that. Luke's face was scrunched and his eyes were almost sad. It seems to me his time away from DEATH had affected him more than I knew. I didn't like not knowing everything, it didn't feel good. Frank looked back and forth between Luke and I with confusion.

"You two are doing the mind thing again," Frank asked, feeling left out.

"Nope, don't worry about it," I stepped back and glared at Luke, "C'mon Frank, let's leave Luke alone." My headache went away. I was done trying to force my way in. It wasn't worth it. I started to walk out of the library.

"Dawn," Luke stood up and started to stutter. He couldn't get out a coherent sentence.

Suddenly, the alarms started to blare. The screeching sound made me cover my ears. Luke looked panicked and Frank was already out of the library running in the direction of the door. I chased after him. He wouldn't be able to open the door, but it wasn't a good idea for him to be near it either. I Flashed in front of Frank holding my arms out. He looked like he was in some kind of trance, as he tried to push me out of the way.

"Frank! Stop it!" I pushed him back. Frank's eyes were going crazy. The sirens were still blaring at full blast. I covered his ears after many attempts of trying to get to the door. Once they were covered his eyes began to change back to normal. He shook his head looking very confused. I put his hands over his ears and indicated not to move them. I pulled him into Harrison's office. Harrison was frantically trying to shut the alarms off. He went from computer to computer typing and hitting buttons over and over again.

"What's happening?!" I screamed at Harrison. He looked up at me and shook his head. He was looking at the cameras that pointed to the entrance becoming completely still. Harrison put his hand on a scanner and a blue map of DEATH like a holograph popped up along his desk. He zoomed in on the Boundary near the entrance and there were bodies trying to force their way in. Frank was wincing as the sirens continued to blare. Luke was silently in the back of my head asking what was going on.

"*We have to do something,*" I said to Luke, flicking my head towards a hopeless Harrison.

"*What are you gonna do? There's nothing to be done. They can't break down the Boundary!*" He yelled in my head. Luke from what I could tell was also in pain from the sirens. It must have to do with his Changer hearing. I don't know what is up with Frank. He was still clutching his ears trying to keep it together. He looked like he wanted to say something, but then doubled over to the floor. I went to his side helping him on his feet.

"Dawn, these aren't my sirens!" Harrison explained trying to figure out what to do. I stepped towards him and it showed someone was overriding our system with not just hacking, but someone using their abilities. Their ability was stealing all our technology from us.

"We're going to lose all control soon," Harrison's voice was strained. The noise was affecting him too. I had to figure out how to stop it.

"*I've rounded everyone up? What do you want to do boss?*" Luke asked.

"*Is everyone being affected by the noise?*" I noticed Frank had now fallen to the floor again. I ran to him.

"*Yeah, no one has the strength to Flash out of here,*" Luke said. I could tell his head was hurting and others around him were in a state like Frank. I felt pain, but I was still standing, so was Luke. I wonder why? We needed to get everyone out of here. Harrison was rushing around still clicking and pushing buttons to try to make things work. Nothing he was doing was working. Harrison didn't even look up at me. Frank was still doubled over holding his ears. I picked him up slowly.

"Harrison, we need to get everyone out of here, now!" I started to walk Frank out of his office. Harrison collapsed on his desk.

"*Luke, we need to get everyone to the roof. The Boundary hasn't fallen yet so we'll still be protected. Harrison's not good, he can't do anything. I'm going to Flash Harrison and Frank up there. You lead everyone to the stairs!*" I ordered.

Luke didn't respond; he went right to work. I motioned to Frank to hold my hand and touched Harrison's back. I concentrated hard. I've never Flashed anyone but myself, especially not two people. I felt heat come off my hands and feed through Harrison and Frank's body. I breathed, a swirling feeling in my chest building in my chest until it snapped into place. I felt the wind before my eyes opened and we were up on the roof. Luke was letting more people through the door. As soon as people came through, they gave a sigh of relief and returned to normal. I ran to the edge of the roof, Frank following close behind. What I saw was not what I was expecting, the people trying to take us over looked like us. Frank was standing next to me. He seemed to know what was going on. Frank's eyes turned to slits.

"What's wrong?" I asked.

"Those are Packers, Guardians I worked for. They're this gang that sells and uses Changers for profit," Frank almost growled out. I looked at him astonished.

Guardians are supposed to protect Changers. This was so wrong. Frank looked like he was ready to attack. I grabbed his shoulder and felt a spark then something yanked me back.

***

"Well well well, boys, looks like we got ourselves a new recruit," An attractive teenage boy with spiky hair and a glistening smile stood over a young Frank. Frank couldn't even move, you could tell he was shaking. He was on his knees with his head bowed like this guy was royalty or something.

"What?" Frank asked, slowly lifting his head. He looked up with pleading eyes and a face that was so bruised he could only see out of one eye. The teenage boy knelt to Frank and licked his thumb. He traced it all around Frank's face from the tip of his chin to his black eyes. The bruises vanished as he moved on to the next part of Frank's face.

"I am your savior now. You belong to me. Do what I say and no harm shall come to you," He said to Frank with a sickly sweet smooth voice. The boy stood up and pulled Frank up with him.

"Boys, meet the fresh meat!" The boy turned around to his posse of hooting and hollering teenage males. One girl stood out of the crowd, she was petite, it looked like the wind could take her away. The face she had on was strong and all knowing. It reminded me of Jada's eyes. She stood with her arms crossed unmoving and her silver muddy hair flew back and forth as the boys around her pushed their way to get to Frank. She looked towards me, but I knew she wasn't looking at me, but those eyes were piercing. Was she looking at me? No, not possible.

***

I was yanked back. Frank looked very concerned for me. He gave me a little shake and squeezed my arm.

"Dawn? Are they doing something to you?" He panicked.

I looked at the Gate again. The Boundary was shaking. It was about to collapse. I saw the spiky hair teenage boy was in the vision. I also saw the girl who looked much older. She had her hands outstretched and her eyes were glowing. She was using her abilities to hack us.

"I'm fine. Frank, do you have any idea how to stop her?" I asked and pointed to the girl from the vision. Frank looked sad, but slowly shook his head. He looked at me as if asking if it was okay for what he was about to do. I grabbed his hand and gave it a little squeeze. We both jumped off the roof and headed toward the intruders. I created a shield in front of us as I saw they were preparing. The lead boy took a step in front of the girl with a devious smile. There were two other guys with weapons ready to swing. Frank and I stopped right in front of the shaky Boundary.

The boy crossed his arms, "Heyyy Frankie boy! I see that you thought you could escape us," He said, putting his hands against the Boundary. He glared at Frank with such intensity. "Look King, I paid my debt. I'm starting new. There is no reason for this," Frank said, surprisingly calm. He didn't lose his focus on King, the lead boy, as he moved towards the Boundary.

"Eyre, this is what he wants. Why do you think he keeps you around as his only girl in the Packer-,"

Frank pauses before saying, "Family. You mean nothing to him just like I meant nothing. As soon as it's between his life and yours he'll always choose himself first."

I looked at the girl with the silver hair. Eyre. She doesn't even acknowledge Frank as he says words I'd imagine carry weight. The Boundary starts to shake more.

"Luke on my signal everyone uses their ability to create a new shield, but not before I tell you," I feel Luke nodding his head, listening to what's going on, and updating Harrison who I sense is not happy.

"King, these are people you do not want to mess with. These are real Guardians. The ones sent to protect the very thing you want to destroy," Frank doesn't raise his voice he just slowly steps closer to the Boundary. King doesn't make a move, he stands his ground in front of Eyre.

"We'll see how good they are when this shield falls. Tell me, Frank, was it worth betraying your brothers for this?" He extends his arms as the Boundary begins to fall. Eyre's hands fall to her side and her eyes return to normal. Frank meets her eyes and she shows no emotion. Frank steps back as King steps through.

"Now!" I yell at Luke and strengthen the shield on Frank. Lights of all different colors shoot from the roof and begin to create a new Boundary, but the Packers are already inside of it. The Boundary won't be created in time to avoid a fight. It would only be temporary too, we'd have to capture them. Two boys surrounded me while King and Frank were still standing facing off. The two boys came for me and I wasn't

able to concentrate on them and the shield on Frank. Frank looked at me, reassuring me to drop the shield. I let it fall.

"I'm really going to enjoy this," King gritted his teeth. He threw the first punch that Frank blocked as the two boys tried to enclose me. I Flashed out and the boys knocked into each other. I let a little laugh escape. The boys turned around and ran toward me. I threw a kick to the one's chest and punched the other in the throat. That didn't seem to affect them. They grabbed both my arms and I tried to break it, but their specialty must be strength dwindling because I could feel it leave my body. I saw Frank and King still at it with Eyre just standing behind them completely still. Frank tripped King and sent him flying to the ground. I tried to break free, but the more I struggled the more strength they took. Frank reached for Eyre, but King grabbed him and threw him back to the ground. Frank got up to help me, but King put him in a choke hold.

"How's that feel, little Prince?" King said, tightening his hold on Frank. I needed to help him, but no matter what I tried, these boys' grip was too strong.

Suddenly, I felt a whoosh behind me. I smiled at that comforting presence.

"Hey boys," Luke caught them off guard and they turned around giving me a split second to get out. I jumped in the air feeling my strength return, as their hands released me and they fell to the ground. I looked at Luke questioning him why he isn't with the others. He gave me a look that said Harrison's got it. I didn't doubt that.

"*Luke don't touch them,*" I said, giving him a smile, warning him as he joined me back to back.

"*So a little duet of Flash dance seems good to me,*" He laughed as the boys gathered their bearings and came after us. We Flashed out of the way. The Packers growled as Luke and I appeared behind them. Before they could spin back around, Luke passed me a pair of ability diminishing handcuffs, able to hold the strongest of demons. I Flashed on one boy's neck as Luke hooked the handcuffs on. The Packer fell to his knees wincing. I Flashed over to the other one, but he knew what was coming and blocked me. He stood over me and went to pick me up over his head. I Flashed out of sight and cuffed him fast. He too fell to his knees. Luke Flashed both boys up to the roof. I turned around and Frank wasn't doing well. King had him pinned under his foot

"Lil Frankie, back where he belongs. Under my rule! I gave you everything. I made you and this is how you thank me!" He pushed harder into Frank. Frank gasped. I looked around and Eyre still hadn't moved. I got a stupid idea, but it was now or never. I Flashed over to Eyre and put a knife to her throat. She didn't even flinch.

"Hey King!" I yelled. Eyre didn't struggle or make a noise. It was like she was under some kind of trance. King slowly turned, putting more pressure on Frank. Frank's eyes widened as he saw what I was doing to Eyre. I wanted to tell him not to worry, but I had to make it look real.

"Dawn," Frank choked out.

"Urgh, who are you?" King asked, frustrated. He knew he couldn't let Eyre die or he'd lose control of DEATH, he wasn't going to let that happen.

"I'm Dawn Shadows. I want to make a deal with you, but first let Frank go. You're outnumbered and we already have two of your boys. Once the Boundary is complete you'll be forced out of here in a very painful way," I said, tightening my hold on Eyre. Frank looked at King then back at me.

"Hahaha, I like her, Frankie. She's even more diabolical than you. I could use that. Hmmm...Shadows I know that name," He released his foot from Frank's chest and Frank coughed rolling onto his knees. I tried to keep myself together after he said he knew my name. He was probably just baiting me. King stepped toward me.

"You want to make a deal with the devil? Give it your best shot," He said with the most chilling smile I'd ever seen.

"You give us back control and we owe you a favor we have to pay back. If not I kill Eyre to get control and we send you and all the Packers to Galrich prison for crimes against the Guardian oath," I say with confidence and try to match his smile. King laughed and looked at Frank who was struggling to get up. Frank looked horrified. He didn't know what I was doing.

"Dawn, no you can't, you don't know what kind of deal you're making," Frank said, coming to his feet. King turned back to me and smiled.

"Why would I care if you kill her? My abilities could easily heal her," King laughed. Frank was mostly recovered as he stood tall trying to find a way to come at him. I shook my head at him.

"Yes Frankie, listen to her. She's smart don't mess this up," King didn't even look at him, he kept his eye contact with me.

"That's right. You can heal her, but tell me could you heal her heart?" I moved my knife from her neck to her chest. King looked at me, his face turning into a sneer.

"Do it. I'm not making any deal with filthy Guardian royalty ," He whispered. I was shocked. He fell for it. Eyre's eyes began to glow. The people on the roof began to stop making a new Boundary. Eyre was giving us back control. She was definitely hurt by King's words.

"Like I said, can you heal her heart because I think you hurt her feelings," I let go of Eyre as she started to give us back control.

"What are you doing girl!?" King launched for her and me, but he was too late the Boundary sprang back and King fell to his knees screaming. The Boundary was starting to tear him apart. Unless he was welcomed in he would die and so would Eyre.

"*Luke get Harrison to welcome them. We have to arrest them,*" I pleaded, holding Eyre. I threw cuffs to Frank and he strapped them on King.

"Who's the boss now, Master King?" Frank spit. King stopped screaming. He let his head hang. Suddenly, Eyre began to disappear.

"What is going on? No!" I tried to grab onto her. I heard a small laugh in the air.

"Goodbye Miss Shadows, we shall meet again," Eyre said as she vanished into thin air. I looked at Frank who gave a big sigh and shook his head as if he knew this was a possibility. That was probably going to be a problem.

"Well Dawn, this was no prank," He smiled. Frank Flashed King to the roof, as I sat there in the grass bewildered. I had a feeling this was only the beginning.

Chapter 11

Worry

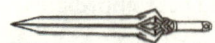

Harrison was pacing like always trying to decide what he wanted to do with Frank and I. Luke stood in the corner with his arms crossed biting his nails here and there. His nervousness was washing through me in waves. I don't think he's ever been in trouble before. I'm not sure what Harrison was going to say. I don't think we should be in trouble. We saved this place for goodness sake. I had to say something.

"Harrison stop pacing," I tried to make him stop. It was getting annoying. Frank looked perfectly calm, in the face anyway. He had his tooth pick back in his mouth, biting down hard, and his hands were balled into fists. I was afraid of what he might do. I wanted to reach out and grab his hand, but thought better of it. I'd have to deal with that later.

"I should report this to Galrich," Harrison reached for a gold button on his desk. Luke and I looked at each other.

"Mr. Grove, do we think that's such a good idea?" Frank asked before I could object, and blinked as he used Harrison's last name. There was no emotion creeping into his voice just like Eyre. He has been trained to get rid of emotion.

"Yeah, does Elder Tallahan even know Luke is back. What stops him from coming back for Luke and I?" I asked, backing Frank up. Harrison looked at me then to Luke who was pulsing his leg up and down. He had his fingers placed on his bottom lip, and I heard distinct crunching that made me want to push his hand away. I decided to put my hand on top of his jittering leg instead. Luke's eyes glanced at me and he took a deep breath lowering his hand.

"I have to report this. I don't have to say anything that Luke has returned. I am not sure what Elder Tallahan's intentions are with you two, but I too would like to know more," Harrison leaned forward on his desk. I didn't expect him to say that. I thought for sure Harrison would be the first to give us away. I didn't have a response. I realized I didn't know how to agree with him. I was always fighting him on something. It felt weird to be on the same side.

"Sir, from what I know is that the Packers whereabouts and mission were known in Galrich and they have done nothing to stop them. They don't care, Sir," Frank's voice started to shake a little with anger. I inhaled. Galrich knows about the Packers and they've done nothing about them?

"I am aware of that, Mr. Summers. From what they have told me is that they were waiting for something big to happen. This might be it so they can press charges and round them up," Harrison pressed the gold button and it started to blink a gold light.

"Luke, I suggest you leave. I will let you know if Tallahan decides to come to visit or anyone from Galrich might, maybe even the Enforcer. Go Luke," Harrison said firmly. The Enforcer is basically Galrich's scapegoat. The Enforcer does all of their dirty work and anyone who sees it never lives to tell the story. Luke looked at me, his head buzzing with all kinds of emotions. He quickly Flashed back to his room.

"As for you two, I need you to help me explain what happened and who we have in custody. Frank I want you to know, you have immunity, they can not hold anything against you for being a Packer, but they might be harsh on you. Can you handle that?"

"Yes, sir," Frank responded with total confidence, his fists still clenched. The button began to raise and a little hologram popped up. It was the perfect image of Elder Tallahan himself. I resisted the urge to glare.

"Ah Harrison, is this urgent? I'm in a bit of a situation right now," Tallahan said, trying to blow him off. He didn't even look at Harrison.

"Yes your excellency, a group of Packers, and their leader almost seized the school. I have Dawn and our newest student Frank Summers to explain what happened. I will tell you there's no cause to worry. We have them in custody here," Harrison explained with the utmost respect.

Elder Tallahan pinched the bridge of his nose. Then let out a frustrated sigh. "Oh very well Mr. Harrison I shall pay you a visit. No need to explain the situation now. I'm glad they were defeated. I do have one question for the former Packer boy, Mr. Summers," Tallahan finally looked up and smiled that weird smile.

Frank cleared his throat. "Yes, your excellency," He responded like Harrison did. I wanted to laugh. Frank was anything, but formal.

"Mr. Summer's, you realize that you were brought to DEATH under one condition. You are my personal informant. Did you have any prior knowledge of this attack?" Frank was an informant? I looked at Frank and he didn't move. Was he ever gonna tell me he was an informant? I glared at him while he didn't acknowledge me.

"No sir, I had no knowledge of this or that it was even on King's radar. I believe this in retaliation to what he perceives as my betrayal, your excellency," Frank replied calmly and coolly.

"Very well Mr. Summers. I shall see you all in 24 hours and Miss Shadows I want that boy found," Elder Tallahan said very seriously and his perfect hologram image looked straight in my eyes before he vanished. The way he said "that boy" worried me. Harrison looked at me and I thought I saw a flash of concern across his face, but it quickly faded.

"Dawn I will inform Luke, you and Mr. Summer's get some rest. You did well," He waved us off as we exited the door. I looked back as the door closed. Harrison put his head in his hands. As we walked down the hall, Frank let out a big sigh.

"Are you ok? You seem really mad?" I asked.

Frank turned around to face me. "No one was supposed to know that I am-," He cut himself off and ran a hand down his face, "Sorry, *was* a Packer. When Luke told me Harrison was looking for someone on the inside, I jumped at the opportunity to get away. King couldn't give a crap about this place before now. He wants something else, is planning something else. It was too easy of a catch. King never does a job unless the whole Packer group is involved. He only brought The Twins and Eyre. She's probably gone back and is taking up leadership right now. Your stunt back there may have angered her, but King has an influence over her like I've never seen," He was panicking, his breath quickening and eyes widening with each sentence his spoke.

"Frank, look, maybe he does, maybe he doesn't, but he's locked up and can't use his abilities. We can't worry right now. Plus who knows how long I'm going to be here for. Elder Tallahan really wants Luke and I in Galrich. I'm not saying this isn't pressing, I'm saying we should be worried about that old creep," I said trying to take his mind off King and the Packers.

"Yeah it's only worrying me more, Galrich should have come after us a long time ago, but they never did. They have plenty of evidence to lock them up, but they haven't. I think they are working for Galrich or Elder Tallahan," Frank whispered like someone was watching us.

I looked at him. He wasn't making sense, but the thing was that he was making perfect sense. Is there corruption in our capital in Guardian leadership? I think I already knew the answer. There was a lot we didn't know and a lot we had to find out.

Chapter 12

Escape of The Not So Rebel Kids

Luke was freaking out, wait no, more than freaking out. He might be going a little insane. Elder Tallahan was coming today to inspect the Packers, but we both knew he wanted us. We sat in my bedroom trying to come up with a plan. Specifically, Luke, Lila, Hailey, Daniel, Frank, and me. This in a way was our own little council.

"They can't take you away! Can they?" Lila squeaked. She looked around. I sat on the foot of my bed, my legs swinging off just hanging before the floor. Frank was sitting in a chair next to my bed chewing that same toothpick and wearing his leather jacket. I wondered how the toothpick stayed intact and if he ever washed that jacket?

Hailey was doing some kind of homework in the opposite corner of Frank, not really paying attention. Daniel was standing by the door as if waiting for someone to break up our little meeting. Then there was Luke. Luke was pacing and muttering nonsense. He was really giving off a Harrison vibe. None of us knew how to answer Lila's question. They all looked as if I had to be the one to give bad news.

"They can sis, and they will if we don't come up with a plan to at least get Luke out of here... again," I said, making my voice sound light.

"I wasn't here for the first time, but the Packers could easily track him out there. They know the whereabouts of about every Changer in the city, but they only go after the biggest prize," Frank said, trying to help. Luke looked at him mortified. I spun to glare.

"I'm sorry, but um- what would the Packers have to do with this? Luke is a Guardian not a Changer," Hailey pointed out in her nervous way, her interest piqued. Frank's eyes widened as he realized not everyone in this room knew about Luke.

"Yeah Frank, stop focusing on the Packers," I pretended to chastise him.

"Sorry my bad," He looked right at Luke, genuinely apologizing.

Luke knew what he had to do. He had to get to Jordan. He could escape with her. Harrison would have to verify it as a mission. Elder Tallahan wouldn't be able to refuse if Luke is on a mission with his protecti due to Guardian law. Keeping it from the others is what he was trying to do, maybe even from me. He didn't want to give the location of Jackson Cassie away. I needed information about my parents and Jackson could give it to me. Was he trying to protect me? He was still clouding his mind.

"Luke has a plan and we are going to do it. Who's ready for a mission?" I said excitedly while Luke looked at me shocked. He knew he'd have to give me the information at some point. This was the perfect excuse. The rest of the guys smiled and nodded their heads, even Hailey looked ready to go. Frank looked at me sensing I was lying. I knew he did, but then he smiled.

"Let's go guys, up and at 'em," He clapped his hands and opened the door as the rest filed out. Hailey was the last and looked like she knew something else was up, but she would never ask.

"After you, ma Lady," Frank bowed his head and gave a smirk. Hailey stuck her nose in the air and stomped out of the room. Frank chuckled and closed the door, leaving Luke and I alone. Luke turned to me, his face still in a state of shock. He was silent.

"You're taking me to see Cassie and I don't care if it's against every loyalty code the wolves have. I need to know, Luke. I need to know where my mom is. She could still be alive." He looked away from me, shaking his head.

"Luke, if you could find out who your parents were wouldn't you do it at all costs?" I pleaded, trying to tug at his heart strings. He shook his head again and ran his fingers through his hair placing his hands on the back of his neck.

"Fine. I'll take you to him, but Dawn you're messing with some dangerous stuff. Jackson Cassie is a strict man. He will do anything to protect his pack. I won't be able to protect you," Luke said in almost a whisper. I nodded my head and smiled.

"Luke, it'll all be okay, you worry too much," I walked over and put a hand on his shoulder. He seemed to relax a little and even smiled.

"What?" I laughed. He looked at me kind of confused.

"Can't you just read my mind Shadows?" He raised his eyebrows. Luke knew exactly what we had to do. We had to create a fake mission file and I had to forge Harrison's signature for the appearance of approval.

"It's just ironic. Who would've thought I was the rebel?" He laughed even harder. I smiled with him and didn't even mind that he was taking my title.

***

I went to visit Harrison because I knew I'd have to get that mission file, but I also knew I had to tell him something that made sense for not just Luke and I, for the rest of the gang's absence too. Taking a big breath before I knocked on his office door.

"Come in," Harrison answered before I opened the door and looked up at me in surprise.

"Oh Dawn, interesting. I usually call you down here. What can I do for you?" He asked. I closed the door and walked closer to his desk. I just looked at him because in all honesty I didn't know what to say. Dawn, the queen of lies seemed to be all out of them, so I did the thing I never thought I'd ever do, especially towards Harrison. I decided to tell the truth, well most of it.

"Harrison, I'm getting Luke out of here, at least until Elder Tallahan is gone. I need you to sign off on a mission. At first I was thinking it had to be for Luke and his protecti to fall under Guardian law so he didn't have to go to Galrich, but now I think it has to be a mission for Frank, Lila, Dan, Hailey, and I to go look for Luke. Elder Tallahan needs proof that we are going along with this and-," I explained as fast as I could, but Harrison cut me off.

"And it is the only way to know for certain what Elder Tallahan's intentions are," He finished my sentence. I stood there shocked. He was exactly right. Harrison looked at me then opened up one of his drawers and placed a white mission form on his desk. He began to write, then after a few minutes, he signed the signature I knew all too well at the bottom. He then clasped his hands together and the form shimmered away.

"I have sent the mission to Galrich's headquarters. Tallahan should hear about it by the time he gets here, and you all should already be gone."

I stood there mouth a gape, not knowing what to say. Harrison actually agreed with me?

"I want Luke found, Dawn, at all costs," He was playing along. I realized that he had pressed the gold button and was recording a message for Elder Tallahan. I smiled. Harrison remained expressionless. I walked to the door. I paused before opening it. I was in shock at how cooperative Harrison was being, I should thank him. The words just couldn't seem to leave my mouth.

"Dawn, be careful," Harrison said. He didn't look me in the eye as he returned to what he was doing before I came in, but there was genuine concern in his voice. I gave a quick nod and ran down to the Training Room where the others were waiting. As I entered, everyone stopped what they were doing and looked at me. Daniel was practically hitting the ceiling. He was jumping up and down so fast filled with excitement. Lila was standing next to him, her arms crossed, she looked angry as usual and ready to go. Frank slung on a backpack, placed the toothpick in his mouth and smiled at me, a perfectly cool smile. Hailey was leaning against the wall. She didn't look nervous or excited; she simply just smiled the tiniest bit. My eyes scanned from her to Luke who was sitting on the floor, his hands folded and his elbows rested on his knees. He was still worried and not completely sure if he was doing the right thing. He was even more surprised that I told Harrison the truth.

"What are we doing just sitting here? Are we ready to go?" Daniel said, running out of the door. Lila followed him yelling at him to slow down. Hailey acting like the mother told Lila that was no way to talk to Daniel heading out the door. Frank came to me and gave me a knife. I slipped it in my pocket. Luke finally stood up and came to join us. He gave Frank a brotherly look. I wasn't sure what it meant.

"You boys ready?" I asked. They looked at each other then at me. We walked right out the front door and past the Boundary. We had escaped. At least that's what it felt like, I looked back at DEATH. I had a different feeling. I wasn't quite sure what it was, maybe sadness, I don't know. It was almost like something was ending. As I scanned the building, at the top of the roof I saw Jada, her red hair was whipping in the wind. Then she disappeared. That couldn't be good.

Chapter 13

Hunting Hunter

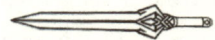

It was weird being out on our own not having to sneak around. We followed Luke all around the place. I wasn't sure where we were going. I set up shields all around us because Luke asked. He was being extra precautious. It was hard to tell what he was thinking, his mind was all over the place. I think he was trying to distract me from what he was really thinking. There he goes, forcing me out again. I'm not sure if he trusts me anymore. If I don't know what he's thinking, can we really be close anymore?

"Trouble in paradise?" Frank came up behind me shifting his eyes to Luke. I laughed. Frank was forever joking. I didn't answer because I didn't need to. Frank was mostly trying to make conversation. I could tell he didn't like the tension between Luke and I. Frank suddenly came to a stop.

"Everyone hide," He whispered, but loud enough that everyone heard him. I grabbed Lila who squirmed at my touch and ducked behind a tree, not the best place, but I wasn't sure what to do. Frank was the next tree over. Luke was holding Daniel back behind a dumpster in a tiny alleyway. Hailey went invisible in exactly the same spot she was when Frank told us to hide. I wish I had that ability. It would make things a lot easier. Surprisingly, she doesn't use it a lot. Then I saw why Frank told us to hide. A couple of Packer boys came running down the sidewalk. They seemed to be looking for something.

"Come on man you said you had one," A boy with sandy hair and grey eyes shoved a boy with black hair and brown eyes.

"I swear! I can smell him," The black haired boy growled. They had a metal trap in their hands waiting for their prey.

"The scent is strong here," The grey eyed boy said and looked around, his eyes squinted like he was going to see something else. I couldn't see where Hailey went. The boys kept looking around and the blacked haired one rounded the tree where Lila and I were. I covered Lila's mouth and got out my knife getting ready for us to be found. I felt something that felt like a hand touch my shoulder. I tensed, but didn't want to move. As the boy rounded the tree, he looked right at me.

"Man there's nothing here I checked everywhere," The boy said looking disappointed.

The boys started to walk away. I waited till they were gone to look behind me. I saw Hailey's blue eyes looking back at mine. She smiled rather sheepishly. Hailey stood up and waved to everyone that the coast was clear.

"Your welcome," she whispered, motioning to everyone. I guess whenever the Packers looked where one of us was hiding Hailey made us invisible. I was very impressed. I've never known Hailey to do anything like that before, she wouldn't even do that in training. It was refreshing to see a different side of her. Frank was walking quite fast in the direction the Packers went. I ran after him, Luke followed close behind. Frank wanted to chase after them and find out what they were doing. He was trying to be the hero to make up for his past mistakes. Luke cut me off. He gave me a look that said I should stop, he'll take care of it. I didn't want to stop though. I guess that's one of my flaws, stepping in things I shouldn't. I looked over at Lila as she was crossing her arms. She was probably mad at me for protecting her which is ironic. She wanted to take care of herself. Lila stomped away. Luke started to head back with Frank and they seemed to be arguing about something. I went over to them.

"Man c'mon I know we're on a mission to protect you and keep you away from Tallahan, but the Packers are doing horrible things. I have to stop them, please, Luke," Frank was begging him. I didn't get why he was even asking permission Luke wasn't the boss.

Luke turned to me glaring, "You know what Dawn, I am the boss right now." I flinched at the hardness of his voice. He turned back to Frank.

"Look, you've always wanted to play hero, but have never followed through," Luke threw his hands in frustration. Frank's eyes widened and he stepped closer to Luke.

"What the hell is that supposed to mean!" Frank yelled.

"Boys, boys, enough," I stepped, pushing them apart. I gave Luke an extra shove for the unnecessary comment. I turned to Frank, his normally bright and mischievous eyes were muted. He slouched away. I turned to Luke and he was glaring at me.

"Luke, what's wrong?" I asked as I threw my hands up exasperatedly letting them flop to my sides, irritation entering my voice. He shook his head, his eyes downcast.

"Dawn, you should have stayed out of it. All of it. Frank wants to go after those Packers. We have a mission. We stick to it," He said as he waved everyone over. I did not appreciate his tone.

"Okay boss man, you know what? Yeah, Frank and I are going after those Packers. We'll meet up with you later," I said with as much salt in my voice as I could. Frank looked at me surprised then grabbed his backpack and grinned at Luke.

"Dawn, wait-," Luke said, grabbing my arm. I yanked it away and spun towards him.

"I think you forget yourself Luke. I protect and support you all the time. Maybe this is a stupid idea. Maybe I shouldn't get involved, but I don't care. So it seems neither do you about a lot of things, apparently-," I stopped myself. Luke looked flabbergasted; he didn't know how to respond. The others were quiet. I don't think they've ever seen Luke and I argue.

"Frank, let's go," I said as Frank and I walked away. I didn't look back, but I could feel Luke's hurt feelings. He still had a block on me from reaching his mind, but I could tell he was fighting the urge to rip into his wolf form. Lila looked at me taking a step forward, but then thought better of it. They all started walking in the opposite direction of us.

***

"There they are," Frank whispered as we hid behind some bushes right outside the Packer camp. I felt funny, almost childish by hiding. The camp was made up of complex patterns of tents that were very uniform. Packers were circling the perimeter in tight formation. Their eyes were as focused as hawks. Frank unzipped his backpack carefully and pulled out a dark object I didn't recognize. It was weirdly shaped, like a deformed spiky ball that was in perpetual motion. It was blurring in Frank's hand like it wanted to escape.

"What is that?" I whispered as he fiddled with it. He looked up from it and shrugged his shoulders. It finally stilled, and one little spike popped out of it. Frank raised his eyebrows twice giving me a smirk as he pricked his finger on it. It happily accepted his blood. My eyes widened and I waited for him to explain.

"You know I don't actually know. But watch this," Frank threw it over the bush. I heard a shout, some movement, then total silence. Frank stood up and I slowly followed his lead. The Packer camp was frozen and in the middle of it all was the black spike pulsating. I don't know how to describe it. It was like time had stopped and all the Packers were not moving; they seemed to be in a trance of some kind. A constant plus was emitting from the object. They were frozen in time.

"I like to call it the Time Stopper, now hurry we only have 5 minutes," Frank said, running through the Packers. He was almost giddy. It was like he had been waiting for this his whole life. I ran after him, not sure what I was getting myself into. As I followed Frank, I noticed the whole camp was buzzing with life. Packers of every age seemed to be in the midst of daily activities. They looked like a family smiling, eating, playing, you would never know that they were cold blooded killers. There were a lot more kids than I was expecting, but there were no girls, just boys. Eyre seemed to be the only female packer. It annoyed me more than anything. Sexists jerks.

"Dawn, we have to keep moving. I gotta get to the Tower to free all the captured," Frank said, pulling my hand. On the way to the Tower, I saw a familiar face.

"Hunter!" I yelled and ran over to him. He was in a cage strapped down with Packers surrounding him. It looked like he was in the middle of trying to break free or maybe not, he didn't look exactly conscious. Frank ran over to me. This was not good. How did he get here? I saw him not that long ago.

"We have to get him out," I said, reaching for the lock on the cage. Frank all of a sudden grabbed my hand.

"Wait! Every time we touch something the less time we have. Time will start to reset itself. We have to wait till I free everyone and then we can save him," Frank said, hitting my arm away.

"What you're saying is we'll have to fight our way out?" I smiled.

Frank laughed, "Yes, but we'll have a lot more back up if I release the other prisoners- I mean Changers."

The Tower looked just like its name. A long grey windowless building that touched the sky. Frank moved quickly, he scanned his hand on a pad that made a door appear, as he did that I could feel the air start to return to normal. Once the door was open, we Flashed inside. There were thousands if not more prisoners locked up in here. I looked at Frank in awe.

"I used to be in charge of the Tower," Frank said, shame hanging on every word. I touched his shoulder, giving him a little nod. I closed my eyes and focused on the Tower. The lock system was complicated, but nothing I couldn't take care of. I let out a big sigh and one by one the locks began to break. As they broke, the guards started to begin to regain movement and the prisoners began to come out of their cells. Our 5 minutes were up, but we had all the time we needed now. A brawl began to ensue.

"These prisoners won't trust me, I locked most of them up. I will go get Hunter, can you lead these guys out of here?" Frank said, running from me.

"With pleasure," I said as a large Packer came barreling towards me. I ducked down and swept his legs out from under him. The prisoners started to fight back too, one by one the Packers were left unconscious. I looked around at all the people being held and they were looking at me.

"Well c'mon," I said, waving them through the doors. They ran all nodding in my direction. As soon as I got everyone to safety, I ran to help Frank. He was still battling the Packers trying to get to Hunter. Hunter was in a cage chained pulling on the bars. Frank had at least five guys on him. I summoned up all my will and felt an energy release from my palms. The Packers on top of Frank were thrown off him. Frank looked at me shocked. I ran over to Hunter and pried open the cage. Hunter's hands were badly burned and as I helped him out I noticed his side was gushing blood. Why wasn't he healing?

"Hey, Dawn," Hunter said weakly, trying to smile. I wrapped his arm around my shoulders. He wasn't going to be conscious for a long time.

"I leave you for one second and you're already in trouble?" I asked, trying to be funny and keep him talking. I could tell he wasn't going to be awake for long.

"Huh, more like I meet you and I'm the most wanted guy in history," He said weakly with a laugh and a wince. I started running, pulling him along.

Frank and I ran as fast as we could. There were Packers beginning to encircle us. I wanted to Flash, but I feared Hunter wouldn't be able to handle the sudden pressure. Frank was ahead of us fighting us out, suddenly a shield started to close the entrance off to us.

"Dawn! They are shutting us in! We aren't going to make it. We need to turn it off!" Frank said as he kicked a Packer off of him. The shield was shutting us in faster and faster. I needed to think of something quickly. The prisoners were just beyond the entrance and were trying to help us by breaking through the shield, but they couldn't penetrate it. The shield closed. We were trapped and Packers were at our every turn.

"Frank, take Hunter. I have an idea," I said, running toward the control center of the camp. It was a red brick with a large antenna at the top. That is where the shield was coming from, if I could manage to break that I could get us out. I Flashed to the top of the building and sure enough the antenna was radiating the shield.

"Dawn Shadows," I heard from behind me as if the wind called me. I whipped around ready to fight. I saw that unmistakable silver hair whipping in the wind. Eyre's unforgettable face looked back at me. Her petite frame made her look so young. She smirked.

"Eyre, see you didn't hide very well," I said, backing up to the antenna. She stepped towards me.

"I said we would meet again, didn't I? I didn't expect it to be so soon, but here we are" She said in her airy voice. She crossed her arms. Then looked down in the direction of Frank. He was fighting off many Packers.

"Lil Frankie, always getting into trouble," She laughed. Then her face turned cold. The unmoving features I saw before.

"Eyre, let us leave," I stepped towards her. She didn't move. It was like she was frozen, but her hair whipped in the wind. I looked down and Frank was not doing well, there were many Packers on top of them. I could see Eyre was looking at Frank and for a second I saw worry cross her face. She suddenly looked more innocent than ever.

"If you care about him, call your boys off," I said. She flicked her eyes over to me and then over to Frank. She was distracted, now was my time. I jumped up into the air towards her and kicked her in the head. She crumpled to the ground as the shield crumpled. I knew as soon as she was on this roof she was responsible for the shield and was just emitting her power through the antenna. I went to go Flash down to Frank when suddenly, Eyre grabbed my ankle and I felt the same sensation I did with Jada, but this time I was pushed forward.

Frank and I were sitting in chairs facing back to back, our hands bound. Frank's head hung low and I was struggling to get out of the ropes. I could tell I was in pain. Frank grabbed my hands and winced. He shook his head. The room was black and the air was damp. I had a feeling that people were watching us. I wanted to help, but all I could do was stand there. I was yanked back to the present.

I gasped as the Packer camp came back into my vision. My head was pounding and my body felt numb. I felt pressure on my chest as I tried to suck in a breath. It felt like I needed to collapse, but I kept myself up. Eyre was still on the ground and had a hold of my ankle.

"He's not safe with you and will never be safe with you," Eyre whispered that worried look lingering in her eyes. Eyre either had the talents of a Seer or she was using my spark of Seer magic to give me a clue. The shield surprisingly did not go back up. She was letting us go. Most importantly she was letting him go. I Flashed down to Frank and grabbed Hunter. We Flashed to where we started our little break out. Hunter was in bad shape and losing blood fast. Frank looked as if he was going to pass out, but was filled with adrenaline from what just happened. He couldn't stop bouncing.

"Frank, I need you to hold Hunter still, I think I have to cauterize the wound," I looked him in the eye and prepared to help Hunter. Frank nodded trying to be serious, but he was joyful and giddy. He did what I told him to do. I rubbed my hands together creating enough heat to burn the skin and then pressed it against Hunter's side. He screamed in pain and his eyes turned a bright yellow.

"Dawn, we have to calm him down. He might change and we can't have him running through these woods with angry Packers looking for blood after what we just did!" Frank panicked, the giddiness gone. I released my hands from his wound and started to stroke his dark locks. I heard a growl in my head. Was I able to communicate telepathically with Hunter? I concentrated hard and could feel a strong connection to Hunter. I began to tell him everything was okay. Hunter's eyes began to close and his body unclenched. I kept up what I was doing and kept his mind calm.

"What? How are you doing that?" Frank asked, confused.

I shook my head, "It turns out a Guardian and their protecti have a connection. I can talk to him in his mind similar to how I talk to Luke. I told him to put his wolfy away."

Frank chuckled, "You really are something else, Shadows." He sat back on the grass and gave a big sigh. He looked so tired and bruised. I was surprised he was still standing after the hits he took.

"Frank, it's okay you can rest now. I will keep watch and we can meet the others wherever they are in the morning. We're not going anywhere with Hunter in this condition anyway," I said, trying to assure Frank that everything would be alright. Frank nodded and started to curl up into a ball on the grass.

"Oh, hey I just want to say-," Frank started.

"Don't mention it," I smiled. He smiled back and closed his eyes, quickly falling asleep. I kept stroking Hunter's hair. He was dreaming in bright colors and peaceful thoughts. As it turned to night, I set up a fire and kept watch. Luke was sleeping. I could feel it. He was worried. I tried to reassure him we were alright and would be seeing him soon. I did not let myself think the only threat we'd be facing in the days to come would be the Packers. If I had only known what Eyre's vision was about, maybe I could actually fall asleep. I laid down and looked at the starry sky. The sounds of Hunter and Frank's breathing calming me down. My eyes began to feel heavy, but I had to fight the urge, someone had to keep a lookout. I sat up and watched the fire dance until the sun came up.

Chapter 14

Stupid Stupid Boys

F rank was the first to wake up. He bolted upright like he had a bad dream and started looking around. I had been just putting out the fire. Hunter was curled up into a ball slightly shivering. I think he has a fever. Changers are supposed to heal fast like Guardians. I only hope that will kick in soon. Frank turned to me with groggy eyes and heaved a sigh of relief.

"I'm sorry. How long have I been out? Shouldn't we go find the others?" He said quickly, getting to his feet.

"Frank, it's ok. We're not going anywhere. Hunter has some sort of infection and his healing needs to kick in. I will let Luke know where we are," I said watching the fire die out and the smoke drift into the air. Frank sat back down and nodded his head. He grabbed his knees to his chest and bit his lip.

"You look worried, something the matter?" I asked. He looked at me and then at Hunter. He shook his head. I kicked his foot.

"C'mon, spit it out," I said with a laugh.

"Okay, okay. You're making me say this, I just want you to remember that," He said, pointing a finger at me. I smiled waiting for him to go on.

He heaved a sigh, "I didn't like it." I gave him a confused look. Frank's eyes flicked to Hunter and then cringed as if waiting for me to slap him. He seemed to fumble with his words before finally speaking again.

"I didn't like how close you were to that *thing*."

"Um- Okay, why?" I asked, containing my knee jerk angry retort and flicked my eyes to Hunter, who leaned against a tree staring at the sky. I'm sure he could hear this entire conversation. Frank shifted uncomfortably.

"My whole life his kind-Changers- have always been the enemy. I don't know anything else. I'm sure everything I know is wrong. Luke is the only Changer I haven't actually tried to harm. I met him at such a young age. It was right before I officially became a Packer. After I joined, I thought he'd forgotten about me, but he came back for me. You sent him to me when you made him vanish after the protecti ceremony. I guess I had been on his mind. King and The Packers are terrible twisted people, but when I saw you stroking Hunter's head last night. I wanted to pull you away and run as far from here as we could. I wanted to hurt him. He paused, his breath quickening, "Dawn, I'm still that monster. I'm a Packer. It's embedded in my blood. That darkness will never leave me," Frank's voice started to break. He was in deep emotional conflicting pain. I didn't know what to say. I just looked at him checking on Hunter. He felt a bit cooler which was a good sign. Frank took a toothpick out of his pocket and stuck it in his mouth. He was back to macho Frank. I was glad he opened up to me and also surprised. I just got some information on Luke's whereabouts when I sent him away from DEATH.

"Frank, listen to me. You are not a bad person. Look at what you did! You saved the people you locked up. You made amends. It's okay that you had a moment of relapse. It's understandable, but the most important thing is that you didn't act on it," I said, trying to sound as wise as I could. Luke was better at making people feel good. The words didn't feel right, but they seemed to do the trick. Frank smiled.

"So that mind thing, does it work from any distance? Can you tell Luke where we are?"

"Oh, you just watch and learn Frankie boy," I said, closing my eyes, opening the block I had put up to keep Luke out. I didn't want him to be worried and I was mad at him for trying to control me.

"*Dawn! Dawn!*" Luke's voice rang through my head. I winced.

"*Ow man, hi to you too. We are okay. I just wanted to tell you where we are,*" I said. Luke was still overcome with worry. I could feel his anger at me for leaving, but I didn't feel like I had to apologize. He had so many questions and was firing them like rapid fire into my brain. I was so tempted to turn him off and just shut the doors, but I kept him in. I didn't answer his questions. I let him know repeatedly where we were and that we were fine. Frank watched me intently waiting for me to tell him they were coming to get us.

"*You know it wouldn't kill you to answer. We are on our way to you,*" Luke finally said.

"*Great, see you soon,*" I said about to shut him out.

"*No wait I-,*" he hesitated, "*Nevermind.*" Luke's presence was gone. He had closed me out. It stung a little, I always felt I was the only one that could do that, but lately Luke wasn't against doing it anymore.

"Soo...?," Frank asked impatiently. I nodded my head and went to check on Hunter. He still had not regained consciousness. I was worried about that, but I knew his body had to heal. Hunter was also a presence in my head. It was like different radio channels I could switch off between Hunter and Luke. The signal for Hunter was weaker than Luke's. I could not hear Hunter's thoughts, but I could feel what he was feeling. I knew he was going to be okay. Frank didn't seem to be as happy as he was when we went to sleep last night. He was on edge waiting for someone or something to attack. He kept looking over his shoulder.

"Frank, you're making me nervous. What's up?" I asked. He shook his head.

"It's not like the Packers to not retaliate right away. I don't know. I thought there'd be more of a fight," Frank gave a nervous laugh.

"Are you kidding? What was the stuff at the camp then?" I said getting up and checking the trees making sure there was no one in them. Frank laughed some more and shook his head. I contemplated telling him about Eyre. I realized I never told him.

"Um- so up on the tower I ran into-," Frank looked up at me.

"Eyre," He said, cutting me off.

"Yeah, how did you know?" I asked, going to sit in front of him.

"I knew Eyre would come back and lead the charge if anything ever happened to King. I think she was more power hungry than I thought," He said with a shrug. He looked away like he was remembering something.

"What's the deal with you and her?" I asked, trying to get his eyes back on me. I remembered what I saw in my vision of Frank first meeting the Packers. Eyre has a soft spot for him. I should probably tell him what I saw, but it wouldn't help anything.

"Well, we were always together like you and Luke. We were King's best soldiers and we understood each other," He said, still avoiding my gaze. It was like he was lost in a memory.

"I messed up with her though, I should've taken her with me. I left her behind," Frank said.

"Why?" I asked tucking my legs in resting my chin on my knees.

"She will always be loyal to King, always. That is one thing we will never understand about each other. She thinks he saved her from a lot of suffering," He said with his voice wavering. I reached my hand out resting it on his hand trying to comfort him. He sniffed and got up to his feet.

"I'm going to do a perimeter sweep just in case and make sure all the Changers we saved are out of the woods. I'll be right back," He said, taking off. I shook my head. Boys. They never want to confront their feelings. I heard a groan. Hunter started to move around. I went to his side as his eyes started to flutter open. He heaved another groan.

"Hey stranger," He said with a weak smile. He started to sit up. "How long have I been out?" Hunter looked around gathering his bearings.

"Oh you know, years," I said with a laugh. He laughed then gave a cough.

"Thank you," He said with seriousness in his eyes.

I shook my head, "It's my job."

"No, I mean I heard you in here," He said, pointing to his head. I suddenly felt embarrassed.

"You kept me here," He said, trying to stand up. I pushed him down and shook my head. Hunter winced.

"Yeah, probably a good idea. How did we get out? I don't remember much," He said, laying back down. I smiled. He looked a lot better, but still weak. My hand was still on his chest and I felt it rise and fall. He has a strong chest and his heartbeat was fast. I started to become fixated on the pulse of his heart.

"Dawn?" Hunter raised an eyebrow. I took my hand off of his chest, blushing. I looked away.

"Sorry, I was curious about your heartbeat and not much to tell you. We got lucky, I guess," I said with a shrug and trying to cover up my staring at him.

"Yeah, Changers have a very fast heartbeat," He said, smiling with those sea green eyes. He gave me a dazzling smile.

I heard a smack in the air and jumped to my feet. Frank Flashed back with Luke and the rest right behind him.

"Dawn!" Lila came rushing toward me and gave me a big hug. I hugged her back and relief rushed over me. Luke looked at me, crossing his arms in disappointment. Hailey had Daniel on her back waiting to leave.

"Look what I found," Frank said with a little bit of anger. Luke growled ready to fight Frank. They started to take steps toward each other. I Flashed over to Luke. We were face to face and his eyes were glowing gold. I grabbed his elbows and shook him.

"*Luke, deep breath,*" I said in his head. He did as I said and his eyes returned to normal. Although, he didn't look like he had any intention of not fighting Frank.

"Are you serious? You two actually want to start with this now. Stop!," Luke still was pushing into my hands trying to get past me. "Okay, you are best friends even though you might not see eye to eye right now. Now back off before I take you both down," I said sternly, giving Luke a shove. He was calming down, but he was having trouble controlling himself. I looked over to Frank who had a toothpick in his mouth and a smirk on his face. I gave him a quick glare which made his smirk fade. He looked over at Hunter.

"The wolfy's up," He said, pointing at him. Hunter stood up.

"Call me that again King's lil-," He said angrily.

"Woah," I cut him off, pulling Frank's hand back.

"Oh no, *please* let him finish that sentence. I would like to see how it goes for him," Frank and Hunter were face to face. I smack the palm of my hand against my head. This was insane; they were all at each other's throats. I Flashed in between them.

"No, no, no!" I screamed.

"This guy is half the reason why my kind has been hunted down, tortured, and killed!" Hunter pushed against my hand. I pushed back.

"Yes, Hunter you're right, but he's not like that anymore," I said as I looked over at Frank who was glaring at Hunter. Frank shook his head. He seemed to remember where he was. Hunter's breathing calmed down a little and I took my hands off of both of them.

Frank sighed, "I'm sorry, old habits die hard, I guess." He swiped his hand through his hair and gave a nervous laugh. Hunter stuffed his hands in his pockets and nodded his head. I could feel Luke's piercing eyes on me. I slowly turned my head. Luke's eyes softened.

"*I was so worried,*" He said, starting to talk in my head.

"*I know. I'd say I'm sorry, but I'm not,*" I responded sassily.

Luke gave a chuckle. The others around us knew we were having a conversation they didn't hear and went about doing their own things.

"*Yeah, but I am. I shouldn't have talked to you that way. I promise from now on things will be different. I'll respect your decisions,*" Luke said in a serious voice.

"Thank you, I'll believe it when I see it," I said and couldn't stop myself from giving him a hug. He squeezed back, tucking his chin down into my neck. We both let out a sigh.

"You're going to have to tell the others eventually about you being a Changer and Guardian," I said. He nodded, but didn't respond as the others grew impatient.

"Hey sis, we have to get a move on," Lila said. I nodded my head as Luke and I pulled apart. Hailey and Daniel were packing gear up so it was easier to carry. Frank was listening to the wind trying to see if there was danger. Lila was looking at me, giving me a little smile. Hunter seemed to be healed a little weak, but ready to go.

"Alright, what's the plan?" I asked, which I immediately regretted.

Luke, Frank, and Hunter all started talking at once. They all had different opinions on what our next move should be. It became a circle of voices.

"No," Luke said to Hunter, "We're trying to get to Cassie's."

"That's what I'm saying-" Hunter began.

"I'm sorry, who are you?" Luke waved off Hunter.

"You both are wrong-" Frank said, trying to get in on the conversation.

"Oh shut up, Frank!" Luke yelled. This started a whole argument between the three. They all wanted to be the leader. The alpha males. I rolled my eyes and suddenly thought of a plan.

Hailey came up to me watching them bicker. I sighed, I wasn't going to step in this time. I didn't have the energy. I pushed myself past Luke's block in his head and grinned triumphantly. I got the location out of his head.

"They really are frustrating aren't they? You already got a plan don't you?" She laughed.

"Yup, you ready to go?" I asked.

"Oh please let's," She said.

I smiled and offered her my hand. Daniel came up and took Hailey's and Lila took mine. I had already seen Cassie's location in Luke's head and could easily Flash there. I was sick of the boys fighting. It was time for me to take charge.

"Goodbye suckers!" I laughed at them. They all looked at me in shock as we Flashed away.

Chapter 15

The Cassie's

Alright so a mental note, don't Flash directly into a wolf's territory unannounced. As soon as we landed on Cassie's land, we were surrounded by wolves. Their eyes were like daggers glowing yellow. They had fur of all different colors and were all different sizes. Daniel didn't seem to notice they thought we were a threat and wanted to go pet one. He was all smiles, the growls did not seem to phase him. Luckily, Hailey had a hold of him or he would've been dinner. I raised my hands up slowly trying to show we were no threat.

"Um- hi- um wolves, I'm here to see Jackson Cassie," I said as the wolves began to close in on us. I put Lila and Daniel behind Hailey and I prepared to fight.

"That's enough!" I heard a gruff voice bellow in the distance. The wolves shook their heads and began to open up the circle around us. Then through the middle came a sharply dressed man. He was dressed in a suit that had a stunning gold trim. He had aging features, but two of them I recognized, caramel hair and green eyes. As he walked, the wolves bowed their heads, this was their Alpha. This was Jackson Cassie. In those forest eyes, there was a lot more pain and coldness than before when I saw him in the visions. He looked at me almost as if he saw a ghost.

"Oh my," He said, his eyes softening. He came closer. Lila began to fidget, ready to pounce, her hands started to make little sparks. I held her arm, giving it a reassuring squeeze. Jackson was now face to face with me. He was searching for something in my eyes. He then looked as realization settled into his eyes.

"You're her daughters," He said, his eyes beginning to tear up. At that moment, the boys had Flashed on either side of us. Luke was out of breath and ready to apologize to Mr. Cassie. Hunter was looking at all the wolves feeling at home, but at the same time guarded. Frank was...well Frank. He was trying to act as cool as a cucumber, his toothpick in his mouth and that leather jacket slung over his shoulder. Mr. Cassie was distracted by this for a little bit as he sized up Frank and Hunter then nodded toward Luke. He immediately turned his attention back towards me.

"Dawn," He said, something about his voice sounded so familiar. Luke's head was buzzing. He had never seen a soft side to Mr. Cassie.. He then looked at Lila. His expression fell for a fraction of a second. He quickly recovered, as he focused on me.

"May your old godfather give you a hug?" He said his arms wide. My eyes widened. Godfather? That couldn't be true otherwise this wouldn't have been our first encounter. I wouldn't have been left with Harrison. Why didn't I remember him? He would've been around for all these years. I didn't know what to do so I just nodded. Mr. Cassie swept me up into a huge hug. Lila was trying to grab at my hand, but I waved her off. He was not a threat. I suddenly felt very safe and that it was okay for me to hug back.

"Welcome," He said as we pulled apart. The wolves began to retreat into the woods. Luke took a step forward and bowed his head.

"I am so sorry sir, Dawn meant no disrespect-," he said trying to explain, but also to save himself from trouble. Mr. Cassie waved him off, not even looking at him.

"It doesn't matter, boy. Now, you run along with your other friends and show them around. My goddaughter and I need to have a long awaited chat," He said in a friendly way, but in a tone that sounded like an order. Luke smiled and nodded. The others looked toward me.

"Go on. I'll be fine," I said, waving them off. Frank and Hunter lingered behind, hovering behind me.

"Boys, I see you are very protective of her, but I would never put her in harm's way. I also think she could take me down by herself if she's anything like her mother," Mr. Cassie said seriously with a hint of humor. That seemed to be enough for Hunter, but Frank was not too convinced.

"Dawn, I don't know why, but I feel like you're safe and that I have to leave you now," Hunter said and started to follow in the direction of the others. His panic shot through me. I just his arm as he walked away trying to reassure him.

Feeling compelled to do something by an Alpha must be a wolf thing. Frank, on the other hand, stood his ground.

"If you don't mind sir, I would like to stay with her?" Frank said, with a nice smile still chewing that darn toothpick.

Mr. Cassie sighed, his facial expression darkening, "Bold of you to ask, even if it is to protect Dawn. I should let my wolves tear you apart, Prince." He let out a growl as he glared daggers at Frank.

Frank took out the tooth pick and tilted his head

"I suggest you don't call me that, sir," He replied coolly like the threat didn't bother him, but I noticed how his fingers slightly curled into a fist.

"You could say my allegiance has shifted," Frank's voice softened as we made eye contact. A slow blush filled my cheeks at the way he looked at me. Like I was the reason for his change of heart. Mr. Cassie seemed to consider this for a moment, the earlier tension dissipating.

"As long as his presence is okay with you, Dawn?" Mr. Cassie inquired.

I nodded, I wasn't sure what to expect from this and having Frank here would be comforting especially since Luke seemed to be under orders. Mr. Cassie began to walk and we followed close behind. The trees suddenly broke away and houses began to emerge. This was the Cassie pack. The houses were quaint and normal. People were bustling about everyday chores and kids played ball in the grass. It was peaceful. It felt homey. Normal.

"Mr. Cassie, I have so many questions-" I began to say.

"Call me Uncle Jackson. I understand, we will get to all of them I promise," He said as people around bowed to their knees as he passed by. It was like he was royalty. I looked at Frank and he gave a big shrug. I knew alphas had power, but I didn't think it would be like this. We finally came to a house. No, not a house, a mansion. It was a beautiful white with roses surrounding the whole front yard. It stood in the back far away from the other homes. Jackson opened the door and we followed him in. The inside was ten times more beautiful than the outside; it was like I had walked into a castle. Jackson sat down at a giant dining room table and motioned for me to do the same. Frank began to sit down pulling the chair out with a cringy screeching noise.

"Ah young man, I do believe you can wait in the living room. It is down the hall and to the left," said politely, but a hint of anger was in his voice. I turned to Frank and he didn't move. I kicked his shin hard. He grunted and looked at me angrily.

"Fine," he said with a mock curtsy in Jackson's direction and stormed out.

"I'm sorry about Frank. He's still getting used to how to act like a Guardian," I said, folding my hands together.

"I'm glad you have people who love you in your corner and would do anything to protect you, like I couldn't," He said with a sad voice. I looked down and didn't know what to say. I had one burning question and decided to just rip off the band aid.

"Do you know what happened to my mother?" I asked, looking directly into his eyes. Jackson visibly winced. This was a sore subject for him. He swallowed and looked at me, his green eyes sad.

"I lost her, as to what actually happened to her I'm not sure," He said quietly. I gritted my teeth, I was starting to get angry. That wasn't an answer.

"Look Uncle Jack or whatever you want me to call you, I need some answers," I started to get salty. Jackson looked away. I could tell there was so much he wanted to say, but just couldn't find the words. After a few minutes in silence, he suddenly looked up.

"If you're anything like your mother, maybe I can show you?" He reached out his hand expecting me to grab his. He was saying my mom could see visions too. I had more in common with her than I ever knew. It was not my favorite thing to do, but I reached out slowly and hovered my hand over his. I looked at him and he smiled. It was genuine, not the Harrison fake smile I was used to. I grabbed his hand and he squeezed mine. That's when I felt that pull back to the past.

***

Opening my eyes there sat my mother and Jackson. She was holding his hand and stroking his back with the other arm. Jackson appeared to be crying.

"Jack, I'll be fine and back in no time you won't even have time to miss me," She said with her sweet voice. Jackson looked up at her, tears streaming down his face.

"That is such a lie, you're choosing him Darcy. You will always choose him," Jackson said and tore his hand away from her. Darcy looked at him in shock. She didn't know how to comfort him. I assumed the "him" Jackson was referring to was my father. She went to touch his shoulder and then thought better of it. She bit her lip and tears started to well up in her eyes.

"I'm sorry Jackson. I love you, but I can't live here anymore," She got up and Flashed away. Jackson was left alone.

The image swirled. I was pulled forward a little bit.

My mother stood in front of a mirror looking at herself. She was in a stunning wedding dress that made her look like an angel. The train went all the way back to where I was standing behind her. I heard a door close behind me. I turned around and there stood Jackson in a black suit, his eyes lit up when he saw her. My mother saw his reflection in the mirror and turned. She was surprised.

"You came?" She said with a huge smile. She rushed towards him and gave him a big hug. Jackson pulled her in close and kissed the top of her head.

"Of course, who else was going to be your maid of honor?" He chuckled. Darcy let go of him and stepped back.

"I thought you were against this wedding. What made you change your mind? Oh, how's the pack?" She said excitedly. I realized Jackson had a little wrapped box in his hands. He set it on the table beside him.

"Darc, slow down. You guys are two of my best friends in the world. Well, at least you still are my best friend," He shrugged and gave a smile. Darcy scrutinized his answer. She was looking for more. Then she noticed the box.

"What's in there?" she asked, shifting her head in the direction of the box. Jackson grabbed it and handed it to her.

"A wedding present," He said, as Darcy grabbed it looking confused. She unwrapped the box and took the top off. She gasped. There in the center was a little pulsating purple heart charm.

"It's meant to go on a chain. I know we haven't been on the best of terms Darc, but I wanted you to know that I'm always here for you, so whenever you hold on to that heart I will know your location. It'll come in handy if you're ever in danger," He said looking down at his shoes.

"It's beautiful, thank you. Aren't I the one who's supposed to protect you?" She asked, trying to catch his eyes, but Jackson didn't look up. He turned away from her.

"Hey," Darcy said, walking over to him and placing a hand on his shoulder, "Look at me." Jackson slowly turned and looked at her, his eyes were glowing in wolf form a little.

"You're angry," She said, but didn't take a step back. Jackson shook his head, his eyes returning back to green.

"There are many emotions that trigger my wolf side," He said, stepping closer to her. Jackson reached out one hand and stroked his fingertips against Darcy's cheek. "Being in love with your former best friend's girl and not being able to do anything about it does the trick," Jackson said, placing both hands on either side of her face. Darcy now

tried to look away. I could tell this was the first time Jackson had said it out loud, but she had always known. He held her gaze.

"Listen to me," He said, searching her eyes, "Don't marry him...please," Jackson said as Darcy began shaking her head and tears started to form in her eyes.

"I have to," She said, pulling his hands off her face and stepping back.

"See that-that right there is what doesn't make sense. You're not doing this for love, what you said just proves it. So why are you marrying him?!" Jackson yelled. Darcy turned around ignoring his question. Jackson began to growl. "Why are you marrying him, Darcy?!"

Darcy whirled around to face him. "Jack-please, don't make me choose" She choked, full on sobbing.

"I will not stand here and let you make this mistake and let the woman I love go until you give me an explanation," Jackson was calming down as he saw Darcy's tear riddled face and he turned to leave. Darcy stepped toward him as his hand turned the doorknob.

"I'm pregnant, okay!" She yelled back. Jackson flinched and looked at her in shock. He knew by Guardian decree that if she was pregnant she had to marry the father or risk execution. The outdated laws were something I felt I needed to change. He turned to face her. They wanted to hug each other, it was clear, but Jackson was done. He opened the door and left, slamming it in my mother's face. I tried to reach out to her, but I was pulled forward again.

In front of me stood the other boy from the visions, his black hair and golden eyes were glaring at Jackson. They looked like they were about to fight. Jackson's eyes were glowing yellow, his mouth pulled back into a sneer. Meanwhile, the other one had a devious smile on his face.

"Alright wolfy, are we doing this or not?" The black haired boy asked, pulling a knife out. I recognized myself in him. My father? Before I could get a better loo at him, Jackson came barreling toward him at full speed surprisingly not changing into wolf form. The other one was prepared for his attack and took him down to his back with one blow. He held the knife against Jackson's neck and knelt one knee on each arm. He dug the knife in further, drawing a little bit of blood from Jackson's neck.

"You mean nothing to her, do you hear me? Nothing!" The black haired boy started off whispering and built to a roar. I heard a very loud snap as Jackson shrieked in pain. He had broken something in Jackson. I couldn't quite make it out, my vision started to blur. My head began a familiar throb, but I tried to step closer and hear what they were saying. As he was on top of Jackson, he held a chain in his other hand and dangled it

in front of his face. I focused more and my vision started to clear up. It was the purple heart Jackson had given my mother in the previous vision. Jackson tried to fight against the hold he had on him, but it was no use.

"You think for a second this will keep you in her life, you're wrong!" He screamed in Jackson's face. He then placed the heart next to his foot. I took a step forward knowing what he was about to do. He lifted his foot and crushed the heart like a bug. There was purple smoke coming off of the glass pieces.

"Now I've broken more than just your heart or was that my wife? No matter... I'm through with you," He said with a chuckle raising the knife up high preparing to kill Jackson. I wanted to help, I wanted to shove him out of the way. My feet couldn't move. I wasn't actually there. My head started to pound.

"No!" I heard a familiar voice scream. Darcy had Flashed in, stealing the knife out of the black haired boy's hand before he could complete the act. He looked up at her and his mood immediately shifted.

"Darcy, I'm so-" before he could finish the sentence my mom Flashed Jackson out of there. The scene shifted a little bit. I was not pulled forward or back. My mom was in the hospital wing of DEATH getting Jackson treated. He was sitting up and his shoulder hung in a sling. Jackson winced as she touched it. She took her hand off and stepped back. She looked about ready to leave when Jackson pulled her arm.

"Darcy, I'm sorry for storming out at the wedding. I came here to tell you that and I was hoping you guys didn't move yet. Then I ran into--and he just started talking about you and I couldn't stop myself," He apologized with as much sincerity as he could. She smiled and nodded her head.

"Well I do have a question for you," She said as she looked down.

"Anything," Jackson said quickly.

"Will you be her godfather?" She asked excitedly, placing a hand on her stomach. Jackson was surprised she knew the gender, but he nodded his head. They looked so happy I wanted to join in with them, but I was yanked forward.

Jackson was reading something outside as the rain poured down. It looked like a poster and he looked angry. I stepped closer to read it too. It was from Galrich.

Darcy Shadows has gone missing under mysterious circumstances. Shadows suspected to be dead. Husband offering an award to anyone that finds her. She is a mother of two girls. Jackson slammed his hand against the wall that the poster was on and tore the poster off. He put his head against the wall in defeat.

"If anyone can find her, it's you," A voice behind Jackson said with great command. When Jackson turned around, he saw that same blacked haired boy, I assume my

father's, golden eyes staring back at him. My father smiled, but his smile wasn't quite right. He looked more twisted than when I saw him in the last vision. His features looked different. He looked less human, if that was even possible. Jackson glared at him.

"You are the reason she left or am I wrong?," He was remembering something. It was something I had seen before with Jada in the Fallen Choices. Wouldn't that mean that didn't actually happen? The vision of my mom leaving behind the two boys. My father? My heart quickened. Then why was his information erased? She was running from something. Was it him?

"This story you're creating is making this a lot harder on her I'm sure. She's trying to protect your family. Why are you so hell bent on destroying that?" Jackson questioned him intensely. Darcy had never told him why she left, but he had a sneaking suspicion it was because of my father, I could tell.

He smirked, "You don't think I've already found her, wolf?" Jackson turned in shock. "I said I would get her back at all costs and that's what I did. I'll leave you with that thought." Jackson went to grab him, but he had already Flashed away.

***

I was torn back to the present where I was holding a much older Jackson Cassie's hand. I felt sweat dripping from my forehead. Frank was back in the room with a seriously worried look on his face. I looked at him then at Jackson. I needed more, this still didn't give me the answers I wanted. I closed my eyes and squeezed his hand again and nothing. I looked up at him angrily.

"Send me back," I choked. It was hard to breathe for some reason. Jackson looked sadly into my eyes.

"Unfortunately, I can not, whatever you saw, is what you'll see again and I don't think your body can handle it," Jackson said, releasing my hand. Frank had his hand on my shoulder. My head felt like it was getting hot over and over again. I could feel my control slipping away. The house started to shake and I knew it was me doing it. I had to breathe. I had to get it under control. The lights flickered intensely and my vision started to blur. Frank tried to shake me out of it. I think he was saying something to me. Jackson then came rushing over and placed his hands on my face. I heard him say my name over and over again.

"Dawn, you are in control. You got this. Don't let this side of you out," I started to hear his voice more clearly then slowly the earth stopped shaking. I took a deep breath.

"I'm sorry," I said standing up. "I need some air." Frank tried to follow me out, but I pushed him away. I ran outside and clutched my chest. I could finally breathe normally again. That trip back to the past really did a number on me. I wanted more answers though and standing outside wasn't helping. I went to go back inside when I felt the most familiar presence in the world. Luke was standing just before the steps not daring to go any further. Again, I wondered if it was a wolf thing?

"You okay?" He asked worriedly as I just looked at him. He knew that was a stupid question. He could see inside my head for goodness sake. It was stupid, but he didn't know what else to say. Luke wasn't technically allowed to come up the steps unless specifically told that he could. He tried to move as close to me as he could and reached out and grabbed my hand. We were silent for a while till my breathing and heart rate slowed. Luke didn't try to talk in my mind. I think he was afraid I would shut him out. We also heard Frank giving Jackson an earful. Jackson didn't technically do anything wrong. I felt for him. He lost my mom in ways I couldn't even imagine. I never really knew her. I had a different kind of pain. The only thing that annoyed me about him is why he stayed away for so long. The Guardian community thinks he's missing. It was like he was hiding from them. Luke had watched what I was shown by Jackson at least three times trying to make sense of them. He didn't let go of my hand. I was grateful he was here even though I was still mad at him. After a while, Jackson came out with a red faced Frank who stormed off not giving Luke and I a glance. I wonder what Jackson said to him?

"Why don't you guys come to the bonfire tonight?" Jackson asked nicely, as he stayed in the doorway. Jackson didn't want to say the wrong thing. He was being careful around me. This only frustrated me more, but there was no use getting upset over it. Luke looked at it as if he had to go anyway and he really wanted to have some company.

"Yeah okay," I said. I wasn't sure what else to say. Jackson smiled and started coming down the steps.

"Luke, why don't you show her around? You may also stay with her all day if that's what you want to do," Jackson said, the second part with a more serious tone. Luke smiled, he was very happy now.

"Thank you so much, sir," He bowed his head. Jackson nodded back then looked at me. I could tell there was more he wanted to tell me, more I didn't know about. He didn't know what to say.

There was one more thing I needed to ask. "Wait! You know Jada Moon?" He seemed a little shocked by my question.

"Yes, we are long time friends and she has helped me in the past," He said. I already knew this, but I wanted to see if he would tell me the truth.

"She helped everyone forget you?" I asked. Jackson shifted uncomfortably. He gave a big sigh.

"Yes, she did," He said hesitantly. I nodded my head not knowing what to say.

"I'll see you all later," Jackson said and walked away before I could ask any more questions. Luke grabbed my other hand and pulled me off the steps up to standing.

"Now that you're here, and Alpha has given me some control today I can tell you whatever you want to know about wolves," Luke said a little giddy, his inner nerd was showing. I suddenly felt something open up in his head, something that had been closed off to me for a long time. It was all his wolf memories, everything he had experienced in wolf form. He loved being a wolf, way more than I ever knew. I always thought he wanted a different life because he had to hide a part of him, but his wolf side wasn't the one he wanted to change. Luke wanted to give up his Guardian side more than anything. I saw images of him running through the woods and his experiences at the Cassie Camp. I also saw a beautiful girl wolf that would pop in every once in a while in his memories. Luke loved the speed, the hunt, and most of all the loyalty.

"Dawn, I know you're taking a lot in right now, but I want you to know I never wanted to keep this from you. I tried to show you this part of me, but when I found out I was a wolf and changed for the first time, a wall went up in my head. It's because Jackson was always my Alpha. I was meant to belong with his pack and blocking this side was his order. He was trying to protect me from the Elders finding out what I am. I understand if you're upset or want to throw me into the-," Luke was droning on and I couldn't take it anymore. I threw myself at him, tackling him to the ground. I smiled.

"For a wolf, you're pretty weak," I teased. Luke arched an eyebrow and flipped me on my back. I laughed so hard tears came out of my eyes.

"Okay , okay," I said, trying to catch my breath. Luke rolled over onto the grass laying beside me. I picked up my head and laid it against his chest. He wrapped one arm around my shoulder.

"I'm not mad at you anymore, dingus," I said, nuzzling my head more into his chest. Luke didn't have to say anything, I could hear him loud and clear. He was happy and where he belonged.

***

Luke showed me all around the "JC Den" as he liked to call it. He introduced me to almost everyone. Luke showed me how he hunts as a wolf and where I could find something to eat.

"Alpha-um sorry habit- Jackson did go missing for a while looking for your mother. He doesn't talk about it and no one knows what actually happened to him. He came back assuming Alpha and has made our society a secret. If people knew he was here all along, he would be arrested," Luke was trying to explain why everyone thinks Jackson is missing. I nodded my head. I guess it makes sense, I would want to run too. Luke was babbling away and I became lost in my thoughts. Was my father the bad guy? Did he hurt my mom? What does this mean for me? Is this why I act the way I do? Is it embedded in my genetics? Luke was too far gone with what he was talking about. I was glad he wasn't interested in my thoughts right now. Luke and I were making our way to the bonfire, the sun was just beginning to set. We spent hours talking about everything he couldn't share with me. The smile on his face was breathtaking. I listened intently to most of it.

"...oh and one time I had to sneak out of DEATH because there was some pack meeting and you caught me, remember?" Luke asked excitedly.

"Oh wow, that's what you were doing? You told me you were studying late at night. I was dumb enough to believe you," I laughed. Luke joined in, when he suddenly stopped dead in his tracks when he saw something. I kept laughing and then looked over to what he was looking at. We were close to the bonfire, I could smell the smoke. In front of us, was that girl that was lingering in his thoughts before. She smiled at me, her eyes were a bright ice blue. She was petite, but looked like a strong presence. Luke became nervous, I could tell. She had a certain effect on him. She ran up and gave me a hug. I gasped in shock.

"Oh I'm sorry! I just have heard so much about you and I'm so glad Lukey can tell you everything now. You don't know how much of a pout he is when...well I suppose you do know. Anywayyyy... I'm Jordan Cassie, next in line for Alpha. Sorry about the hug," She said out of breath at the end, extending her hand. Jordan was gorgeous. She had skin that was literally glowing, that complimented her smile. She wasn't bragging either about being Jackson's daughter. It was just a fact. I could tell from just those few words she said to me she was a genuinely pure person. I took her hand and shook it.

"I'm Dawn Shadows," I said. She smiled and nodded because of course she already knew. Luke was getting fidgety next to me. He wasn't totally comfortable with us meeting. It all felt a bit overwhelming for him. Luke's two worlds were finally colliding. It was going to take some time getting used to it. She made him nervous. This was the girl he had a crush on no doubt about that.

"Hey J, it's been awhile," Luke said. He stepped forward and they embraced for a few seconds. It was a little bit of an awkward hug. Jordan pulled away and gave him a little shove.

"Took you long enough. I have always wanted to meet you, but this one can never break the rules. It's sooo annoying," She said with a little flop of her velvet hair. She looked at me to agree. She knew I would.

"Yeah he's the worst, it's like he's trying to be a-."

"Gelical?" Jordan finished my sentence. I nodded my head. She knew him well. I felt these mixture of feelings within my chest. Jealousy? I didn't have a reason to be jealous. It just hit a nerve. Luke was my best friend, but obviously he had this whole other life I never knew about.

"I was just heading to the bonfire. I would love it if you would join me?" She asked, looking at me with the excitement of a little kid asking for ice cream. Jordan's smile was so contagious I started to smile, when I caught myself it was already too late. I looked at her with my smile and nodded. Luke started to follow us and Jordan stepped in front of him.

"Slow down there bud, I am taking Dawn. This is some much needed girl time. You can head to the bonfire in a few minutes," She shoved him back a little. Luke wasn't mad like I thought he'd be. He just smiled and waited. Luke's mind was wide open now and he was calm. It was something I wasn't used to, everything was so complicated recently, but I'm glad Luke found his home. I followed Jordan throughout the camp. The entire camp was set up strategically for protection and to keep it hidden. The bonfire, as soon as we came in sight of it, was the center of the camp. It stood tall. It wasn't your normal roasting marshmallows bonfire, this was at least 8 feet tall. It was breathtaking.

Jordan saw me admiring it. "This is where our pack gets together every weekend and just has fun. The fire never dies out here. We always keep it lit. It is safe because it is hidden away, so outside of the camp you can't find it. There's shields all around it so the smoke can't escape and give us away," She said. I loved this place. The wolves seemed so free compared to the life I was used to.

"It's amazing," I smiled at her. There were young and old partying around the fire. They had food out buffet style and next to it was a bar. Jordan approached the bar and asked the woman behind it for two of whatever she wanted to give us. The woman nodded and looked me up and down, she knew I did not belong here.

"Don't worry Mama G, she's cool," Jordan said, noticing the woman's tension.

"Ah yes, I think it best your papa don't allow Guardians in, they trouble. Especially this one," Mama G said with a thick accent I couldn't quite place. She started to make two drinks, but still eyed me up and down. Jordan shook her head.

"Mama G is one of our Omega's. She was in the last war which has caused some trust issues. She is old, but don't look it. I think it might be a special ability of hers. She's older than my dad and his right hand. She also makes the best drinks and I can't tell you what's in them I don't even know. She says it's her secret recipe," Jordan said the last part a little louder and thanked Mama G. I nodded towards her and tried to smile, but her eyes changed to silver. I think she was trying to intimidate me. I just politely smiled back. Mama G continued to glare. Jordan started to walk closer to the fire, handing me the drink and I followed close behind, wondering where Luke and the others had gone. The wolves were laughing up a storm. I don't remember the last time I've been around this much fun. Jordan was trying to talk over all of the noise, telling me stories and the in and outs of the camp. I wasn't really listening.

"Dawn! My dad's about to make a speech" I looked and then saw Jackson walking to the center just before the fire. The whole crowd started to become silent. I searched for my friends. Hailey and Lila were on the other side across from Jordan and I, they seemed to have made some friends. I couldn't seem to find Luke, though. Hunter, Frank, and Dan were standing closer to the outside. Dan wanted to go off by himself I could tell because he was struggling against Frank's hand. Hunter was looking around, seeming comfortable, while I could tell Frank's teeth were gritting as all sorts of wolves glared at him. This wasn't the safest place for him with his past and all these wolves seemed to know it. Jackson finally made it to the center of the fire where a riser was out for him to stand on.

He began to speak, "My pack! I have some news. My goddaughter, Dawn Shadows, has come and found me after all these years. She has brought many of her Guardian friends with her, as well as two of our own Changers. I expect you to treat them with the utmost respect. Is that clear?" Cassie questioned everyone. He was a natural leader that much was clear. The aura he emitted demanded presence.

The wolves responded in unison with nodding heads and respectful looks, "YES SIR".

The wolves around me were all different. They all had very unique characteristics that set them apart, yet you could feel their bond in the air. It was almost palpable. I understood what unity really felt like in their presence. It was a family without a doubt. A family of probably more than 600 people, but a family nonetheless. Luke's emotions were so clear in my head I could feel the bond he had with these people, every single one of them. Luke and I had a similar bond. A smile began to creep on my lips. It was a nice feeling to just feel simple happiness and see it among others. It made me want it, but I realized I have it. I know Lila, Dan, Hailey, and Luke are my family, but before it felt like an obligation, now I know it's more than that. Harrison can sometimes be included in that, but I guess my family isn't simple. Hunter and Frank were just joining it. I looked at them across the crowd. Hunter caught my eye and smiled his sea green eyes filling me with an emotion I couldn't quite place. Frank looked in my direction, his teeth were less gritted and he looked more comfortable and that stupid tooth pick was back in his mouth. I felt close with both of them and really related to them. They were fighters. The wolves were fighters. I knew like the wolves I would fight for my family to the death.

Jackson continued, "I want to stress the importance of refraining leaving the camp at night. The Packers are still at large and it is my number one priority to make sure none of you fall into their hands. I also wanted to report to you my scouts reported demon sightings on the outskirts of our shields,". The crowd took in a collective gasp and my body went rigid. Demons were sneaking around outside? We were lucky we hadn't run into them yet. They were a threat, but ever since the war there's been little to no mention of large gatherings of them.

I felt Luke's presence in my mind, *"Dawn, if demons were around here should we have sensed it?"*

"We should have."

It was odd Guardians are supposed to inherently know a trace of a demon, any demon. I couldn't imagine why we hadn't felt it.

"Now, now everyone. It is no cause to worry. A few demons out and about is nothing to be concerned about. I wanted you to be aware so you know why I will be closing off the east half of our border till further notice," Jackson said calmly. I had a sneaking suspicion that he was hiding something. After all, is a great leader ever truly transparent with their followers? No, there's always more to a story. Demons lurking about was news to the Guardians, otherwise, he would have reported it and we would've been sent down to capture them. Which meant, Jackson didn't want the Guardians to know they were around. I didn't know for sure, but I definitely was going to find out. First, I needed more information about my mother's past which meant I had to play nicely.

"Alpha, you do realize we have the Prince here?" One of the wolves called out, referring to Frank. The wolves around me whispered and it became tense. Jackson nodded in the wolf's direction, his face was completely calm, but I could tell he didn't like the outburst.

"Frank is no threat to us. He has made a change and if my goddaughter trusts him then so do I," Jackson said finding my gaze. I could sense the wolves eyes on me. They weren't happy about Frank being here which was understandable. There was some growling around me, but no one made a move for Frank. I looked over at him, but he seemed unfazed.

"He returned me back to my Pack," Another's voice piped up, "He freed all of the prisoners, which included me within the Packer camp. We should be thanking him." This caused arguments of insue, but I was grateful someone spoke up otherwise I would've.

"Enough of this talk!" Jackson spread his arms wide "Let the festivities begin!" This caused cheers, yells, and all kinds of noises to escape from the wolves, all tension from the previous few seconds disappeared. Jordan was still standing next to me. I had forgotten she was there with all the commotion. She whipped around to face me with a bright sun shining smile on her face.

"I think it's time to get this party started!" She said, pulling me by the arm and towards Luke who was pushing through bodies to get to us. Frank and Hunter were making their way towards us too. I tried to find my sister and I realized her and Dan had Flashed on top of the bar. Mama G was smacking their legs with a towel looking very annoyed. Lila was jumping back and forth missing the lashes while Dan was getting hit by every swing. Hailey seemed to be trying to get them down looking very bossy. They seemed to be having fun and weirdly normal. I decided not to worry about them as Jordan tugged me more into the crowd. Luke and the boys reached us.

"Hi, I'm Jordan, Jackson's daughter," She introduces herself to Hunter and Frank.

"Oh wow, good to meet you, I'm Hunter," He said politely. Jordan shook his hand as he extended it. She turned to Frank, her expression suddenly losing its brightness. Frank didn't change his expression or try to introduce himself. Jordan seemed to have some familiarity with him. I guess being the former Packer called Prince, King's right hand man, Frank was known in the Changer community. Jordan quickly tried to hide her sudden change in expression and smiled. It was a little fake.

Frank took the tooth pick out of his mouth and took on a serious face, "I think we need a re-introduction. I'm Frank Summers, a Guardian,". He added a little emphasis on Guardian to make sure she knew he was no longer a threat. He didn't extend a hand knowing she wouldn't take it. Jordan just nodded the fake smile still plastered on her face. The party raged on around us as we were stuck in the awkward air that Frank and Jordan seemed to have created.

Hunter decided to break the ice. "I don't know about you guys, but I could use some time to relax. Let's dance!"

Luke snorted, "I'm not dancing."

"Who said you had a choice?" Jordan grabbed his hand and pulled him into a crowd of dancing wolves. I watched them go and felt a little jealous. Luke would've never let me do that. Hunter ran after them. I could tell he was excited to be around his own kind. When I turned back Frank was walking away from the bonfire, and was almost out of sight. I ran after him instinctively.

"Hey!" I called after him. Frank didn't stop walking. I Flashed in front of him inches from his face. He looked at me. There was a sadness in his eyes, something I hadn't yet seen before from him. He quickly tried to shake it off and put on a devilish grin.

"Shadows, are you following me?" He asked, crossing his arms. I wanted to question him about what I had seen in his eyes, but I thought better of it. I wanted to help make him forget his past.

"Actually, yes," I said, giving him a little shove backwards. He laughed, but it didn't touch his eyes.

"I have a bet for you," I said knowing he couldn't turn it down. He loved to gamble.

"I'm not falling for it, Shadows. You. Are. Not. Getting. Me. To. Dance," He said with another laugh this time his eyes began to soften.

"I admittedly wasn't going to say that, but now that you mentioned it...," I took his shoulder and spun him back to the crowd.

"This is not how bets work. You're cheating!" He yelled at me trying to sound serious, but didn't resist my pushes. The wolves were free spirits. There wasn't any party like a wolf party. Frank and I joined on the outside of where most of the dancing was happening. Frank looked at me uncomfortably, shoving his hand in his pockets still chewing on the toothpick. He was going to have to explain how that's survived this whole time eventually. Now I admit, I wasn't the best dancer, but I had some rhythm. I reached for the toothpick to pull it out of his mouth and he shoved my hand away. He slowly moved his hand to it and removed it from his teeth with a big grin then put it in his front jeans pocket. I laughed and grabbed his hands and started making his body sway, pulling his arms forward and back. He resisted at first but after a few minutes he started to loosen up. We started jumping and shaking our heads like we were at an intense concert. The beat of the music flowed through me and I was all smiles which is something that hasn't happened in a while. Frank grabbed my hand and spun me into him then quickly back out. He then picked me up by my hips and my hands were on his shoulders. As he brought me down, my hands grazed the zipper on his leather jacket. I felt a spark and before I was back on my feet I was yanked forward in time.

***

I didn't comprehend what was happening at first. I was in what looked like DEATH, but it was on fire. I couldn't quite make out everything. It was like watching a video that was pixelated, disjointed and fuzzy. Then clear as day I saw Frank standing next to...me?! I had my hand on his jacket. It looked like I was telling him to stand back. There were figures in front of me, but they were blurred. I couldn't make out their faces. There were words exchanged. I couldn't make out all of them either. That's when I noticed Luke was also in my vision with Hunter. I could tell we were surrounded by blurred figures with no faces. I looked at myself. I was beaten and exhausted, but my face looked dangerous. I noticed I had a shiny weapon in my hand. I didn't recognize it, because it wasn't mine. I dropped the weapon and raised my hands. The hidden figures moved forward seizing Frank and I. I wanted to shout, wanting to do something, but my voice faltered. I finally heard Luke screaming, "No, Dawn!" The picture became more fuzzy. I tried to run to Luke's voice, but I was thrown back to the present.

***

I gasped as my feet touched land and reality came back into my vision. My head hurt. This whole going back and forth in time was not the best for my body. I wondered if Jada had gone through the same thing. Frank was still holding my hips and my hands were on his shoulders bracing myself. He looked very worried and was trying to say something to me, but my ears were ringing. Frank didn't know what was going on. I could tell he was trying to get Luke to come over to us. I shook my head trying to make the ringing stop. I noticed my legs were wobbly.

"Dawn? Can you hear me?" Frank tried to yell over the music. I nodded my head as the ringing was going away. Luke came out of the group of people with Jordan and Hunter at his heels. Frank had somehow picked me up and we were walking away from the party.

"What is going on?" Frank asked Luke. That's when I felt Luke's presence in my head. I groaned. I didn't want him to see what I just saw.

"She was somehow triggered to be sent to the future. She's okay, I think she's just in shock," Luke explained to everyone. He didn't acknowledge what he saw in my head, but he did seem scared by it.

"Let's get her to my house," I heard Jordan say. She was making people move out of the way so Frank could carry me. I was thankful they were so concerned, but I was fine. My body was just very drained from the journey in time I just took. The last thing I felt was my skin hitting blankets. My vision was blurring again and then everything went black.

Chapter 16

My Beginning

My mother was walking toward me. I could see her clear as day. I scanned my eyes over her and tried to see where we were, but all around her was blurry. Those blue eyes, wavy dark hair, and smile I missed so much were looking down at me. She was stroking my hair. Am I dreaming? I must be dreaming. It felt so real though, I could actually feel her touch. I wanted to say something, but words would not form. I was speechless. I wanted to cry, scream, laugh, but I couldn't use my voice. My mom got up to her feet and started to walk away from me. I tried to stand, but I couldn't move. She was leaving me. This wasn't right. This couldn't happen again. She looked back at me and blew me a kiss, as white light consumed her.

***

I bolted straight up sweat dripping down my forehead. A deep yearning for my mom settled in my chest. My eyes began to well with tears and I blinked trying to not let myself cry. I realized I was in a lavish bedroom sitting on a king's size bed. It was dark in the room with very little light pouring in from the window in front of me. I suddenly heard what sounded like a choking noise. Luke was sitting in a chair to my right snoring very loudly. I relaxed a little bit. I was inside Jackson Cassie's house. I looked down towards my feet and Lila was snuggled up wrapped in a blanket from head to toe fast asleep. How long had I been out? I looked to my left, sensing Luke and Lila weren't the only ones here. Frank was also in a chair sleeping with his toothpick dangling from his mouth. Hunter was across the room lying on the carpeted floor with a pillow under his head in a ball near the big window. Daniel was in a circular chair next to where Hunter was lying, that seemed to swallow up his whole body sleeping peacefully. Hailey was sitting on the windowsill, and I noticed she was awake. She turned her head and looked at me. She gave an excited smile and hopped off the sill carefully avoiding a sleeping Hunter. She slowly made her way to the bed and got in it next to me making sure she didn't bounce it too much so Lila wouldn't wake up.

"I'm glad you're awake. You gave us all a scare," Hailey whispered.

My voice rasped, "I'm sorry." I tried clearing my throat.

"So it's true you can see the past and future?" She asked. I nodded my head. I couldn't remember the last time Hailey and I had an actual conversation.

"Wow, is it scary?" Hailey looked at me while getting a little closer.

"No, not scary," I whispered, "It's more crazy and weird and utterly exhilarating." I hadn't really thought how I felt about being able to travel through time, but the words just came pouring out. Hailey nodded her head and bit her lip, deep in thought.

"I'm sorry," she said so quietly I could barely make it out.

"Why?" I asked.

"Well...," she paused and then gave a sigh, "I've always been sort of jealous of you."

My eyes widened in shock. The perfect Miss Hailey was jealous of me? I didn't know what to say.

"I've never liked you because of it. You are always so brave and intimidating. I've never known how to talk to you," She continued after I didn't respond. I looked at her, still shocked. I thought about what she was saying. We have never been close, but I didn't think it was either one of our faults. We were just so different. She was waiting for me to respond while I caught better glimpses of her face from the light of the moon pouring through the window. I never noticed before how strikingly beautiful Hailey's features are. She had deep grey eyes that were so full of knowledge. It complimented her dark caramel skin and curly black hair.

"Hailey, you don't have to be jealous of me. You already have brains, beauty, not to mention that invisibility power of yours. It quite literally saved all of our lives," I said with a smile. Hailey smiled back at me, but I could tell she didn't believe me.

"We all have our insecurities and fears, Dawn. I've felt like I've been...stuck in your shadow my whole life. I've felt invisible. My own power caused me fear. Not anymore and it's a nice feeling," Hailey gave a little sigh of relief. I felt bad that I caused her some insecurity. I knew I wasn't always nice to her, but I never knew how much it affected her till now. I reached my arms out to her wanting to give her a hug. We embraced for a quick second.

When we broke apart, Hailey looked to Luke "He's a Changer and a Guardian." It wasn't a question. I nodded my head.

"He could have told all of us. We wouldn't have said anything," Hailey said with a tilt of her head.

"I told him that a thousand times, he was afraid he'd be looked at differently. Not to mention the more people who knew the greater the chance of the Elders finding out," I explained as Luke let out a chorkling snore that made me smile. Hailey nodded.

"I don't think Danny and Lila have noticed yet," She said with a shrug. It didn't matter if they did or not. Hailey let out a giggle after a moment.

"I pray for Luke when Lila finds out," She said, containing her laughter.

"She'll set him on fire, while we'll get the popcorn," I grinned. Hailey clamped a hand over her mouth as silent laughter rocked her body. I laughed with her, not caring as much who I woke up. We sat there for a moment looking at our friends...our family.

"Well we should get some more sleep," Hailey whispered, getting off the bed carefully. I nodded. My body still felt drained. I didn't know how that was still possible when I was out for hours. I watched Hailey get back up on the windowsill, as I laid back down. I was out as soon as my head hit the pillow.

***

We have been at Jackson's for a little over a week now and I am nowhere closer to getting the answers I need about my mother or father. Jackson seemed to always be busy or "out on patrol" whenever I tried to talk to him. He was starting to give me suspicious vibes, as much as I wanted to trust him, I didn't know if I should. It felt like he was keeping secrets from me. When I did see him, he calculated his words carefully. Luke did not share my concerns. Jackson was Luke's alpha, so it made sense that he didn't want to believe he was anything but amazing. Luke was happier than

I've ever seen him. He was telling real jokes that were actually funny. He told everyone about his secret. They didn't even seem surprised. Lila didn't even throw a fireball at his head to Hailey and I's surprise. Luke was also spending most of his time trying to impress Jordan. I have to admit it made me jealous. I didn't feel as important to him anymore. I felt like I was being replaced or better yet eclipsed by her sunshine. I mean I couldn't blame Luke for liking her, I even wanted to be friends with her, she was the ultimate girl next door everyone wanted to be around her. She would light up any room she walked into. I think I had the opposite effect; the wolves' moods darkened when I was around. I was starting to wonder if that was one of my abilities?

Luke told me I was crazy, but I wasn't so sure. I could feel in his head that I made his mood shift too. He always said it was because he constantly worried for me. I put it off because of my reckless tendencies in the past, but maybe it was more than that. I have been keeping Luke out of my head. I didn't want to know how much he was worried about the vision I saw. I couldn't explain it and it only made it worse to worry about something that might not happen. I wasn't bonding well with the others at camp either. It was like the wolves thought of me as a threat. I couldn't blame them, I was an outsider invading their territory. I would act the same way if they just barged into DEATH. Hunter was the only one that was unaffected by my presence. He liked having me around. We had spent a good amount of time together since my incident. Frank on the other hand was walking on eggshells around me. He was worried he would trigger another vision, especially after Luke had mentioned he had triggered a vision before. When I saw him the day after, he politely nodded his head and strode off in the other direction. I of course was very frustrated by his behavior, but I decided to give him space. He was already on edge here fighting his Packer tendencies.

Hunter and I would go on long walks around the outskirts of the Packs border. I wanted to go on the walks because I was suspicious of those so-called demons Jackson said were lurking around this side of the camp. I knew we weren't allowed to be here, but it didn't make any sense that we didn't feel the presence of any demons. I remember the sensation vividly since I came in contact with my first demon. It was when the Elders brought us in and released a captured demon on us. My skin felt like it was sizzling and the hair on my arms stood straight up. My mind became hyperactive and my heart seemed to beat out of my chest. Guardians are able to feel a demon within a 5 mile radius. The time we've been at Cassie's I haven't felt anything. I was afraid there was something I was missing. When I told the others about my concerns, Hunter was the only one who took me seriously. He agreed to investigate with me, although we have found nothing yet. The trees around us were an inviting green. Various animals hid in their crafted homes avoiding us. As I looked down at my feet, they were encircled with spiders. I have noticed a ton of spiders recently.

"Dawn, I believe you about there being something up around here," Hunter said as we were walking around the perimeter ripping me from my thoughts. My eyes shifted and my brows furrowed.

"Well thank you, you seem to be the only one," I said with a laugh. I was beginning to think I was just being paranoid. Hunter and I walked in silence for a few more minutes. He seemed nervous about something, his head was buzzing.

"Out with it. What's on your mind, Loves?" I said, giving him a little shove. I still couldn't figure out how Hunter and I were connected. I was the only one that could reach out to him though. He wasn't able to get inside my head. He tried a couple of times and said it hurt his head. He could feel the connection and feel me in his head, but could not do anything with it. It was a one way channel that only worked when I activated it.

He gave a big sigh, "Jackson wants me to officially join the Pack."

"I'm a little rusty on wolf facts. What does that mean for you?" I asked, wondering why he was so nervous about it.

"As a wolf, once you pledge yourself to a Pack your decisions are no longer your own. You have some free will, but you can't go against the Alphas wishes. Jackson is a pretty strong Alpha. I have trouble resisting his orders even without a Pledge," He said as we walked. This is why Luke struggled, but Luke didn't seem to have an issue with this aspect. He just thought of it as the most loyal thing anyone could ever achieve.

"Jackson isn't forcing you is he, because if he is I'll-"

"No, no," He said, "It is completely up to me. He was very nice about it. He only asked because he knows how tough my situation is. My parents are gone. I have a little brother Tyler. He is staying with some friends of mine completely safe, for now. I haven't really told anyone about him. I want him to have a normal life as long as he can. I told Jackson I can't take the Pledge until Tyler turns for the first time. Although, I am not sure ever taking the Pledge is the best idea," He said his tone growing serious. He had mentioned Tyler to me when we first met. If he was anything like Hunter, he'd be fine on his own.

"I get it. I would never give up my free will. I like going against the rules too much," I said trying to lighten the mood.

"Ah, yes you do. I wouldn't be standing next to you right now if you didn't," He said looking into my eyes. Hunter's eyes were like looking into the ocean. They were green with flashes of blue. I could look at them all day watching them change. I realized we had come to a stop. I cleared my throat, breaking the awkward prolonged eye contact and blushing. I started walking again. We were still a long way from the main part of camp.

"That's my job. Hey, I never asked how you got yourself in that mess. How did you run into the Packers?" I asked.

Hunter gave me a little smirk and ran his hand through his hair. "I went looking for them and got in over my head."

I was shocked. Although, it was a very me move. "Why would you do that?"

"I had been watching their moves for a while. I heard King was going to attack DEATH because Prince," I quirked my eyebrow when he used that nickname. "Sorry, Frank had defected. I wanted to help you guys out, but when I got there you guys were already taking them inside. Then I followed Eyre's scent all the way to their camp. I figured I would just go in and cause a little bit of trouble and then get out. When I took my first step to enter the camp, Eyre found me. She said she needed me to show her strength and prove she could lead the Packers until King broke out. She created this screeching sound and I passed out. I don't remember much of what happened after that. I just remember waking up and seeing you," He explained. Eyre was going to be more trouble than I thought. She was a little too unpredictable. Frank also had a strong connection with her. Hunter was waiting for me to respond, but I was deep in thought. I was thinking about King and if he really could escape. Harrison had not tried to make contact with us since we left. I think he was worried about Elder Talahan finding out this was a fake mission. I wanted to ask Jackson if I could try to contact Harrison to make sure King was still in prison when I suddenly felt pressure in my head. Luke was trying to break past the block I put up. I was getting better at keeping him out. I let it down.

"Hey, what's up?"

"Jackson asked me to get you, he wants to talk to you. Also, Dawn I'm not going to tell Jackson you're on the East side with Hunter," Luke said in my head, sounding concerned. Hunter looked at me confused.

"C'mon we've been busted," I said to Hunter. We made our way back to the Cassie Mansion.

***

As Hunter and I walked up to the mansion, Luke and the others were all out front on the steps waiting for us.

Luke made his way toward me as he said, "Jackson said he wanted everyone out of the house. I think he wants to talk to you privately about your mother," his eyes growing nervous. I took a step back. I wanted answers, but maybe I didn't actually want to know them. I hadn't bothered Jackson about it since we got here. I shook my doubt off quickly. I needed to know. I went right past Luke and the others straight into the beautiful house. Jackson stood in the front hall waiting for me. He looked perfectly calm.

"Ah Dawn, I see you got my message. Your mind connection abilities to Luke must come in handy," He said, trying to make small talk.

"Your power over him must come in handy too," I responded meanly. Why was I being defensive? Jackson was trying to help me. I could see it, but I just couldn't trust him. Jackson lifted his eyebrows. He looked almost confused.

"I have never invoked the Pledge against Luke and I never intend to. Luke does what I say purely because he wants to. Yes, it's true I do have some influence with my words, but I choose them very carefully. I don't want to take anyone's free will away," He said, trying to smile at me. I crossed my arms, rolling my eyes. Why was I being such a brat? I couldn't help it. I didn't want to trust him because I didn't know how. Jackson motioned for me to join him in the dining area where we had our first conversation about his and my mother's past. I walked into the room taking a seat while he sat across from me at the large table. I didn't think he wanted to sit next to me for fear that I would reject his attempt to get close to me. He looked at me and then down at his hands. He was trying to find a way to get out what he wanted to say, as I stayed silent watching him squirm.

He heaved a sigh, "I'm sure you're wondering why I asked everyone to leave the house?" I was, I trusted them with my life, well maybe not Jordan, but we really haven't had a chance to get to know each other. He already knew that Luke and I couldn't keep things from each other for long. I sat back and crossed my arms waiting for an explanation.

"You can invite them in if you wish, I just thought you might not want them to know everything, yet," He said, keeping his face expressionless. I suppose he was right. I didn't know what he was going to say and he just confirmed I didn't want people to know.

"I'm okay with them outside," I said, trying to keep the nerves I was feeling out of my voice. I could tell Jackson knew I was nervous despite my efforts to come off strong.

"I'm feeling the same way, Dawn. I am a coward. I have been running for so long. When you came to me, it was like my past flooded back. It was just too much to deal with, that's why I've been avoiding you. I'm not sure if I'm ready to completely face it, but it's time for me to stop running," He said, his eyes teary. He was working hard to hold them back. I couldn't help, but feel for him. He continued with a shaky breath, "In order for you to understand I have to start at the beginning, which I believe you already know. Guardians weren't always put into a school and trained. The Elders started the school based on five child Guardians."

"Darcy, Elianna, Amidra, Thomas, and Harrison," I said, trying to help him out as best as I could.

"Yes, after the Creator and Djinn war, Guardians were spread all over the world. They still are of course, DEATH is fairly new. The DEATH children were Guardian prodigies. The more they fought the stronger they got. They were an unbeatable team even at such a young age. The Guardians were already tasked with protecting other species humans, Changers, Deceased, and Seers. The Elders decided these special five would start a program where each Guardian gets a specific person to protect, a protecti. That's when your mother met me, we were the same age as you. I was an angry young wolf that had a knack for getting in trouble. She was the most intelligent, brave-hearted, and beautiful girl I ever met. We became fast friends and after a few years we were best friends. I'm sure you've already guessed I fell in love with her. She on the other hand had eyes for another," Jackson paused sadness taking over his face. I remember back to the visions he had shown me. I knew just how much he loved her. She had chosen my elusive father who no one seemed to know about or even acknowledge his existence. I didn't ask more questions. I just let Jackson compose himself.

"Thomas Shadows, your father, was a mysterious man. He had jet black hair and dark eyes. I only ever saw him smile in Darcy's presence. The tricky thing about him, Dawn, is no one can remember him. I don't think I even know his real name, Thomas definitely isn't it. The Elders covered it up by placing Thomas in the school's name. I can't remember why either. I discussed this with Jada. The way I was able to do it was to more or less erase specific moments in time where I did something important. Thomas is a completely different situation. We should be able to recover the events, but with Thomas it's like he didn't even exist," Jackson said. I could tell he was struggling to hang onto the details he did have. That's why my father's name was crossed out in the files and I couldn't find any information about him. I looked down at my hands on the table. Was my past always going to stay a mystery? I bit my lip and drew in a shaky breath. Jackson kept with his tale.

"It wasn't until I showed you the past that I began to remember bits and pieces. I remembered I was friends with him for a short period of time. We acted like the best of brothers. I think mostly we did it for Darcy. He always made me feel unsettled, but his charisma was unparalleled. I think," Jackson's eyes looked like they were looking at something far off in the distance. He shook his head after a moment.

"Do you know much about the creation of the Guardian race?" Jackson asked, shaking his head, his voice growing in urgency, switching quickly from my father. The more he talked about him the more he seemed to struggle to get the words out

.

"It's the first thing we learn in H.O.G.S class. We were created from humans and the blood of the Gelical Michael," I surprised myself. I didn't think I actually paid attention in class, maybe Luke had rubbed off on me.

"Yes, but I think we can agree that you've seen, from the Packers, that not all Guardians are out to better the world. The first generation of Guardians were imbued with unimaginable powers, as time went on the gelical blood became diluted and Guardians began to have control over only a few specific abilities. Darcy and I were sent out on a mission because there were Guardian disappearances happening all over the world. When we finally found these Guardians, they weren't like themselves, they were dark beings that fed off their own fear, as well as, the fear of others. We tried our best to thwart them and for a long time we thought we did. We had no idea that they were special and not all of them were outright evil. They had infiltrated our society," Jackson said, his voice lowering like he was afraid he was being watched. I have never heard of this before. It was likely the Guardians at Galrich wanted it covered up. It made them look weak.

"The years went by and Darcy became closer with Thomas. Their abilities together were so powerful and soon they fell in love. What I didn't know is that Thomas was more than just a Guardian. After their marriage, Thomas' personality became darker, his appearance changed. I remember his eyes drained of any trace of brown. He would go on mysterious missions and disappear for days. Darcy told me he had told her a secret. He wasn't a Guardian more like he was one of the dark Guardians we had been tasked to handle. He became their leader," Jackson said, his forest eyes darkening. The lines on his forehead became more pronounced.

"What do you mean?" My mind started reeling. It was what I suspected, my father wasn't a good person. How could he not be a Guardian? I didn't understand what Jackson meant by that. If my mom and him had discovered a different type of Guardian what did that make them? Jackson's eyes began to water and he sucked in a breath.

"Dawn, your mother knew that he was something more. She was in love with him, but that love blinded her from the truth for a long time. It wasn't till after you were born she recognized what he was and what it truly meant. He was tricking her and hiding things from her. Thomas became obsessed with power and the rise of a more powerful Guardian race," He said. I looked into his eyes waiting for him to go on, watching as he struggled in silence. Jackson bit his lip, then went to talk, letting out an indecipherable mumble as he wiped his hand over his face.

If my father wasn't fully Guardian, then what could he be that was so scary Jackson didn't want to say it out loud? My breathing quickened and my palms became sweaty.

"Your mother- you know- she tried to stop him. She did everything in her power to put an end to his plans. She never wanted you to be alone. She loved you very much, Dawn, I want you to remember that. Your father loved you too, in his own twisted way. He always said that everything he did, he did for you," Jackson was talking fast and grasping at anything he could tell me. I felt like I was paralyzed. What didn't he want to tell me?

"Jackson, what was my father?" I whispered.

"Dawn, in order to honor your mother I feel it's best to keep that detail out of this. It does not affect you," He said, coming around to my side of the table and kneeling beside me.

"You have to tell me, please, Uncle Jack, please," My voice came out raspy as I pleaded with my supposed family member. I couldn't be kept in the dark any longer. My father's past was obviously important. If I learned anything from DEATH, it was that our past wasn't to be forgotten.

"Dawn, it doesn't change who you are, it doesn't matter. It doesn't-," Jackson started to say, grabbing my hands.

"JACKSON I NEED TO KNOW!" My rage flared as I dropped his hands and sprung from the chair. My power surged, something inside of me trying to push its way out. I walked away from him towards the end of the dining table. Jackson looked surprised by my reaction. He stood up slowly from his kneeling position and walked towards me. It was then I realized how tall he was and how small I am compared to him. I suddenly felt like the kid I was supposed to be. He put a hand on my shoulder and I looked down feeling bad for yelling at him.

"Look at me, Dawn," He said in a commanding, but soft voice. I looked at him and I saw tears streaming down his face.

"He was," Jackson swallowed, braving himself for the next words he was about to say, "a demon."

I gasped. Jackson had just broken my entire identity. I understood why he didn't want to tell me because he knew what I now know. I'm half demon.

Chapter 17

Dankra

T he world around me felt like it didn't exist. I was numb. I knew Jackson was trying to get my attention. I didn't remember sinking to my knees. My breath was coming out in a short rapid pace while my heart felt like it was beating out of my chest. Am I having a panic attack? I should be stronger than this.

"Dawn!"

Luke was in front of my face now trying to get my attention. When did he get in the house? Crap. I had dropped the block. He knew everything now. What would he think of me?

"Dawn, you're okay," Luke said in my head. I vaguely realized he was shaking my shoulders. I felt his presence in my head. He was trying to make sense of what I had just been told.

"Jackson, what did you do?" Luke growled. Jackson had caught me and was now holding me up. He responded to Luke, but I didn't hear it. My head was buzzing. I needed to calm down, but I didn't know how. I don't think this was my power trying to take control and burst out like when Jackson had shown me his past. This was just me having a breakdown and it wasn't something I was used to. Luke's face started to become more clear.

"Hey D, breathe. It'll be okay, just breathe. Can you do that for me?" He asked. Luke's hands were on either side of my face now. Rubbing his thumbs on my cheeks trying to keep my eyes on his.

"I'm-I'm a monster," I tried to get out. I was glad I didn't say it out loud. Luke shook his head and wiped a tear off my face. I didn't even realize I was crying till now.

"Give me a break, Shadows, you're not that cool," Luke tried to make a joke. I wanted to scowl at him, but a little smirk tugged at the corner of my lips. His arms scooped me into his body while he held me. My breath started to slow as Luke rocked me in his arms while I let out years of emotions. I wanted to speak to my mother more than anything. She should be the one to explain this to me. I wanted to scream at my father for betraying her.

Jackson was standing over Luke and I, looking helpless. I could tell he wanted to do more for me. He didn't like seeing me in pain. I needed to get myself under control. This reaction I was having wasn't fair to Jackson. I had asked for this. I wanted to bury myself in Luke's arms, but there was still more to the story. I knew there was. Jackson knelt on the floor by Luke and I. Waiting. I couldn't tell how long Luke had been holding me. My breathing finally calmed down while Luke watched my face with an intense stare.

"Dawn, maybe you don't have to know more," Luke said with a breathless voice and furrowed brows. He gave my shoulders a squeeze not taking his eyes off Jackson. I'm half Guardian and half demon. There's no record of this anywhere. I needed to find out as much as possible so I could understand it better.

"There's more," I said looking at Jackson not moving from Luke's embrace. I wasn't asking him. He slowly nodded.

"Your mother is from a direct line of the first Guardians and your father is from the first Guardians who drank demon blood which mixed with their abilities and Gelical lineage. This created something called Dankra, a fear demon," Jackson said. Luke didn't let go of me. He just listened silently.

"What does that mean exactly?" I asked, my voice getting a little bit stronger. Jackson shook his head like he'd rather not tell me, but he went on.

"They draw power from their own fears. They quite literally become their greatest fear. It's what makes them so dangerously powerful. They are controlled by fear, but at the same time they are stripped of it. The longer a Guardian is a Dankra the more they lose their emotions and connection to any trace of human life," Jackson continued, his voice blunt and serious. Luke suddenly had a thought in his head.

"The Dankra have been roaming the outskirts of camp," He thought, rubbing circles on my back. I was confused. We should still be able to sense them though.

"Jackson, are those the demons that have been trying to get into camp? We can't sense them because they're half Guardian and it suppresses our demon censors?" Luke asked, although he knew he had figured it out.

"Yes, I believe they are. Why are they here? I wish I knew. It could be that they know Dawn is half Dankra and Thomas is looking for her. It could be they know who I am and Thomas is after me," Jackson said, with an amazingly calm voice.

Luke tensed. He didn't like the idea of the demons being after me specifically. "Why do they want Dawn now after all this time?"

Jackson sighed. He didn't want to answer the question. I knew why. My bloodline was perfect. That's why Thomas married my mom. She was descended from the first Guardian line and he was descended from the first Dankra. As to the timing, I was starting to become a fully realized Guardian. They wanted to move against the Elders and Galrich.

"It's simple. I could be their most dangerous enemy or most powerful ally. They're after me because I'm the perfect weapon against the Guardians," I answered Luke before Jackson could. Jackson just stared at me. Luke gave me a quick hug. He was thinking of images of tearing those demons to shreds. The only problem was, I was technically one of them. Wait, I wasn't the only one. I realized how selfish I was being. I should be worried about my sister. Was she half demon too? Luke winced at the thought of it.

"What about Lila?" I whispered not wanting to know the answer. Jackson smirked a little. I wanted to slap it off of him. This was serious. My sister was too young to know how to deal with this, especially with her quick to anger issues.

"I've been meaning to talk to her and you about that. Thomas is not Lila's father," Jackson said, his eyes growing soft. I looked into his green eyes, trying to make sense of what he just told me. They looked oddly familiar to my sisters. I gasped. It made perfect sense.

"Are you her father?" Jackson looked at me straight in the eyes and nodded. I sunk further into Luke's arms as they went slack. He was shell shocked and looked at Jackson in a way I've never seen before. I couldn't tell if he was mad or maybe impressed? He was thinking too fast for me to keep up.

"Your mom and I had a complicated relationship. When she started realizing what your father was, she wanted to leave him. There was a time where she and I ran away with you. It was only a few months, but we were both so lonely. I had just lost my wife during a Dankra raid leaving Jordan motherless. Darcy had sought me out to give her condolences. Then after a while we found our way back to each other. It seemed too perfect for awhile, but as soon as we found out your mom was pregnant with Lila it became a different story. She had to keep up her marriage with him as a ruse to try and destroy his empire from the inside, so we could be truly rid of him. We knew he would find us eventually. Shortly after Lila was born, Thomas was convinced she was not his because she had no Dankra blood. He sent the Dankra to kill Lila, but your mom convinced them that Lila was actually his daughter. I don't know how, but it gave me enough time to get you both out of there. I was able to escape with Lila and you, but I lost your mother in the process. That was the last day I saw her," Jackson explained through his pain that echoed in his voice. I couldn't comprehend what I was hearing, but I was glad Lila would not have to deal with the demon craziness. I feared for Jackson though Lila was going to burn him alive when she found out. I needed to move on from this topic. I would have to deal with it later.

"Do we know why I haven't shown signs of being a Dankra?" I asked Jackson.

He stood up slowly. I pushed against Luke's chest. I was okay now and it was time for me to stop being a baby. It was interesting to me that I didn't even know I was half demon. I guess some part of me knew there was more to my story.

"I helped your mother block your Dankra abilities. It was very complicated. Before I tell you, I need you to understand we had to take all necessary precautions. We needed to give you more connection to your Guardian side, tip the scales so to speak," Jackson explained. I was scared of what he was going to say. I didn't know what lengths they had to go to. Luke stood next to me crossing his arms. He seemed upset with Jackson. I would have never expected this attitude towards his Alpha a couple days ago. He looked at Luke and then back at me.

"We had to use old, powerful, and illegal magic," Jackson continued. Luke growled. I looked at him startled. He was clouding his thoughts, but I don't think it was on purpose. Jackson had set him off about something.

"Your mother and I placed something deep inside you, as well as", He paused, "Luke," Jackson gestured to him ignoring his increasing anger. I gasped. He was talking about the Bound! My mom and Jackson had placed it in us. Luke knew what he had been talking about before he even said that. Luke took a step towards Jackson and I grabbed his wrist.

"Luke we need to hear him out," I didn't understand why he was so mad about this. He was the one who said he wanted the Bound to be true.

"Dawn, the only way to complete a Bound is to have access to one of the children's parents," I looked at Luke and suddenly remembered what Jada had told me. She didn't think the Bound could be possible because we didn't even know who Luke's parents were. Jackson wasn't only holding my family secrets he had Luke's as well.

"Luke, calm down now," Jackson's voice grew in volume. He was giving Luke an order he couldn't resist. Luke shuttered, but stepped back, keeping a hold of my hand.

"Jackson, you owe Luke an explanation," I said.

"I wish I could tell you more about your parents Luke, but I can't. Your mother came to me. She was a Guardian who did not attend DEATH. She said she couldn't care for you and I took you into my care. She needed someone who could also understand a Changer. We had no idea you would become both a Guardian and a wolf. I asked her to help us with the Bound before she left, she gave me permission and some of her blood to perform it. I'm sorry she wouldn't even give me her name," Jackson let out a sigh. Luke was more angry than I've ever seen him. He was holding it in though because Jackson had ordered him to calm down. I was holding on to his hand for dear life, afraid he would lose control. Jackson just looked at us not knowing what more to say.

"It was the only way to protect her, Luke. We needed to hide her from him as best as we could," Jackson said. He misunderstood. Luke wasn't mad about the Bound. He was mad that Jackson, who he considered to be like a father to him, lied. He was hurt and I knew how he felt.

"I'm sorry, Luke," I said in his mind. He looked me in the eyes and surprisingly gave me a smile.

"It's alright, Dawn. I get to say I told you so," Luke actually laughed out loud. Jackson looked between us, confused. I laughed too. I'm happy Luke was right about the Bound. It could make us potentially unstoppable. Luke turned back to Jackson and tried not to glare.

"I really am sorry, kid," Jackson said, putting a hand on Luke's shoulder. I could tell it was nice for him to know where he came from, but it still stung that his mother didn't want him.

"It was for the best," I said to him, giving his hand a little squeeze.

"Yes, who knew I'd end up tied to a half demon," Luke said, trying to make it a joke.

"Too early there bud," I winced then I gave him a little shove. Luke smiled at me apologetically. He then sighed and turned to Jackson.

"I know you were doing your best. I'm sorry for reacting the way I did," Luke said, but his face was blank. He was still having trouble forgiving him. It would take some time.

"Ah, thank you. Before you forgive me, there's one more thing you should know," Jackson said, weirdly blushing.

"Of course there is," I said with an exasperated sigh.

Jackson scratched the back of his neck, embarrassed. Luke crossed his arms.

"The magic is old like I said. It used to be used for arranged marriages. So in order to keep the Bound and keep Dawn's Dankra side in check. You two will have to get married someday," Jackson almost whispered the last part. My mouth fell open. Luke and I immediately dropped our hands. Well, this was awkward.

***

Luke and I sat outside Jackson's mansion staring off into space. The camp looked so peaceful at night. There was some light peeking through the trees. The light of the moon was bouncing off of Luke's concentrated face. We didn't know what to say to each other. Jackson said he would help me find another way to keep my demon side suppressed, but he didn't think there was any other way. Luke and I are so young. We should be able to choose who we fall in love with and marry that person. I didn't even know if I wanted to get married. I wanted Luke to have that choice more than anything, I was the reason he was in this mess. I didn't care if it broke the Bound and let out this super dangerous side of me. Jackson didn't say that it would immediately make me evil. I just wouldn't be able to control my abilities as much as I do now. He also said it would be an extremely painful process to break. He wasn't sure if we'd both survive at the end of it and I'd just have to find a way where Luke and I both stayed alive. It wasn't fair that this decision was forced upon us. Although, I will admit it was nice to have our connection explained.

"*The more I think about it the more it makes sense,*" Luke said in my head. He didn't feel like talking out loud for fear of the others hearing us. I'd rather not have to tell my friends that Luke and I were in some whacked engagement since we were babies. I didn't quite understand what Luke was talking about. I guess he's talking about our connection.

"*It explains a lot,*" I said thinking about Elder Tallahan's obsession with us. Luke shook his head and gave a sigh. He grabbed my hand. I was so used to his touch, but now it made me feel awkward.

"*Not that. I figured out that we had a Bound a long time ago. The marriage part of it makes sense,*" He said seriously. I didn't know what to say. Did he actually think that was a good idea?

"*Easy D, I'm not saying it isn't crazy. It is. It's beyond crazy. I'm saying the way the Bound is formed it makes sense for people who have it to end up together,*" He explained himself fast. He was scaring me. Did he want to marry me in the future? He knows I'm not sure if I want that.

"*Luke, you're not stuck with me. You can date whoever you want and marry whoever you want. I'm not going to ever stand in your way,*" I said trying to catch his eyes. He was looking down, avoiding mine and looked a little disappointed. He bit his lip. He was thinking fast that I couldn't quite make it out. I knew Luke well enough to know he would do anything to protect me. I wasn't letting him give up his entire future just to make sure I stayed who I was. I'll figure out another way. I had to.

"*I mean I do love you, Dawn. I didn't think it was in that way or would ever be that way, but maybe it will be. It's supposed to be. I know you think of me as a brother, but that could change,*" Luke said, finally meeting my eyes. He was still holding on to my hand. Frank's words rang in my ears, "This guy has been in love with you forever." Is this why he wanted the Bound? I pulled my hand back and laid it in my lap.

"*We're sixteen!*" I shrieked in his head. He covered his ears. I wasn't even sorry I was loud. Did he understand what he just said?

"*Yes, Dawn I know what I said. I'm just saying they're worse things than being destined to marry your best friend. What's the point of fighting the inevitable?*" Luke smiled at me. I guess he was right. That didn't mean I wanted to marry him.

"*Ouch, I'm hurt*" He chuckled at my thought. I did sense he wasn't completely joking. I hurt his feelings a little bit. Curse this telepathic connection.

I sighed, "*Sorry, but you know what I mean.*" If this was the only solution, would I be able to go through with it? Could I fall for Luke? The way he talked about it made it seem like we were going to no matter what happened. The Bound would make it impossible not to fall for him. My brain can't handle all this.

"*You're just saying that to make me not feel guilty about messing up your entire existence. You're too nice for your own good,*" I said trying to shut down any thought in my mind about being in a relationship with Luke. Luke laughed. I thought he had a crush on Jordan. I was so excited to help him ask her out.

"Oh, no you were not, you liar," Luke shoved my shoulder. I laughed. I liked Jordan. I just had felt a little forgotten with her around. That didn't mean I didn't support Luke.

"I am not lying! I really am going to help you," defending myself. He rolled his eyes at me. He didn't want my help with Jordan. He wasn't even sure of his feelings for her. I smiled at him. I just wanted him to be able to be happy.

"I think we have more important things to focus on then my little crush right now. Are you gonna freak out every time I give you a hug now?," Luke teased and put his arm around my shoulders. I laughed. I had no reason to freak out about this. We had years to worry about it. If the Bound was able to keep my demon side at bay this long, it could hold on for a few more years. I rested my head on his shoulder and looked up at the stars. Luke dropped his head lightly on mine.

He finally spoke out loud. "I am happy, Dawn and I don't think I would be if you weren't in my life," Luke whispered. I felt my cheeks grow a little hot. I felt the same way. He was my best friend and sometimes the most annoying person I knew, but I didn't think I could survive without him. It sounded so cheesy in my head. I didn't respond because Luke could hear and see how much he meant to me. I decided to change the subject, thinking in my head about telling Lila all this new information. I thought it was weird that she wasn't a Changer since Jackson was her father.

"I thought the same thing, but they're cases of Changers having completely human babies. Lila probably still has the genes just not enough for her to be able to transform or she's a late bloomer," Luke answered my question. He was very interested in how Lila was only a Guardian. I really wish I didn't have to tell her.

"Ah, good luck with that," Luke said with a chuckle and pulled my shoulders in closer. I decided I wasn't going to say anything to Lila until we were back at DEATH. It would be easier that way. Luke and I stared at the night sky listening to each other's thoughts until both of our eyes began to get heavy.

***

"Woah," Frank said. We were sitting at the bar at another bonfire celebration. I had just told him everything about what Jackson had told me. He had cornered me earlier today knowing that something was up. I was glad he was done avoiding me. I missed talking to him. I've never seen him at a loss for words. I thought he'd at least make some uncomfortable joke, instead he looked deep in thought. I wondered what was going through his head. Was he scared of me now? I mean I was scared of me. I looked down at my drink Mama G had given me. I think I figured out it was a mixture of lemonade and some kind of other fruity juice. I looked around me, the bonfire party was in full swing. I liked looking at all of the wolves. It was interesting to watch their movements. They all seemed so in sync. Luke was dancing with Jordan, the two of them made a great pair. I wonder if Luke will tell her? Distracting myself enough from Frank's silence, I looked back at him when he was looking at me with a confused look.

"Summers, you're looking at me like you saw a ghost," I tried to laugh, but I was afraid of the way he was looking at me.

"No, sorry. It just suddenly made sense why King liked you so much," Frank said, still deep in thought. I winced. Did he think I was like King? He saw my reaction and immediately started back tracking.

"No Dawn, I meant he probably sensed you would be a great Packer. He's been trying to recruit demons for years," Frank said, staring off into space. I wasn't surprised. I barely knew King, but I'm sure if he found out my lineage he'd be after me the first chance he got. Frank seemed bothered by something else.

"Frank, spit it out," I said, getting frustrated. Frank shifted uncomfortably. I shoved his shoulder.

"Okay, geez. King has been in contact with the Dankra for a couple months now," I stood up. Frank did say King's capture was too easy. DEATH is a fortress only knocked by Eyre. King could've been wanting to be captured the whole time.

"I'm sorry I didn't tell you. I honestly had no idea that the Dankra were demons. They look so much like us. I should've told you sooner," Frank looked down at his hands. I stood in front of him and my fists balled. It wasn't that I was mad at Frank. I was worried that the Dankra had found a way to invade DEATH through King. We needed to get a message to Harrison.

"Already on my way to talk to Jackson," Luke's voice rang in my head. I looked over at him and saw he had Flashed away from a confused Jordan. I thanked Luke and looked at Frank whose head was in his hands. He seemed so disappointed with himself. I put my hand on his shoulder trying to comfort him.

"It's okay. Luke is on his way now to get a message to Harrison, if there was anything going on we would've heard about it by now," I said, trying to sound positive for Frank. Although, I was mainly trying to convince myself that King being in contact with the Dankra was just a coincidence. Frank looked up at me and nodded. I missed overly confident Frank right about now.

"Jackson said he has a way to contact Harrison, get to the mansion," Luke's voice said in my head. I grabbed on to Frank's jacket and Flashed him and I to the mansion.

"Shadows, I could've done that myself. I hate the feeling of being forcefully teleported," Frank grumbled. I stuck my tongue out at him. I liked that I had figured out how to Flash myself and others. It definitely confused both Frank and Luke. We walked into the mansion where Luke was standing with Jackson. Catching them in the middle of a conversation.

"That's not a good idea, Luke. If it's one thing I've learned you can't force-," Jackson was saying as Frank and I entered what looked like his study. Luke cut him off with a glare. Jackson gave him an apologetic look. They were definitely talking about me. I decided it wasn't important to ask about it.

"We can contact Harrison?" I asked Jackson. He nodded and pressed a golden button on his desk that looked like the one Harrison had to contact Galrich. Frank took a seat popping his toothpick back in his mouth. Luke also took a seat right in front of Jackson's desk. I decided to stand as I watched the button flicker waiting for Harrison to answer with anticipation. To my surprise, Jada's enchanting hologram face appeared before us. She looked oddly flustered.

"Jada?" I asked. She turned to me and smiled.

"Hi, little warrior. I'm a little unfamiliar with the way holograph communication works," Jada laughed nervously. She was acting odd. I wanted to ask her what was wrong, but if someone else was in there with her we could give away our location.

"Harrison's not here right now, Dawn," She said, still keeping her voice light. The way her eyes were fidgeting upward told me she definitely wasn't alone. I needed to say something. I just didn't know what to say. Luke was trying to stay out of the picture in case it was the Elders we were worrying about. Jackson was also trying to keep his image out of the holograph's sight. That made me think the Dankra had infiltrated DEATH even more. Jada looked at me and plastered on a smile.

"Was there something you needed?" Jada said, still having a fake cheery voice on. How could I make her tell me what was going on without asking directly? I decided to try something, but it was unclear if Jada would follow along.

"Luke, write everything she says down," I said in his mind. He gave me a confused look, but grabbed paper off of Jackson's desk being careful so Jada couldn't see him. He nodded to me that he was ready.

"Oh yeah sorry it's more of a Harrison question. Where's Harrison?" I asked, matching her voice. Jada smiled at me.

"He is currently in Galrich with Elder Tallahan and the captured Packers," Her eyes shifted upward again. It took everything I had not to Flash to Jada and help her from whoever was threatening her.

"Right, I forgot. I'm glad to hear they did not escape," I said, trying to choose my words carefully.

"Dawn, honey, DEATH prisons have never been escaped," She laughed smoothly and I tried to join in.

"I just wanted Harrison to know that Frank and I discovered Eyre took over for King," I said, trying to sound serious. I wasn't even sure if Jada knew who Eyre was.

She played along, "That is concerning. I will tell him as soon as he gets back. He has his communication devices shut off. This information might even get the head Packer, what's his name, to confess to his crimes. Oh that's right, King." The nervousness in her voice was creeping in again. She looked up and her face fell for just a second and then smiled at me.

"Dawn, I do have to go oversee the annual demon simulation. I do wish you were here to help," She said, pretending to be overwhelmed with teaching DEATH students. I smiled at her.

"That's funny, I can't teach. It was good talking to you Jada," I said knowing she was about to hang up.

"Yes, see you when you get back," Her eyes stared at me intently, questioning if I got what she was saying. I had no idea what was going on but I hope I could figure it out. Jada's face disappeared and I was now staring at a confused Jackson. Luke was looking at what he had written. Frank cleared his throat.

"Any of you feel like there's more she's not telling us," Frank said what we hadn't said out loud. Luke handed me what he had written and I read it out loud to them. Jackson's eyebrows knitted together.

"She might be using some kind of code?" Frank asked, looking for confirmation. I laughed. He was stating the obvious, but not being helpful.

"Well no kidding, Frank," Luke snorted. Frank threw his hands up in frustration. I looked at the words again. It clicked.

"I think she was going off of every last word I was saying," I whispered, slamming the paper on Jackson's desk. I picked up a pen and circled Jada's last word of every sentence.

"Packers. Escaped. King. Help. Back," I said as I looked at the words . If this was what she was trying to tell us, we needed to get there now. Frank crossed his foot over his knee flicking the toothpick in his mouth. He looked a little more like his usual self.

"We need a plan," Luke said. Jackson looked at me then back at Luke.

"Is it possible we're just reading into this?" Jackson said. It was possible, but my gut was telling me there was trouble. Harrison would never leave DEATH. The Elders wouldn't allow him to because he was in charge of taking care of so many next generation of Guardians. King had to have escaped and was taking over my home. I looked at Frank and he smiled at me. I gave him a glare back. He was starting to annoy me. The shift in emotions was hard to follow.

"If King is behind this, I'm going to enjoy being the one to stop it," Frank said, getting up slowly out of his chair, his eyes screaming for revenge. Luke let out a sigh like he's heard it before. I usually like when Frank is able to get under Luke's skin, but right now we need to act more seriously. I do not need Frank going in there all hot headed and unfocused, but he probably was the best option for taking down King.

"Frank this isn't about you," I crossed over to him and pulled on the collar of his leather jacket pulling him down to my height, "You better keep yourself in check." Frank's smile widened as I glared at him. He didn't move his gaze as he removed the toothpick from his mouth and put it in his pocket. I pulled on his jacket again and shoved him backwards hard enough to make him stumble, but his smile never faded. I turned to Jackson who was standing behind me, his forest eyes deep in thought.

"Get your team ready, Dawn. I will send Jordan and a couple of my best fighters with you. As much as, I would love to be there. I can't risk being seen. Harrison and Jada know about me, but if the Elders are anywhere near I can not go," He said. I had expected as much, but that didn't stop me from being disappointed. Jackson was supposed to be the loving protecting adult, but he will always be hiding from his past.

"I thought you said you were done running," I said, crossing my arms challenging him. He smiled at my sassiness, but still tensed a little bit. Luke shoved his hands in his pockets and looked down. He was always embarrassed by my lack of respect for authority. Jackson walked up to me and patted a hand on my shoulder and strode out of the room. I scoffed. Coward. These Packers needed to be stopped, especially if they were working for the Dankra. I heard three smacks of air behind me. Lila, Dan, and Hailey were standing in the room. Lila ran up to me and gave me a hug. I smiled at the unexpected outburst of affection. Hailey slowly came to join, wrapping her arms around me and Lila. Dan came up and joined in too. I looked at Luke in confusion. He looked at me and shrugged trying to act innocent. They pulled away from me. Lila gave me a shove.

"Did you think you could just keep it a secret that you're half demon?" Lila asked, flame sputtering from her balled fists. I winced and looked at her in shock. I looked at Luke. How dare he? He was putting his hands up in defense, when Hunter and Jordan suddenly ran into the room. Hunter looked out of breath like he had just sprinted here. Jordan was wide eyed with a freshly cut lip.

I forgot about Luke for a second, overwhelmed by Hunter's feelings. They weren't about me. It was panic that was pounding the inside of my brain as I took a step toward Hunter. We all looked at them waiting for an explanation.

"We just came from fighting off demons at the border. I told Jackson on his way out, he told me to tell you we need to get to DEATH now!" Hunter blurted out in a panic.

I looked at everyone. They were all looking to me to tell them what to do. I didn't know who made me in charge. It certainly wasn't me. We didn't have a plan. We'd be going in completely blind. Jackson may need our help defending the camp. As much as I wanted to be I wasn't ready to lead a mission like I thought I was. Luke came over to my side.

"*You can do this,*" Luke said in my head, raising a blond eyebrow at me. He knew I was nervous, but still gave me a beautifully confident smile. I looked at him and nodded, feeling a little frozen in place. I looked at my friends. No. My family. Lila gave me a sharp nod. Her caramel hair almost looked bright orange as her fists began to ignite with fire. Frank simply twirled a knife in his hands lightly bouncing on his feet itching for a fight. Hailey looked completely like her sweet self, but a hint of danger sparked through her deep golden brown eyes. Dan looked super excited holding on to Hailey's hand. Jordan gave me a reassuring smile, her eyes shifting to the door most likely wanting to fight a long side Jakson, but she stayed with us. She knew we needed to move fast. I looked at Hunter, his confidence in me was so potent even I started to believe I could do this.

"Alright Hunter and Jordan grab on to me," I said, giving them my hands. One by one everyone started to grab hands. Before I rallied my power, I thought I saw a little spider web forming rapidly on the door. There was no time to worry about that now. I closed my eyes, concentrating my energy into Hunter and Jordan's palms feeling the warm power inside me. I know I could handle Flashing both of them. I let out a breath and took one more look around me. It was time to go. I closed my eyes. Snap!

We all Flashed to DEATH. I opened my eyes and let out a gasp and dropped Hunter and Jordan's hands.

Orange and red danced before me, DEATH was on fire.

Chapter 18

Under Attack

We stood outside where the Boundary formerly was. The shield was completely down. I shook my head in disbelief. The top of DEATH was completely cased in raging flames. It mimicked the feeling of rage in my heart. We needed to get in there and get everyone out. I started running towards the entrance and the others followed. We couldn't Flash in especially with the chance of being caught in the fire. I suddenly heard high pitched shrieks from the sky. I looked up as a demon with wings came swooping at me. I threw my hand out sending a blast of my energy, sending the creature tumbling.

"Dawn! All around us," Luke said in my head. I looked around. We were surrounded by the same winged demons. They came out of the sky one by one circling our little group. As I took a closer look, these demons were not Dankra, they looked nothing like us. They had scaly grey skin, a wide wing span, and dangerous curved fangs. I took out my knife from my belt and readied myself as the creatures came closer, shrieking more and more. Their claws digging into the ground. We had never fought anything like this before, I'm sure Luke knew the actual name of these demons, but if he did he said nothing.

"I got this! " Lila said to all of us over the demons shrieking. I tried to yell in objection, but another ear piercing shriek from the demons drowned it out. She took a deep breath and closed her eyes. When she opened them, they were orange with flickers of red. She turned to me giving me a look that said don't freak out and the moment she let go of her breath she ignited in flames. I gasped, she was brilliant. The way her hair became fire itself, she had been waiting to explode into her true fiery self. The demons were closing in on us, claws scratching at the earth.

Lila clapped her hands together and pushed them out. The demons all around us wailed as they were caught in balls of massive fire. One by one they turned to ash. Frank let out a long whistle as we all stared in shock at my little sister. My sister sucked in a breath and her skin returned to normal, only her fists remained on fire. Lila's eyes turned back to their enchanting green, for a second I saw Jackson's green eyes look back at me with a mischievous gleam. I wasn't sure it was my place, to tell her that we were half sisters. Not that it mattered to me. There was no time now. The sound of DEATH crumbling was even worse than the sight. The thunderous crack as the fire began to eat away at it made my heart skip a beat. I didn't know what had happened to everyone inside. We especially needed to get to Jada. As we kept running to the entrance, more and more demons attacked. I tackled one to the ground slamming my knife down into its chest. I looked up and saw Jordan shifting into wolf form jumping up catching a demon in mid air and tearing it apart. I was impressed with her ferociousness. The sunny Jordan I knew was way different than the one before my eyes. I was suddenly lifted into the air with big claws wrapped around my right arm. I let out a growl planning on Flashing back to the ground, when a long spear came barreling at the demon. It screamed and let go of me. I Flashed in midair landing safely crouched on the ground. I turned to look who threw the spear and Daniel looked at me with a shrug. I could've almost laughed. One of Daniel's abilities, conjuring weapons from thin air. It came in handy, when he could use it properly. We were so close to the entrance now. It was just a few feet away. Hunter in his wolf form attacked a demon who was blocking the entrance. He ripped off his head and threw it at my feet. Show off. I could feel his pride.

"Dawn, we'll hold them off. You do what you need to do. We'll join you as soon as we can," Luke's voice rang in my head. I was glad to hear his voice. It was a small comfort in the midst of all this messiness. I looked back at him for just a split second. I had not seen him turn into wolf form at all during this fight. It surprised me. He smiled at me as he stabbed another demon.

"I can't expose I'm a wolf out in the open like this and if I'm going to fight for my home I'm doing it as a Guardian," Luke said quickly as he shielded himself from a demon striking at his head. I finally got up the steps where the door used to be. It had been completely knocked down. I stopped as I crossed the threshold. The hall

was silent, not a demon in sight. I had to keep moving. I ran past every room on my way to Harrison's office making sure no one was trapped inside. There was no one. That worried me more. I finally made it to Harrison's office and the door was closed. I kicked it down.

"Ah didn't I tell you? " King's smug voice crooned. Jada was gagged and tied to Harrison's chair. She lifted her head slightly. I could see her face was bruised, something I hadn't seen in the hologram. King was flanked by the Twins that Luke and I had fought before. Their muscles clenched as I entered ready to fight me. King on the other hand, seemed relaxed as he picked up a knife from the desk and twirled it in his fingers.

"I knew the Seer had somehow informed Dawn. I told you, right boys?" King asked, looking at the brothers. The brothers didn't respond, they just glared at me. I put up a shield around myself as King stopped twirling the knife and pointed it at me. I smiled back at him, daring him to throw it.

"I knew I liked you. You have grit and great survival instincts. You'd think you were raised on the streets," King said, moving the knife to Jada's neck. I stepped forward hissing.

"I wouldn't do that if I were you," I said, trying to sound intimidating. I looked at Jada and she shook her head at me. She was right. I wish she could see how I could win and just tell me what to do. I couldn't attack now, I needed to wait for an opening. The Twins walked around Harrison's desk to either side of me ready to grab me in case I made a move. It was much easier to fight these two from a distance. I could Flash them both outside, but I had no idea what effect their abilities would have on me. If they were both touching me, I might not even be able to stand. It would also leave Jada with King. I had no idea if she could even fight. King smirked as he pressed the knife against Jada's neck more, wincing as it drew a trickle of blood. King started to laugh, keeping my feet planted firmly on the ground, squeezing my fists to the point of pain as I fought the urge to lunge at him.

"Seers can't heal right?" He says looking between Jada and I for confirmation. My lips pulled back into a snarl. King responded with a handsomely beautiful smile. He gave a nod to the Twins and they grabbed my shoulders. I tried not to show how much their touch bothered me. I could feel my muscles weakening. My strength fed into the Twins. I couldn't keep my knees from buckling. I gritted my teeth as I felt myself lurch forward. The Twins kept me standing, their large hands crushing my shoulders. I wonder if they had names or if King even bothered giving them any. King traced a finger down Jada's face while still keeping the knife at her neck. Jada stared straight ahead with no emotion on her face, I wondered how she stayed so calm. I tried to move, but more strength was leaving my body as I swayed a little bit. I needed to know what to do and fast. Jada looked at me, her deep purple eyes looked confident. She did not fear King. I hoped she had a plan because I knew as long as the Twins had hold of me I wasn't saving Jada anytime soon. Luke was still fighting the demons outside and even if I called to him and he marched in here to save Jada and me, the demons would follow. I don't think we could handle King and the demons. I have a feeling King is a much more skilled fighter than what he displayed when we captured him.

"I've always been interested in Seers, too bad they were all wiped out. Were you *there* when your people were slaughtered by my master?" King whispered to Jada, but loud enough so I could hear it. I looked at Jada in surprise, she still showed no emotion. My father had murdered all the Seers? She had never told me and probably never planned to. I tried to shake out of the Twin's hold. They gripped tighter causing a wince to leave my mouth.

"Boys, we were ordered not to hurt... what is it you call her?" King looked at Jada who stared forward, "Oh yes, *little warrior*." King removed the knife from Jada's neck. I didn't know why. If he was smart, he'd Flash us both out of here now. He made his way over to me. Good. I hope he got closer so I could head butt him. He gave a look to the Twins and they pushed me to the floor. I tried to fight them off, but I felt like a noodle. Jada didn't move. King came closer and knelt down by my face.

"I can't hurt you or your little sister, who is currently destroying all of my demon legion," King said, his eyes looking right through mine. I smiled at the thought of my sister taking out his army. I looked back at his eyes, dark and deadly, devoid of all emotion. Then it became clear. King wasn't just a Packer or a Guardian.

"You're Dankra," I hissed at him. He chuckled, confirming my suspicions. I wanted to lurch forward and punch his face, but I still couldn't move. My entire body was drained of strength. He stood up and made his way back to Jada. There had to be a reason why she got me here and why she wasn't trying to escape. She still stared straight ahead.

"Boys, the Guardians outside are annoying me. Go, I can handle these two. Your abilities should last long enough to keep her down," King ordered his lackeys, giving me a smug look. They released me, but my strength still did not return like the last time I fought them. I slumped forward, my hands barely catching me. I gritted my teeth and tried to keep my eyes on King. Jada was staring forward trying not to look at me. I decided it was time to get some information and stall till I got my strength back, although I was not certain if it would even return.

"So, oh great King, my father made you a Dankra?" I asked, sarcasm dripping with every word, trying to push myself to stand. My knees still shook. King looked at me amused. He tilted his head giving me another handsome smile.

"No," He brushed a strand of Jada's hair with his knife, "I'm his son," King said nonchalantly. I groaned. Of course. What is it with all this secret family nonsense?

"I thought my mother was the first," I said, wanting to throw him into a wall. I pushed myself against the door frame still not being able to stand.

"True, I'm not the first of our kind. He loved your mother, that much is true. He needed to try before he tried with your mother. He didn't want to kill her, so I was the experiment. You were the success, for lack of a better word. He's also spawned a few more, but they died from the power that existed inside of them. It ripped them apart from the inside out. We are the only two who have survived. Although, I wonder if you will once whatever it is suppressing your Dankra side is taken care of," King explained flatly, twirling a piece of Jada's hair around his finger. She didn't shy away from him, keeping her eyes straight forward. My father did not know about the Bound. I needed to keep it that way, he'd kill Luke without hesitation.

"So you infiltrated DEATH to claim it for Thomas?" I said, pushing myself up to stand. King raised an eyebrow as I brought up a name that obviously wasn't our fathers, but he understood.

"What? Can't call him dear old dad?" King chuckled and opened a drawer in Harrison's desk pulling out power dampening cuffs. Crap. I finally was standing without the door frame support, but my knees were still shaking. King approached me, his dark eyes dangerous. I looked at Jada, but she still did not move. I glared at her. I can't believe she's doing nothing.

"Sure, I'll call him dear old dad, when he can get up the nerve to capture me himself," I spit at King's feet. He smiled and grabbed at my hands. I pulled them away and rear back my right hand, slapping him in the face as hard as I could, which wasn't very hard with the lack of strength. I wobbled at the effort, but stayed standing. King kept his head to the side for a moment, chuckling. My red handprint showed triumphantly on his cheek. He turned back to me, his eyes wild.

"You know little sister, I like you. Maybe someday you'll grow to like me too," He went to grab at my hands again, the cuffs open and ready to drain my power completely. I swung again, but missed and fell to my knees. He chuckled again and knelt down. I tried looking at Jada. I think she was...smiling? I couldn't tell with the gag on her. She winked at me, her purple eyes grew brighter, as a ripple of energy passed out of her emitting all around the room. The feeling of it was overwhelming, but when I looked back at King he didn't seem to notice. He didn't even move. King was frozen with the cuffs just before my hands.

Jada had stopped time.

I blinked in surprise. Jada mumbled my name trying to push the piece of cloth out of her mouth, but failing. I got up to my feet, my strength wasn't fully back, but at least I could walk. Jada's purple eyes flicked down to her strapped hands and then back at me. I stared at her in shock while she tried to grunt my name, snapping me out of it. I untied her mouth and hands. She sighed in relief, although her forehead was beaded with sweat.

"Very good little warrior, I saw multiple possibilities...well let's just say you said the right things," She wheezed out. Her eyes were still shining a brighter purple. The energy causing time to stop was still pulsating out of her. She swayed a little bit. I caught her.

"Are you okay? How did you-I don't even. You stopped time!" I screeched at her. She smiled up through her bruised and strained face, as she righted herself to a standing position. She didn't look so good.

"I'm fine. I just- I can't hold this for much longer. I'll take care of King. You have to go help your friends, I saw-," Jada stopped and swallowed, giving me a little shove out of the room. Of course, she wasn't going to say what she saw. I shook my head and crossed my arms about to ask anyway. I also wasn't going to leave her alone with my supposed sadistic half brother.

"Dawn you silly girl, you really think I grew up at DEATH and didn't learn how to take care of myself. I was the first in my class to knock out Harrison. Now go!" Jada said, snapping the cuffs on a frozen King. She shoved me out before I could ask her what she saw. Time started to move again. I felt it in my bones. Jada couldn't hold it any longer. I didn't ask her where Harrison was or how everyone had gotten out. I didn't need to worry about that though. Jada said I needed to help everyone else and I would heed that warning. I Flashed outside. Luke and Frank were fighting the Twins. They were keeping their distance only going in for very calculated hits. The Twins were trying to get to Lila who was decimating King's demon forces with her fire. I Flashed to Luke's side just before one of the Twins got his hands on him. The Twin hesitated for a split second, shocked I had gotten away from King. Luke and I took advantage of his pause, I kicked his legs out from under him while Luke hit the hilt of his knife into his temple. The Twin slumped to the charred ground completely unconscious. Luke grinned at me, but it quickly faded as we heard Hailey shouting.

"Danny!" I snapped my head to her distressed voice.

Jordan was next to her in her human form, a hand on her side as she leaned against Hailey. She was looking up at the sky with a look of horror on her face, as she tried to keep Jordan standing. I saw a demon carrying Daniel away. He was unconscious. I didn't even think about what I was going to do. I Flashed on top of the demon stabbing it in the back. It roared and let go of Daniel. It twisted around, flinging me off before I could reach him. Its talons dug into my shoulder as I fell trying to grab on to me. I tried to Flash to Daniel in mid air, but it wasn't working. When I tried again I missed him and we kept falling. My vision was blurring. I couldn't muster up the power to Flash. Lila was suddenly in the air with us, her feet encased in fire propelling her into the sky. She lowered Daniel to the ground. I caught Luke's face as he saw I was still falling. He was trying to figure out how he could Flash to me in the air and get us both to the ground. I'd Flash again, but the scratch from the demon had done something to me. I could feel it. I was almost to the ground when I stretched my hands before I hit the grass making a weak shield to protect me from most of the impact. When I released it, I rolled on the grass and made my way to standing letting out a groan. I could feel the demon's poison in me, but I didn't care. I needed to access my powers no matter what the demon poison did to me. I Flashed over to my sister while creating a shield around us. Demons were trying to break through it. There were too many of them, two hundred, at least, even if Lila had destroyed half of them. Lila still had Daniel in her arms breathing. Hailey was holding up Jordan who looked like she was going to pass out, all the color drained from her face.

"He's okay," Lila said, giving me a look as if to say I saved him and you did not. If we weren't surrounded by demons, I'd give her hell for that tone. Frank came towards us, his face covered in dirt dragging the Twins, who were both unconscious, by the collars of their shirts. I focused on him, allowing him to pass through the shield. He threw them both at my feet with a look of triumph on his face. I half expected him to put his toothpick I knew was in his pocket back in his mouth, but he just stared at me with a dark expression I only saw when he talked about King.

"I'm sorry, Dawn. I was fighting the demon, but it bit me and Daniel tried to help me, but it just took him," Jordan apologized. Her voice sounded weak and panicked. If the demon bit her, the poison was already circulating in her bloodstream. She had minutes before she lost consciousness.

"It isn't your fault. We need to get you out of here," I said looking around at the demons closing in on my shield. Frank knelt next to me.

"Where is he?" Frank hissed. I have never seen his face so serious. I knew he was talking about King.

"Jada is taking care of him," I said, looking around us to make sure none of the demons had broken through. I felt every one of their attempts like they were running into my own body. I gritted my teeth. I needed to keep it up. Frank put a hand on my shoulder. He could tell it was hard for me. I ignored him as best as I could. Luke and Hunter were still outside the shield keeping as many of the creatures away as they could. They needed to get in my shield, they couldn't keep them out forever and we needed a plan.

"*Luke get in here,*" I said in his head while I created a small opening for Hunter and him. I knew I didn't have the energy to expand it. The demon poison burning my shoulder and soon I'd have no powers. Luke launched into the hole, as Hunter ripped off a demon's head who was coming for the opening and quickly backed into it. He was still in his wolf form, his sea green eyes rolled over me making sure I was okay. I nodded at him. He could feel me being drained from the demons repeatedly pounding on the shield. I winced.

"Dawn, I think I can make everyone invisible. I've never tried this many people at one time, but I can give it a shot," Hailey shouted at me over the demons shrieking. I looked at her. Her beautiful dark curly hair was matted with blood. I couldn't tell if it was hers or not.

"No, not all of us."

"But I-"

"You make Daniel, Jordan, and yourself invisible," I said, trying to make my voice sound commanding and turned to my sister, "When I let my shield down, you turn these suckers into ash. Lila as soon as you take care of these demons and Hailey if you see an opening you both run like hell. Understood?"

I expected her to fight me, and mentally started thinking of my argument, but Hailey sighed. She opened her arms as Lila gave me a dangerous smile then slid an unconscious Daniel over to her. Frank was looking irritated. He wanted more than anything to get to King and get his revenge, his hands shaking.

"Hey, Summers," I said, snapping my fingers in his face. He snarled as he saw my shield weaken, "You make sure none of the demons get to Hailey, got that?" He just nodded his head, his jaw tightening. He was losing control. He needed to focus on something in order to reign it in. I looked at Luke. He looked tired and beaten, but also gave off a strong presence that was the only thing holding me together. Hunter's loud growl snapped me out of my trance. The demons were breaking through my shield. Hailey quickly made herself, Jordan, and Daniel invisible.

"Here we go!" I shouted and looked at Lila. She stood up on her feet taking in another deep breath, her eyes turning back to orange. I knew she was ready and let my shield snap with a grunt feeling my power slam back into me. Lila screamed as flames erupted out of her. The fire created a wall around us. The demons who tried to fly in quickly turned the other direction screaming as their flesh seared. The demons were retreating. I smiled. We were winning. DEATH wasn't lost after all.

It got quiet. There was a creepy crawling sound as spiders surrounded us. Should've known that was suspicious. Two shadowy figures stepped into view. Lila didn't let her wall of fire down yet, a woman's giggle made its way to my ears. A charred figure walked straight through Lila's fire. It looked like a woman. Lila took a step back in surprise. When she emerged from the fire, she was blackened from head to toe, lava ran through the cracks of her burned skin. The woman's giggle came again from the creature that stood before us. The eyes were staring at me. They were completely red. It closed its eyes and slowly the woman's skin started to turn normal. The char falling off her body and the lava retreated into her skin. Suddenly, the terrifying creature became a stunning redheaded Dankra woman. She was dressed in a show stopping red gown that looked like it was literally sewn into her. The woman smirked at me.

"Dawn," she rasped. Her voice sounded like she had been swallowing the fire she created. Lila let down her wall of flame and I readied myself for a fight, but she was determined to start it. She punched her fist out sending flame straight at the woman's head. The Dankra woman let it hit her. It simply melted into her skin as she gave a horrifically gorgeous smile. Luke stiffened and Hunter whined. Frank took a step forward, but I shot him a look. He backed off. The others were still invisible. We needed to make sure they stayed undetected.

"That won't work, sweet Lila, though I do say I'm impressed," She sent out that chilling giggle again. I didn't know what to do. The spiders around us began to close in, making a barrier between us and the Dankra. I finally found my voice.

"Who are you?" I asked. The woman curtsied, her red dress tightening around her skin.

"Amidra Carson, at your service," Her voice sounded like smoke. My eyes widened. That couldn't be.

"You were one of the four original DEATH students that went missing," Luke said in shock as one of the shadowy figures made their way towards us.

"That we are! " A woman's voice chimed through the air, as she came to stand next to Amidra. She had dark blue hair shaved on the sides and silver black eyes that glowered at me.

"You're Elianna Beatrice," I whispered. The woman smiled, but it didn't touch her eyes.

"You work for... my father," I almost choked on the word. They didn't answer.

Amidra turned toward Elianna, "Don't kill them, just do what we came to do."

Elianna extended her hand at me as hundreds of needles sprang from her fingernails. I narrowly avoided them.

"That's the best you got?" I seethed at them. Elianna raised a challenging eyebrow at me. I looked around at my friends. Luke was pinned to the ground with a long needle hovering over his neck. Frank was on his hands and knees in front of where an invisible Hailey was, needles sticking out his back. Hunter was picking out needles from his side with his teeth growling at Elianna. Lila and I were the only ones not hit. They were sent to take us both. I needed to get them out of here.

"Luke I'm going to try and get everyone out of here like I did with you after the Elders. I'll send you back to Cassie's," I said in his head.

"Dawn, no-" I put the block up again and focused on Luke. My powers embraced him as he disappeared in black smoke. My powers found Hailey's invisibility and wrapped around anyone she was using it on. They disappeared too. Frank was the next to go. Then Hunter disappeared. The world began to spin and I fell to my knees. I was drained and couldn't do it anymore. I turned my head toward Lila, my vision swam. She needed to run. Elianna curled her fist in anger, needles popping out of her skin.

"Lila, get out of here!" I shouted at my sister. She just glared at Amidra and Amidra smiled. The skin around her mouth cracking. Spiders wrapped around Lila's hands constricting her. I reached for Lila, trying to make my power cooperate.

"We will not go with you!" I screamed, standing in front of Lila.

"We're not here for you," She rasped and lifted her hand. My sister yelped. I turned around, as a cloud of smoke engulfed her. It wasn't me. I tried to lunge for her, but she was gone. Where did she go?

"Knock her out," Elianna almost sang. I didn't even realize The Twins had gotten back up to their feet.

I didn't even have time to turn around as the world became dark.

***

My eyes fluttered open, something fuzzy was carrying me. The feeling of someone worried woke me. I was laying on wolf Hunter's back, his chestnut hair tickling my nose. I realized he was forcing his emotions into my head. He had figured it out. I tried to speak, but nothing came out. My entire body felt like it was on fire. Hunter whined, he must have felt my pain. I closed my eyes again realizing what had just happened. They took my sister, but left me. It didn't make sense. Amidra and Elianna. King and The Twins. Dankra. If it was my sister they were after today and not me why did King try to capture me? Lila was with them because of me. I needed to get her back. The images of everything that happened played in my mind on a nightmarish loop. King's twisted expression. Jada stopping time. Luke's horror struck eyes. Hunter's growls. Daniel's little body in my arms. Amidra's charred skin. Elianna's sharp nails. Frank's back. Lila's flame. I tried to fight through the fog that trapped me in a deep sleep. I didn't remember Hunter changing back into his human form, but when I opened my eyes again I was back at Jackson's mansion, in the same room I woke up in after Frank triggered my vision. My shoulder was still in pain, but the rest of my body felt okay. I looked at my protecti and Hunter sighed in relief.

"I ran back as soon as I realized what you did," He paused, his eyes watering, "Dawn, I couldn't find Lila. I couldn't even pick up her scent. I'm sorry," He grabbed my hand. I swallowed and looked away from him. I didn't want to tell him I failed. Hunter waited patiently. The only sound in the room was his racing heart.

"They took her," I whispered. Hunter squeezed my hand. Tears streamed down my face. I quickly tried to reign it in. My protecti's eyes closed in understanding. I sat up and took a ragged breath in trying to control my tears. It took me a minute to realize Hunter's arms had wrapped around me and I leaned into his chest. He stroked my hair and I stiffened. I was only used to this kind of affection from Luke. Hunter noticed and pulled away, but slipped his hand back into mine.

"I-um so Jada got King. Jackson has him chained to a prison wall with power damping cuffs on. I saw him and he was in rage screaming about being your brother," Hunter said, awkwardly trying to change the subject. I winced at that.

"Yeah, my family tree is a bit complicated," I said, still holding Hunter's hand. He put his other hand on top of our joined hands waiting for me to tell him more. I tried not to blush. Then I realized there was more to be worried about. I ripped my hand out of his getting to my feet, walking over to the mirror. I had healed alright. The demon's poison had definitely slowed it down. I flinched. Jordan's gushing side and Frank's bloodied back came to my mind.

"The others are ...?" I asked, whipping my head back towards Hunter. He stood with his hands in his pockets nodding before I could finish.

"They're fine. Daniel hasn't regained consciousness, but he should be up soon. Jordan's healing was slowed like yours. I saw her an hour ago already helping rebuild some of what the Dankra destroyed around camp. And Frank... well you should've heard the words he uttered when they pulled the needles out. Hailey cursed him right back for jumping in front of her," He chuckled. I tried to smile, but failed. Hunter stepped closer to me.

"Luke is with Jackson and Harrison. Jackson and the pack were able to keep the camp safe. Harrison got all the other students out; they're all here," He continued putting an arm on my shoulder as I balled my hands into fists. I didn't have any more time to just stand here. It was time for me to stop being weak. I looked in the mirror. My eyes looked darker, almost like King's. I blinked and they were back to their normal gold.

I cleared my throat. "Time to talk to my favorite person," I said walking out of the room without looking back at Hunter.

***

"You are not going!" Harrison said in his fatherly voice. He seemed off, like he was hiding something. I just didn't know what. We were inside Jackson's house staring each other down. I had gathered everyone and told them what happened to Lila and that we needed a plan to get her back. Jackson, Jada, and Harrison were all shocked at the mention of Amidra and Elianna. Harrison gave me a stern look. He wanted only the adults to take care of this. Jada was standing next to Harrison looking mysterious as ever. I hadn't asked her what actually happened with King or how she captured him. I was just glad she was okay. The bruises on her face still lingered. I was told I was passed out for two days. I wanted to scream at them for not going after my sister already, but I guess the attack here made it difficult. Jada gave Harrsion an annoyed look and I was glad she was feeling the same way as me.

"Yes, I am. Try and stop me if you want," I snickered. I started packing up gear that they had salvaged from the fire. Harrison wanted me to sit here and wait for the grown ups to decide what to do. My sister's life was on the line and I was going to be the one to get her back. I didn't care if it was a trap.

Luke was talking to Jackson in the corner of the room. He was trying to figure out the best way to get past the Dankra's forces. He hadn't said a word to me since I woke up which meant he was extremely mad at me. Jackson couldn't figure out how my father was able to track me. The Dankra they captured said their boss had no idea he was alive, and they were sent for me. The Dankra were exterminated as soon as they gave information, which I didn't feel good about. Jackson was adamant it was the right decision. It was decided that when we were going to search for Lila, Jackson had to stay behind with his pack. It was better if my father thought he was still dead. Although, I knew he wanted more than anything to go after his daughter.

"Listen to me, Dawn!" Harrison grabbed my hands and took my pack from me, his bottom lip shook. My entire body froze at that brief glimpse of his tough exterior breaking.

"Dawn," His voice wavered, "You're not ready for-".

"What I don't understand is how they got past the Boundary?" Jada cut him off, her eyes losing focus for a second then coming to land on Harrison.

"King might have been able to dismantle it, but it was fine when I was taken. You said you had it under control. We looked like we were going to be able to fight them off till all of our security systems failed. You said it was Eyre, but Hunter picked up no trace of her scent when he went back for Dawn," Jada's voice sounded monotone. Harrison dropped my hands, taking a steadying breath, refusing to meet Jada's eyes. I looked at Harrison in shock. Jada couldn't be alluding to... Harrison would never do that to us. He would never give up DEATH to the Dankra. He might be heartless, overpowering, and a jerk, but he was loyal to us. He was my family. Luke came to stand by me, his hands balling in fists getting what Jada was hinting at. Frank and Hunter quickly moved to either side of Harrison making sure he couldn't go anywhere. I wanted to tell the boys to back down, I didn't need their protection, but I couldn't form the words. I turned to see Hailey silently crying, looking at Harrison's guilt ridden face, while Daniel clung to her side. He had woken up a few minutes after I did. He still looked weak. Jackson moved towards him looking ready to attack, but Jada stepped in his way. She looked at Jackson deep in the eyes and he grabbed the back of his neck and stepped away from her. Jada turned to Harrison and put her hands on either side of his face. He tried to avoid her eyes, but she could see right through him. She forced him to look at her.

"Tell me what you did," She said in a commanding, but soft voice. He shook his head from her iron grip, but couldn't look away from her fiery eyes.

"Tell me!" She screamed at him, tears starting to run down her face. I knew then that Jada had already seen what Harrison did. She needed to know if it was real.

"I let her and the rest of them in. She released King and The Twins. I was promised no one would get taken or hurt. She said if I gave over D.E.A.T.H he would give Darcy back. I needed to see if she was alive," Harrison admitted his betrayal. I felt my eyes water. I shook them away as rage took over my entire body instead. Jackson stumbled backwards at the mention of my mother's name. There could be a chance that the Dankra weren't lying and she was still with them like Amidra and Elianna. That didn't mean she wasn't a Dankra herself or that she was the same person. I wanted to punch Harrison and throw him through Jackson's perfect mansion into the ground. At the same time, if I had been offered the chance to see my mother again I'd take it, no matter what the consequences were. Luke took my hand and held me back. He too was furious, but we needed more information and Jada seemed like the only one that could get him talking.

"Why Harry? Why would you fall for that? You know I haven't seen her future since her disappearance," Jada whispered, grabbing on to his face again. Harrison grabbed her hands and leaned into them.

"It was impulse. I thought I could fix this and fix things with you," Harrison said, his voice cracking as he searched Jada's eyes for a response. Jada yanked her hands from his face and stepped back looking at him in disappointment.

"Who's her?" I managed to choke out. Amidra? Elianna? I wasn't expecting the Dankra he was in contact with to be my father. He was using others to do his dirty work.

"One of his favorite students," Jada said coldly.

"Sioena Kellnet," He answered my question avoiding Jada's eyes he continued, "She is an elder in training, or I thought she was. She came with Tallahan to DEATH to inspect the Packers and she stayed behind. She told me Darcy was alive. Sioena was a student at DEATH. I taught her everything she knows. She told me how she met your father and made the transformation. She's been disguising herself this whole time. She said if I left DEATH unprotected she'd give me time to get everyone out. When I saw all the demons I shut off the security systems and got everyone out as fast as I could. I was coming back for Jada when I saw Hunter running around searching for Lila. Then you on the ground," Harrison explained, lowering his eyes. I knew I hated Sioena for a reason and it wasn't just her judgemental attitude.

"So you what? Just took down the shield and hid in the corner like a coward?" I asked, stepping closer to him, my voice growing in volume. He flinched. Harrison had betrayed all of us. I understand that he thought he was doing the right thing, but that didn't change anything. Hunter and Frank were still making sure Harrison stayed where he was. I knew he would never hurt us, but it couldn't hurt to be cautious. Harrison's also a very skilled fighter. If he wanted us dead we'd be dead already. I looked around the room. Hailey was holding a crying Daniel trying to comfort him. He was upset that he had let Lila be taken, although it wasn't his fault. Jackson looked like he was about to throw up at the mention of my mom's name and the capture of his daughter who didn't even know she was his daughter. I could tell it still left him reeling. Luke was still next to me trying to figure out how we were going to get in and out of DEATH without being seen by the Dankra. There seemed like no possible way. We'd have to fight our way in and out. Jada was still staring at her ex in disbelief. I'm sure it was hard for her to deal with Harrison right now, especially because he did it to get her back. I didn't know what to say next. Harrison fell to his knees in front of Jada.

"Please forgive me," He whispered. Jada shook her head, his voice breaking her daze. She knelt down with him.

"I'm going to help these brave children, most of which you raised, fight these monsters and get Lila back safely. I think you should stay out of this. You've done enough," Jada said sharply, but still took his hand in hers. She felt bad for him. Surprisingly, I felt bad for him too. I could see now all Harrison tried to do my entire life was keep us safe. He wasn't the best at it, but I didn't help him out all that much either. I also got a sense that Jada knew something more about what would happen if Harrison came with us, but I knew better than to ask her about it. Harrison looked like he wanted to say something, but before he could Jada got up and walked out. Jackson followed after her.

"The Dankra are inside what's left of DEATH. It is possible Lila is somewhere else, but I think that is the best place to start. They will be expecting us. The only way to make this work is to make them think Dawn is going alone. Sioena will be expecting all of us, if Dawn can get in and distract as many Dankra as possible, we can slip in and get Lila," Luke said walking in front of everyone. He was right. The Dankra wanted me and they would go to any lengths to get me on their side.

Frank chimed in, "There's no way they'll think Dawn is completely acting by herself one of us will need to go with her," Frank pointed at Luke then back at himself. I looked at Harrison who had been still and silent since Jada left. The others seemed to be ignoring his presence, so I did too.

"Why does it have to be either of you?" Hailey asked, surprising everyone. She was right, it didn't have to be Luke or Frank. Luke looked at her confused. He wanted more than anything to be the one by my side protecting me, but that's not what needed to be done. They needed to believe I was surrendering myself over to them.

"I'm not trying to be overprotective, Dawn," Luke said in my head. The others noticed what he was doing.

"That is unfair guys. We deserve to be included in this conversation," Frank said angrily, crossing his arms. Luke looked like he was going to yell at Frank, but Hunter spoke before he could.

"I think it would be best if I go with Dawn. Sioena knows I'm her protecti, but she's too familiar with Luke. She'll be expecting him. She obviously knows Frank because of her connection to King. I'll be something unexpected and possibly enough to throw them off," He shoved his hands in his pockets looking at me. Luke looked at me too. I knew he would be offended if I said it was a good idea, but it was.

"Well that's just great," Luke said, throwing his hands in the air. He already knew I had decided Hunter should come with me. Frank looked at him confused.

I sighed, "You're right, Hunter. It's decided. You are coming with me. Daniel is staying behind at the Jackson camp and the rest of you get prepared to do some more fighting." Frank scoffed and Luke groaned. They were being babies about this. Hailey nodded like she thought it was a good idea for Hunter to come with me too. She looked strong. There was more to Hailey than I ever knew. If I made it out of this, we were going to talk more.

"Once Hunter and I are in, Luke will lead the rest of you around the back of DEATH. If I'm right, they'll most likely try to take Hunter out of the equation and put him into the prisons down in the basement. Hunter will help you guys locate Lila from there," I didn't want them to hear my unconfidence about Lila's whereabouts. I don't know what I would do if they had decided not to keep Lila alive. I couldn't even think about it. Luke put his hand on my shoulder.

"We will get her back," Luke said, trying to sound confident. I forced a smile and nodded.

"Well, who's ready to kick some demon ass!" Frank yelled. We uncomfortably laughed at him. The others started to exit the room. I stared at a paralyzed Harrison not knowing what to do about him.

"I will tell Jada and Jackson our plan," Luke said, flicking his eyes towards Harrison then back at me, as he walked out. He knew I wanted to talk to him. I stared at him waiting for him to say something.

"I don't know what you want me to say, Dawn," Harrison finally spoke.

"I want you to say that you thought what you did was the only way to protect us. I want you to say that you didn't take the easy way out. I want you to say that you had evidence that my mother was alive and not just the word of a lying demon. I want you to say that this wasn't you being selfish!" I said fast, my voice getting louder with every sentence. Harrison looked at me then at the floor.

"I can't," Harrison said, looking into my eyes tears streaming down his face. This was the only emotion I've seen from him ever. There was a small part of me that wanted to reach out and hug him, but the anger in me was stronger. I turned to walk out.

"Dawn, wait," Harrison said. I turned back around as he was finally getting off his knees. "I want you to know that I love you and the others. I'm sorry if I didn't show it. Please be careful," He said pleading with me. I didn't know what to say. I was shocked by what he just said. I had to get away from him so I could cry without him seeing.

"You might love us, but it doesn't change anything," I choked out and ran out of the room.

Chapter 19

Not Ready

As I raced down the hall, I was not paying attention to my surroundings. A familiar arm yanked me into a corner of the hallway and pushed me against the wall. Luke's blue eyes looked into mine. He put a hand over my mouth. Tears still streamed down my face, but I glared at him.

"Don't bite me, okay. Just listen," Luke said in my head, his hand stayed on my mouth. That's when I heard voices coming from the room right next to us.

"We can't just let these kids walk into a fight you know they can't win," Jackson's strong, but sad voice thudded through my ears. I looked at Luke and he shook his head.

"I haven't been able to see anything, Jack," Jada's calm voice responded. Jackson growled and I heard a crash.

"Throwing chairs won't help anything," Jada said with a chuckle.

"What about the key you found? The prophecy *you* told?" Jackson whispered trying to get himself under control. The piece of paper was still in my pocket.

"It's up to Dawn now. I can't tell you anything even if I want to," Jada responded. I squirmed against Luke. What did she mean? Jackson was pacing now, his footsteps making the floorboards squeak.

"Dawn, if you go in there we won't get any more information out of them, just be patient," Luke said, still keeping his hand on my mouth. I glared at him and sighed.

"Can you at least take your hand off my mouth?" Luke grinned and slowly removed his hand from my mouth, but kept his body weight pushing me against the wall. He knew I could easily push him off, but it was keeping us hidden.

"Your pacing isn't helping anyone," I could hear the smirk in Jada's voice. Jackson grumbled something unintelligible.

"Will the prophecy come true?" Jackson said after a long time of silence between them. Jada sighed. I knew her answer before she even said it.

"I can't tell you that either, but you knew that when I came to you," Jada said as I heard her steps, probably towards Jackson. I never knew what led to Jada showing up on our doorstep covered in blood.

"You had to go through King's Packer camp to get it back. I thought it was just because they caught you with my wolves, but we should've known he was Dankra. He has Thomas' eyes," Jackson said.

"You'd think the adults in our lives would stop keeping secrets," Luke's anger rippled through him, his eyes turning yellow. I grabbed his shaking hand that was resting on my hip. He took a deep breath.

"Yes we should have, my Seer abilities are endless, yet I'm controlled by the rules of time. I'm sworn to protect it at any cost," Jada's voice broke a little. She knew what was going to happen every second of every day. I can't imagine what that might be like. I would hate that.

"Dawn has strong Seer magic," Jackson said.

"The future is her fear, Jack," Jada said seriously. My fear. I inhaled that's why she only wanted me to see the past. She didn't know how much I could actually do. The more I saw the future the more my Dankra side wasn't suppressed.

"We've seen no signs the Bound isn't doing its job," Jackson said exasperated.

"Dawn being able to see the future is a sign," Jada stated. There was no question in her voice. The Seer spark came from my mother, but my innate fear of the future made it connected to my Dankra side. Luke slid his hand to my back supporting my shaking body, even with the Bound there was no telling if I could keep the monster in me suppressed. I dropped my head onto his chest.

"The ability is a part of her; she isn't going to stop using it. The Bound will hold and will be solidified when she marries Luke," Jackson said so quietly I could barely hear him. I suddenly felt very aware of Luke's body pressed up against mine. I raised my head off his chest. He noticed me stiffen, but did not move, as I shifted uncomfortably. He was caught up in listening to them. There was silence.

"If there's anything I know about our little warrior, her connection to Luke was important before she even knew what it was for. Yes, that boy is her other half, but I see many futures for her. It comes down to one decision. She has to be the one to choose it. It can not be forced upon her like Harrison and you have tried for all of her life. That is not what Darcy would want," Jada said, her voice growing more serious. Jackson didn't respond. There was a little more movement in the room, one of them sat in a chair.

"Speaking of Harrison. He let my daughter be kidnapped. I hope you know that if she doesn't make it back, I hold him responsible. I will not hesitate to give him the punishment he deserves," Jackson hissed. I've never heard him this angry. Luke was even surprised by the tone of his voice, but he was feeling the same way about Harrison.

"You can't judge him for wanting her back, Jack. I do not forgive him for what he did, but you have to see why. We thought for years she might have become a Dankra... with Amidra and Elianna in the mix...," Jada paused, "It might not be a bad theory," Her voice emotionless. Jackson cleared his throat.

"How are you with all this? Two of your former flames conspiring with the enemy?" Jackson asked, genuine care in his voice. He must have read something on Jada's face we couldn't see. Wait. Two? Luke shrugged.

"Oh Jackson don't meddle. If you want me to admit that I loved Harrison, more than Amidra I can not. Harrison was my first. Amidra I thought was going to be my last. I let them both go a long time ago," Jackson grunted as she said that. She was obviously lying, "You on the other hand have never let go. I don't know whether to feel bad for you or admire you," Jada said, her voice still emotionless even though I detected a little bit of sass. Jackson growled, but it wasn't threatening.

"We better get back to the kids, Moony," Jackson said with a little bit of worry. Jada scoffed.

"I always hated that nickname, but yes doggie you're right," Jada laughed. They started to come out of the room. Luke tensed. I grabbed both sides of his face getting ready to Flash us away. When suddenly, images popped into my head. Luke was thinking about leaning in until our lips touched. He was thinking about kissing me. I froze. I didn't know what to do. I'm not ready for kissing. I'm just a kid. My body didn't want to move though. It didn't want to tell him to stop. Luke blushed as he realized he hadn't blocked his thoughts from me.

"*Dawn, I don't know what that was. That was nothing,*" Luke said but his feet stayed planted in place. I didn't remove my hands from his face as I searched his bright soft blue eyes. I realized I liked those images Luke had created. Luke lowered his head waiting just above my lips. I sucked in a breath and leaned in as well. We shouldn't be crossing this line. I just needed to feel what it felt like just once. Luke's eyes flicked back down to mine in question. Should I stop this? Yes. But do I want to? Luke's hand cupped my cheek. I didn't move, as his lips hovered over mine.

"Ahem," A voice made us both jump. Luke and I pulled apart and looked to see Hailey across the hall. She smiled.

"I'm sorry. I am, but I couldn't just stand here any longer without letting you guys know. I made myself invisible to listen to them and then I saw you guys. When they came out of the room, they would've seen you so I cast my power on you guys. I-er noticed you both were...distracted," Her smile got bigger, but I just blinked at her.

Luke smiled back completely unphased, "Thanks Hailey. I didn't know you didn't have to be touching a person to make them invisible." He looked completely calm. I tried to get into his head, but he had blocked me out again. I crossed my arms annoyed with his sudden need to hide his feelings.

"I've been practicing. All of us are going to the campfire to get ready," She said. I could tell she felt awkward at what she just saw and wanted to leave as soon as possible.

"Sounds good we'll be there in a second," I responded, but my voice was weak. She nodded and skipped down the rest of the hall to the front door. I turned to Luke. He smiled, too confidently. That's it. I slammed him into the wall.

"You try that again. And your hair won't be the only pain I've caused you," I said angrily and out loud so he really got the message. Luke blushed and looked at his feet. Then back up at me. He was giving me puppy dog eyes. I hissed.

"*Nice try, wolf.*" I didn't want to be mean to him, but it was like second nature. I didn't want him to think I had feelings for him in that way. Did I have feelings for him? I couldn't think about that.

"Okay, okay. How about this? You stop trying to sacrifice yourself and I'll never do that again. Also if you think the only pain you've caused me is giving me a bad haircut you're sorely mistaken," He said with a wink, giving me a shove backwards and then Flashed from my grip. Urgh. What had just happened? Do I cause him pain? I slid down the wall. Jada and Jackson were still keeping things from us. I couldn't even be worried about that. All I could think about was what Luke had painted in his mind. What had almost happened, if Hailey hadn't intervened. I'd have to thank her for that later. Luke left me with feelings I couldn't grasp. The worst of all was the wanting that rose up in my heart.

***

After I got myself together, everyone was at the campfire. We decided I would Flash to DEATH with Hunter and then the rest would follow shortly after. Jada was going with them too. She would help them get in and then do whatever was necessary to ensure we got out. That is what she said in many other words, but I honestly was only half listening. Luke kept me out of his head and stayed silent the whole conversation avoiding my gaze. Idiot.

Jackson said we had to stay for one last bonfire. So I sat at the bar, with Momma G staring at me. I could tell she scented I was more than a Guardian. The most amazing thing about Momma G was her silver hair. She was supposed to be frail boned, but she looked as strong as any of the other wolves here.

"If yer wondering how old I am, half-demon, don't try to guess because you won't," She replied with a heavy accent. I smiled at her. I think she smiled back in her own way, which was to glare at me. I didn't care; she knew I was staring as she cleaned the glasses spotless. I turned around to see my friends and I spotted Daniel. He was looking a little better sitting by the bonfire next to some wolves his age by the looks of it. I even saw him laugh. It filled my chest with warmth. Luke and Jordan were sitting on the other side of the fire. Jordan's hair bounced as she was no doubt telling the most animated and intriguing story ever. Luke listened intently while taking a sip of his drink. The other wolves around her were completely mesmerized. I pushed down the tang of jealousy that went through me. Luke had blocked me out entirely since we eavesdropped on Jada and Jackson. I hadn't tried to open up to him either. I think we were both embarrassed. I tore my eyes away from him. Hailey was looking at me as I caught her gaze. She was leaning against a tree. Hailey shook her head, her curls brushed over her face, chuckling no doubt at how I was staring at Luke. I shook my head right back, sticking my tongue out at her and she did the same. I couldn't help, but laugh. It was nice to see Hailey coming out of her shell. Next, I stretched my neck looking for my protecti. Hunter stood on the outskirts of the gathering looking up at the stars feeling overwhelmed. I sent a feeling of comfort to him. He perked up meeting my eyes. I couldn't stop my blush as his feelings about me ran down our connection.

"Ah my eyes, Shadows blushing," Frank Summers' voice thundered over the fire and chit chat. I turned to him, his toothpick resting comfortably in his mouth. He crossed his arms. I rolled my eyes at him and gestured for him to sit next to me. He plopped down with a grunt.

"Something you wanted?" I asked, acting annoyed. He laughed and took his tooth pick out of his mouth.

"Yes, actually. I know you don't want to tell me what you saw when you had your vision," I shifted uncomfortably, "I'm sure I actually don't want to know, but I need to know something." I shivered at the memory of the vision. Frank waited with his brown golden eyes intense. I sighed.

"I saw you and I at DEATH. We got taken away by hooded figures," I whispered. The laughter and joy pulsating through the air couldn't break the tension that passed between Frank and I. He sucked in a breath.

"Was it the Dankra?" He asked.

"I don't know," I said even though now I was pretty sure it was. Frank brushed a hand through his hair. Then looked down at his hands. I paused for a moment not wanting to scare him. He knew I was lying.

"Hey, I can't read your mind like your bestie or feel your emotions like Mr. Dreamy eyes. So can you just let me in for a second?" I could tell he was trying to be funny and I tried to smile.

"You think Hunter has dreamy eyes?" I asked with a grin. Frank rolled his eyes at me.

"Answer the question Shadows," He crossed his arms as I gave a big sigh.

"Yes, it was Dankra and I'm pretty sure it will happen tomorrow." Frank nodded at me, his eyes welled with tears for a second and then quickly avoided my gaze. I opened my mouth to tell him what Eyre had told me at the Packer camp, but the words didn't come. I should tell him to stay away from me. He deserved better than my selfishness.

"Good. You take me with you, Shadows. They'll want me anyway," He said, pulling out his toothpick and sticking it in between his teeth.

"Oh really? Why is that?" I asked, reaching for the tooth pick. He effortlessly dodged me.

"I-um- I think-um- it's hazy, but I think King had the Packers drinking demon blood. I think he was preparing to make us into Dankra," Frank looked at me with realization in his eyes. This was the first time he had told that to anyone. I could tell his hands were shaking soI grabbed them. He took a deep breath, then looked up at me and his expression made me want to cry.

"Does that mean... I could be...?" He swallowed, unable to finish his sentence. I don't know how it works exactly. King would know more.

"Have you been to see King?" I asked, gritting my teeth. My battle with him would come, I hope sooner than later. Frank snorted.

"They wouldn't let me in, with good reason. I don't think he'd be breathing right now if they did," Frank growled. I patted his shoulder. Jackson had said Guardians consumed demon blood to become Dankra. I couldn't lie to Frank he'd see right through it.

"Yes, Jackson said that's how the first Guardians became Dankra. King and I are the only ones born with it that I know of. I don't know how the transition is completed," I said in as soft of a voice as I could. Frank only nodded. I had confirmed what he already knew.

Frank looked so defeated as his head hung. He needed a distraction and I needed to talk to someone about this. I sighed, someone should know about this incident.

"I almost kissed Luke!" I blurted out then clamped my hand on my mouth half expecting the whole pack to turn to me in shock, but everyone kept dancing and didn't even pay attention to Frank and I. Frank turned his head to me slowly and his eyes widened.

"Are you serious?" Frank said inching closer to me with a half smile on his lips. I nodded and bit my lip.

"That's all the info you're gonna give me?" Frank said, crossing his arms laughing. I couldn't help, but laugh with him even though my chest felt like it was going to explode. I was glad Frank had relaxed a little bit. I glanced at Luke. He was still talking to Jordan. I ripped my gaze back towards Frank who had now stopped laughing. He punched me in the shoulder. I sighed and told him the whole story with as much detail as I could. He played the role of the listener well when he wanted to, but barely showed any reaction. When I was done, he laughed again so hard that he fell off his chair. I waited till he got back on it.

"I'm sorry, I just can't believe Luke thought he could kiss you, before I-". The boy be crazy," Frank could barely get his words out; he was laughing so hard. I glared at him. He stopped abruptly at my look. I was also extremely shocked he's never kissed anyone before, but decided against asking him about it. I just blinked at him.

"Sorry, again," His smile was devilish.

"You can not tell Luke I told you. Got that," I said, grabbing on to his arm a little too roughly. He raised his eyebrows. The light from the campfire danced in his eyes.

"Got it, Commander Heartbreaker," Frank said with a little bow of his head. Then smiled that dangerous, but intriguing smile that made me want to punch him in the face.

"I'm serious," I squeezed his arm. Frank snorted at my comment, unphased by my nails digging into his arm.

"I will not say anything to Wolfy Locks. I promise," Frank said, his smile now sincere. I smiled back. Then blushed.

"There it is again. It's weird. Stop doing that," Frank said at the sight of my blushing. I growled at him. He put his hands up in defense. I sighed and rested my head on his shoulder.

"What are we gonna do?" I was partly asking about Luke, but partly asking about the monster that lived in both of us ready to escape at any minute. Frank stiffened. I looked back up at him. My distraction was over. I watched him watch the action going on around us. Frank didn't answer me. He didn't have any snide comments or jokes to make this situation bearable and neither did I. He thought he had escaped his past, but like me he was far from not being defined by it. I sat with him watching the campfire swirl in the air and the people that danced, sang, talked and laughed.. I looked at Frank and he too was admiring the other's joy. I sighed and grabbed his hand pulling him to standing. Our definition of right and wrong and everything we were ever taught might be torn apart, but we could still dance. He smiled as I dragged him into the crowd of people. We danced until we had forgotten what we had to face tomorrow.

***

I woke up at the crack of me...dawn and walked out of the mansion. Jordan was waiting for me on the steps. Hunter and Jackson had told me they were keeping King in one of their holding cells on the west side of camp. I asked Jordan if she would be willing to take me to see him during last night's festivities. I didn't tell Luke. She told me I wasn't technically allowed, but if I followed her to the holding cells tomorrow morning, when she had watch duty, she wouldn't stop me. Jordan pretended she didn't see me as I followed her throughout the quiet, sleeping camp. We came to a dark cottage type house. She looked around and finally beckoned me to follow. As I entered the house, there were two wolves sitting at a table talking quietly as we walked in. They stiffened at my presence. They were both dark haired and muscley.

The one wore a green sweatshirt and torn up jeans. The other wore a black muscle tee. I recognized the one with the green sweatshirt from the first bonfire here. He stood up for Frank.

Jordan rolled her eyes and said in an Alpha's voice, "Gillard and Kyle, Dawn and I have next watch on the prisoner. Come back in an hour."

The one in the green sweatshirt looked to his companion who shrugged.

"She's not supposed to be here, J," He avoided my gaze. Jordan crossed her arms and sunk into her right hip.

"Gill, will you please just leave. We just got you back and I wouldn't want to damage that pretty face of yours," She batted her eyelashes at him. The one in the muscle tee growled, Kyle I assume, but Gillard let out a chuckle like he was familiar with how much Jordan can ness up his face. He stood to his feet finally looking at me. Kyle simply followed him.

"Thanks for the save lil demon. I owe you one," Gillard said while he walked out. Kyle just gave me a stern nod and followed. Jordan watched them go before turning to me.

"I used to date Gill. He's a total softy, but is next in line for First Omega. He got captured by Frank actually. I spent months trying to figure out how to get into that camp," She said, leading me to a set of stairs.

"Why'd you two break up?" I asked, Jordan turned to me pausing on the stairs giving me a shocked look, "Sorry if that's too personal." She giggled.

"No, I just wasn't expecting you to ask. I decided I wasn't what he was looking for," Jordan said. There seemed to be more to the story, but I didn't press further. She led me down two more flights of stairs where we made it to the basement. It had four iron prison cells and King was in the first one chained to the wall with power dampening cuffs. He slowly lifted his head and I could see his face was bruised. He was sporting a freshly bruised black eye, probably given to him by one of the two wolves that just left. It looked like it was healing, but slower than normal. He chuckled and coughed as his black eyes met my own.

"I'll be waiting upstairs if you need anything," Jordan said, not taking her eyes off King until she strode out.

"I wasn't sure if you'd come see me," King smiled weakly, his voice raspy, but amused. I walked close to the iron bars. He shifted onto his knees.

"Why did Amidra and Elianna let you get captured?" I asked, keeping my voice neutral. King laughed again.

"Of all the things to ask me, little sister, that's the best you can come up with? Do you think Amidra and Elianna were alone?" King shifted again, uncomfortable. I considered his question remembering the other figure, I couldn't make out their face. Were they responsible for the spiders?

"Answer the question and maybe I can persuade Jackson to get you chained to a cot," I gave him a devilish smile. King laughed.

"Amidra is jealous of me and Elianna wants me dead or wants to marry me you can never tell with her," He shrugged. I was surprised at his answer. It held some truth, but it wasn't the reason.

"You're telling me that they would just let their master's son get captured?" King only glared at me. I could tell King wanted our father's approval more than anything.

I pushed on, "Or was it because you pissed off dad?" King's eyes grew darker, but quickly recovered.

"I'll answer if you answer me first," He grunted in pain. I only glared at him and he continued, "Do you feel the darkness?" My hands balled into fists. King noticed and smiled. I could lie. It would be so easy, but King could see right through me. I looked inside myself to that part that felt blocked off. It beckoned to be set loose, to take me over.

"I feel it everyday," I whispered. King nodded in understanding, his smile fading for a quick moment.

"Our father sent me ahead of the General as a distraction. She sent the others," He answered, bored.

"Are you talking about Sioena?" I asked, grabbing on to the bars so he couldn't see my shaking hands.

"Yes," He coughed, "They'll come for me, eventually." King's voice sounded hesitant, thick with emotion he couldn't hide, his dark eyes grew softer and glistened. He looked down at his cuffs. I stepped back and went to walk out. There was nothing more I needed from him.

"That's all you wanted to know, little sister? I have lots more information. If you're going to survive Initiation, you have to get better at interrogating," King said, his voice growing softer. I scoffed, turning back to him.

"Sioena doesn't fail. She will bring you in and break you. You have to accept who you are. Ask Jada if she's seen it," King's voice was barely above a whisper. I smiled and decided to ignore his comment about Jada.

"She doesn't know who she's dealing with," I said and added, "Goodbye brother."

King yelled after me, "I'll see you when you come to aide in my escape, little warrior!" The sound of his terrifying laughter made the hairs on the back of my neck stand up.

My hands were shaking with anger as I practically ran up the stairs past Jordan and out the door. I fell to my knees and kept the dark part of me suppressed as I felt it open just a little bit.

***

I walked toward the burnt pieces of my home. DEATH was no longer on fire, but the leftover embers still lingered. Smoke swirled high in the sky. It surrounded me, making me feel like I was choking, but I kept silent. Hunter followed close behind me in his human form. We wanted to make it look like we were surrendering, even though I would prefer his wolf form because the connection between us was stronger while he's changed. When we Flashed in just before where the Boundary used to be, I expected there to be demons everywhere, but it was barren. Although I could feel they were near, which meant there were others beside Dankra here. We came with no weapons. It was Frank's idea to sell the ruse as much as we could. Luke hated everything about it, but that made me agree even more. I didn't need him to defend myself anyway. I looked up into the cloud of smoke, the sight of it pulling me out of my thoughts. There they were. The flying demons we had fought three days before were circling DEATH waiting for us no doubt. My power felt like it was crackling beneath my skin. We were almost at the door as Hunter was surprisingly calm next to me. I didn't dare look at him, the feeling of getting him to safety was too strong. We had a plan, but if something went wrong I was getting them all out of here no matter what happened to me in the process. The flapping of the demons' wings sounded like thunder as I was about to walk right up to the front door. I stopped at the top step and sighed. Hunter looked around stiffening.

"Alright! I'm here!" I screamed jumping up and down not caring if this was a bad idea. It was stupid. Hunter tried to grab my arms as I flung them around, but I hit his hands away. The next thing I knew talons were scooping Hunter and I up. The demon was larger than the ones we fought a couple days ago. It flew with incredible speed. The wind stung my eyes and whipped through my hair. We made it to the top of the destroyed roof. I looked at Hunter and his eyes widened at the sight. We plummeted straight through the opening in the roof when the demon let go of

Hunter and I. I tried not to scream as I fell through the air. I heard Hunter's shouts as he tried to gain control of his flailing body. I pushed my arms to my sides, closed my legs and propelled myself to Hunter. I made it a foot above him when he was only about ten feet from the ground. My shield exploded out of me towards Hunter on instinct, wrapping him in a protective layer. He landed hands sprawled out legs in the air as the shield stopped the full impact a few inches from the ground. I extended my hands out doing the same thing. The hit on the shield was still rough as the impact knocked the air out of me. I let my shield drop as I gasped for breath getting to my feet. I stumbled forward bracing my hands on my knees. Hunter was instantly at my side, his hand on my back. I waved him off, getting myself standing, my breath returning to normal.

"Thanks for the shield. Remind me to never go on a mission with you again, after this," Hunter said, shivering looking up at the hole we fell through.

"What, not a fan of heights?" I said with a laugh. He responded, but I was too busy looking at our surroundings. We were in what was left of the Training Room. There were demons around, but none of them were visible. My skin was on fire. It was dark all around us with very little light pushing through the smoke above us. The sun had seemed to cease to exist around DEATH. We were definitely being watched.

"Miss Shadows, I apologize for that fall. Sway demons are quite hard to control," A slinky voice sounded from the darkness around us. I stiffened and turned around. Hunter stood beside me, his eyes turning yellow as he tried to see in the dark. My eyes adjusted as a familiar figure stepped out into the dim light.

"Sioena," I whispered. The figure who stood before me was not the same as the woman who played the role of Elder Talahan's personal assistant and Elder in training. She was utterly terrifying and stunning at the same time much like Amidra. A true Dankra. My eyes immediately went to the snake tattoos that slithered up each of her arms. They were more than tattoos they seemed...alive, they pushed against her skin, the once flat scales, raised and shimmering. Every move she made they squirmed and writhed. Sioena's eyes were purple slits as she flicked her gaze over me. She wore a black gooey dress that looked melted into her and moved on its own. Her hair was spiked; it looked like tiny knives protruding from her head. The only thing that remained the same was the annoyance that took over me as I looked at her.

"Very good. Here I was thinking you wouldn't recognize me. I'm glad I made an impression."

Sioena took another step forward into the light. As the beams hit her skin, I could see tiny scales running all over her body, a tint of green amplifying the scales' appearance.

Sioena hissed a laugh, "Like what you see? It's amazing what a little demon blood will do."

I only glared. Hunter growled next to me, his muscles threatening to rip into wolf form. I sent a calming feeling to him and he relaxed the tiniest bit.

"Oh right!" Sioena threw her head back and a rattle escaped her throat, "You know I was expecting your other blond wolf boyfriend. What's his name? Luke. It would be so much more poetic to take his life in exchange for your sister. Unfortunately, I'm under strict orders not to kill anyone," Sioena sighed dramatically, giving us a fair pouty lip moving with too much grace towards us. I balled my hands into fists.

"I'm here to make a deal," I said, stepping in front of Hunter. Sioena's snake eyes looked into mine.

"A deal is not in our interest," She hissed and twitched her head to the side. A tooth smile revealed her venomous fangs. I stood my ground as I saw more Dankra started approaching. They were cloaked like the ones in my vision. The Sway demons, Sioena had called them, stayed in the air, awaiting orders. A circle of blue fire erupted around Hunter and I, as Amidra stepped out of the shadows. The lava in her veins danced beneath her skin giving it a glow as she took position to the right of Sioena. Amidra's skin was half smoldering as she stood controlling the fire around us with her eyes. I didn't dare try to get out of the flames. We had to make sure all the Dankra eyes were on us.

"Let me take care of the wolf, please General?" Elianna's windchime voice pierced my ears. She emerged to Sioena's left, her nails extended into sharp points.

Sioena's snakelike laugh echoed throughout the Training Room, "You know he wouldn't like that Elianna." Elianna's face fell for a minute and then fear crossed her face. My father had his hooks in each and every one of these former Guardians. Hunter took two steps towards the edge of the fire. I grabbed at his hand, but he pulled away.

"We are here to exchange Lila for me," Hunter said clearly with no emotion. I put on the best shocked expression I could.

"Hunter, what do you think you're doing?" I hissed at him.

Sioena took a step closer to Amidra's flame that kept Hunter and I in place. I could probably get out of it, but they needed to think I was afraid. Sioena looked at me with her snake eyes searching my very soul.

"Amidra," She said with a silent order in her voice, not taking her eyes off me. The flames died down. The Dankra closed in on us more. Hundreds and hundreds of spiders surrounded each group of Dankra. Acting as a barrier to them. I still could only make out Sioena, Elianna, and Amidra's faces. They were the only ones not cloaked. There was an obvious rank among the Dankra and Sioena was at the top. She strode past Hunter, her body slinking with every step. I watched in horror as she grabbed my right wrist with her scaly hand. I balled my fist so hard that my symbol became more prominent. I gritted my teeth as she licked her forked tongue over it.

"One of the most powerful Guardians I've ever felt," Her eyes grew more into slits as she yanked me to her. Sioena's lips were now pressed to my ear, "Tell me. Can you feel your demon side?" I shivered as she said the words that will haunt me everyday. At the enjoyment of the dormant power, I did sometimes feel ready to escape. I felt Hunter's angry ripple through me, as he lunged for Sioena. Sioena in no time had her hand around his neck. I didn't even feel her step away from me. She clenched harder as Hunter struggled and I panicked.

"Stop, please," I whimpered, watching Hunter's sea green eyes widened in pain, as Sioena lifted him in the air. She hissed and her tongue flicked out, as she dropped Hunter to the floor pivoting around to me. Hunter fell to his knees gasping. I wanted to go to him. Sioena snapped her fingers and two Dankra began dragging Hunter away, while two others seized my arms. I didn't move. Hunter had a job to do and it seems like Sioena's playing right into our hands.

"Put the dog with the sister," Sioena said, never taking her eyes off me. I watched with horror on my face as my protecti was dragged away. Hunter sent a feeling of confidence to me and I tried not to smile.

"I need time alone with our new recruit," Sioena said, coming over to me stroking her nails down my face. The Dankra, including Elianna and Amidra, all disappeared into the shadows. The spiders dissolved with them as Sioena began circling me. I stood with my head up looking at her dead in her purple snake eyes.

"What are you staring at?" I spat at her, crossing my arms sassily sitting into my right hip. She smiled thinly, her scales softening.

"I am figuring out just how much of you is a demon," Sioena whispered, dangerously flicking her tongue out again. I glared.

"That's really nice. What did you find?" I said with a chuckle.

"Fifty percent give or take," She stopped in front of my face again. I was surprised she answered my question. There might be a possibility I could get more information out of her.

"I know that. Tell me something more interesting. Or better yet, release my sister. I will go with you quietly," I said with a serious tone.

Sioena hissed, "I thought you'd be more fun. You are the master's daughter after all." I almost puked at that. The way she said master referring to my father. There was way more than just admiration in her voice.

"Oh yes, what about my father?" I said, trying to reach out to Luke so he could hear every word. He was present in my mind the moment I let down my block.

"*We're in. Keep her busy,*" Luke's voice sounded in my head soothing my tense state. Sioena watched me intently. Did she know about the Bound? Does she know about Luke and I's connection?

"Your father will see you soon," Sioena said, putting one hand on her hip and the other waving me off. A dismissal of my question.

"Give me my sister," I wanted to scream in her face. I needed to slam her infuriating face into the ground, but Luke needed more time. Sioena's purple slit eyes darkened as she looked deep into mine. I shivered again as I felt that power. The other side of me is trying to break out. I couldn't control the gasp that escaped my lips.

A genuine smile spread across Sioena's face, "That's it. I found it. Let it go and your sister can go free. She's not what the master wants anyway. He made an error asking King to go after you. He's arrogant and stupid. Amidra and Elianna came just in time thinking of a more...delicious way to seduce you into embracing your true self," I flinched at her words and the way the snakes in her arms began to move. Luke needed to hurry, I was about to lose it on Sioena.

"If you're debating whether you could take me, you could always try. I might not be able to actually kill you, but I can make you hurt like hell. Not to mention I've been itching for a fight. Pretending to be Talahan's lackey again was super annoying. I had to resist the urge to rip his throat out everyday," She let out a long hiss, as she walked toward me and I backed up with every step she took. I couldn't take this anymore. I Flashed to the other side of her, but before I could even strike, Sioena Flashed me to the far end of the room, her hand wrapped around my neck pinning me to the wall. My legs dangled as she held me against the wall in the same way she held Hunter before. I glared and grabbed at the hand around my throat, almost choking.

"Poor little Guardian," She rattled a sick laugh as her purple eyes grew into perfect slits. The scales on her face became more defined. Sioena's forked tongue flicked out. I couldn't talk. I couldn't breathe as she whispered in my ear, the stench of her breath hit me. Blood and venom.

"You wouldn't be in this situation if that wimp Harrison didn't bring down the Boundary for my army to enter. So easily persuaded. He always was my favorite teacher, so easily manipulated," The snakes in her arms started to move down towards me. I grunted in anger at the mention of Harrison. I was the only one who was allowed to talk about him like that.

"*Dawn, give her hell,*" Luke encouraged in my mind, somewhat muted as I tried to stay conscious. I took that as a sign that they had gotten to Lila. Hunter had done his job. I smiled slightly. Sioena gave me a confused look, her nails clamped down into my neck. I winced. She leaned in closer. Ah yes, thank you. I slammed my head into her, for the split second she was dazed and let go of me. I dropped to the floor quickly getting back on my feet. I heard the rattle come from her before I saw her approaching me, mouth wide open, jaw extended, and fangs out ready to strike. I acted on instinct, my fist swung with as much force as I could muster and hit her straight in the jaw. Crack! I heard her jaw snap under my knuckles like ice cracking. She fell to the floor. I stared at her. I knew she would heal soon and I needed to find the others before she gained consciousness. As I looked at her, the snakes on her arms slithered to her detached jaw and bit into it. It snapped back into place. They were healing her. I grew frustrated as I realized she wouldn't be knocked out for much longer. I started running into the direction the other Dankra took Hunter. I could feel eyes on me. Why aren't they attacking? I made it out of the Training Room to what was left of the first floor hallway.

"*Where are you?*" I said to Luke while rounding the corner hoping the entrance to the basement prisons was still there. Luke was shutting me out. Why was he doing that? He picks the best moments to infuriate me. I heard a loud crash, voices, and fighting as I approached the hallway with the basement entrance. A Sway demon blocked my path. I jumped on his back and snapped its neck. As the demon fell, someone grabbed me. I turned around. Luke's blue eyes stared back at me. I sighed in relief, my anger leaving me for just a split second. Luke's lip was busted open and he had scratches all down his arms, but other than that he looked okay. The others stood behind them pretty much in the same shape. My sister was in Hunter's arms. She gave me a weak smile. I pushed past Luke to her and hugged her as she let out a wince. I ran my hand over her face. She was completely soaked from head to toe. I sighed. They've been putting out her flame. Her skin was as cold as ice.

"Dawn, stop crying, I'm okay. This one won't let me walk," Lila said weakly, slapping her hand against Hunter's chest. I wasn't convinced. Hunter gave her a grin. Hailey came up to me.

"We have to keep moving if we want to make it out of here alive," I nodded. She was right. I looked around confused.

"Where's Jada and Frank?" I whirled around to Luke. He opened his mouth to answer me, but a voice echoed throughout the hall interrupting him.

"Bring it on Dankra! I haven't had a good fight in months!" Frank's footsteps approached fast as he rounded the corner with Amidra and Elianna. I jumped in front of Lila and Hunter. Frank tucked and rolled as fire flew past his head. He got up next to me.

"Hey Shadows, you were missing the fun," He said, his eyes dark. He looked different somehow. He was definitely in his element. I suppose so was I.

"I like him! Can we keep him? I can sense he's one of us. One of King's pets. They're my favorites," Elianna squealed and Amidra breathless. Amidra simply stared at me. She moved her red eyes over me from head to toe. I couldn't tell what she was trying to decipher. I looked at Frank and his jaw tightened. Elianna just confirmed what we already knew. They could sense it in his blood like Sioena did with me. They didn't attack. I stepped forward.

"Amidra, let us go. You were my mom's friend once. Think about what she would want. Don't let my father control you," Amidra's facial expression didn't change as the fire beneath her skin began to build. Elianna giggled as molten lava began tearing at the floor beneath us.

"*We gotta go!*" I shouted in Luke's head. Hailey was nowhere to be seen. She had probably gone invisible. I grabbed Hunter preparing to Flash when suddenly the lava stopped. Hailey and Jada appeared directly in front of Amidra. Hailey had a knife to Elianna's throat. Elianna didn't move a muscle to my surprise.

"Been a long time," Jada whispered to a shocked Amidra. Amidra's eyes softened just the tiniest bit. She choked out a gasp. She definitely recognized her.

"You're dead. You're not real," Amidra said, fire igniting from her fists. I looked at Luke. He shrugged. Did Jada think she could bring out Amidra's Guardian side? The side connected to anything but fear. Jackson said that once a Dankra it was nearly impossible to become a Guardian again. Whatever Jada was doing was not a part of the original plan. She was wasting precious time. We have to get out. Jada smiled softly at her and put a hand on Amidra's cheek. Jada flinched as it burnt her skin, but kept it on her face.

"I'm very much alive, my love," Jada said, wincing as she put her hand on Amidra's cheek again. Amidra stumbled back with a growl. Elianna smiled and her hand moved to Hailey's knife, flicking it away with her long sharp nails. Hailey Flashed to my side just as Elianna let loose her needles towards her. Elianna was now fully in her Dankra form, her skin covered in needles. They popped through her black leather clothes making her look like a porcupine. It broke Amidra out of her trance and she shifted into her charcoal. Jada stepped back, she didn't want to fight her. The molten lava started melting the floor again.

"You kids go! I got this!" Jada said to us. I wanted to help her fight them, but she was right. We needed to get Lila out of here and to Jackson's camp. Flames exploded out of Amidra. Jada outstretched her hand and her purple eyes glowed as she slowed down time moving out of the flames path. Elianna attacked us, needles bursting out of her skin. I put a shield up and they bounced off with ease. Jada gave me a swift pleading look and I nodded at her.

"Come on!" I yelled at my friends Flashing to what used to be the entrance. Demons of all shapes and sizes blocked our way. The hooded Dankra stood next to them. It made me wonder if they could order different demons around to do their bidding. I didn't even think as I grabbed onto Hunter and Lila and Flashed them to the Training Room.

"How did you get Lila out?" I asked Luke who was fighting off the demons at the entrance with Frank and Hailey.

"Hunter and Hailey did most of it. Knocked out the Dankra that took him and got the key to Lila's cell. Jada led us in through the back entrance. We fought our way to the prison when the entrance collapsed. Hailey made herself invisible and went through the block. She got Hunter and Lila out. Jordan's outside ripping apart demon after demon ," Luke Flashed into the Training Room with Hunter, Hailey, and Frank at the ready. Lila looked too weak to do anything. I wasn't sure if she had demon poison in her veins. Jada came running in looking drained.

"I've held them off as long as I could. We need to figure a way out of here." Dankra appeared from the shadows. They had us surrounded. This wasn't good. Dankra restrained each of my friends. Hunter's muscles clenched as he fought hard to keep hold of my sister, while a Dankra had its arm wrapped around his throat in a choke hold. Luke growled as two Dankra threw an unconscious Jordan at my feet. I instantly knelt down beside her. She was alive, but her breathing was shallow. My anger was more than I could handle. I stood up facing the two Dankra that had been carrying Jordan. I Flashed behind them, jumped in the air knocking one down with a kick to the head.

"Dawn!" Hailey yelled at me half her body invisible as she threw a knife. I caught it with ease and plunged it into Dankra's heart. Hailey ran to Jordan and made them invisible. I Flashed on top of the demons holding Hunter down, slicing my way through them. Lila was squirming in Hunter's arms.

"I'm fine! Let me help!" She screamed at Hunter and me. I didn't respond. We had come in with a plan that wasn't going to work. Lila pushed out of Hunter's arms stumbling to her feet, as I screamed her name I was slammed to the ground. I gasped as a Dankra had a knee on my stomach and hands on my shoulders. I looked at Lila, whose eyes started to grow orange. She screamed as fire exploded out of her, incinerating the hooded figures all around, including the one on top of me. Lila swayed and fell to her knees as I Flashed over to her. A slow clap sounded from behind us and I turned. Sioena walked toward us fully healed. The snakes that were on her arm had moved to biting into her jaw. They curled around her neck looking as if they were suffocating her.

"Impressive. I don't say that often," She said with a crooked smile crossing her scaly arms. I smiled back.

"How's the jaw?" I asked. Sioena merely scoffed. I think she found me amusing when all I wanted to do was rip her head off. Lila was struggling to stand so I helped her up, her legs shaking with every movement.

"Little miss sparky doesn't look too good," Sioena hissed. Lila swayed and Luke was instantly on the other side of her. Hailey and Jordan must still be invisible. I looked as Hunter and Frank came in line with us.

"Did she forget to mention that courtesy of a little demon poison I engineered, Lila can't use her powers without them poisoning her from the inside out?" Sioena looked at Lila. Lila glared even though she could barely keep her eyes open.

"Sorry sis," She said weakly. Lila had only taken care of about eight Dankra with her explosion. The rest of them stood around us. I was going to rip Sioena into little pieces with my bare hands.

"Kill the Seer. Grab the girl. Do what you want with the others," Sioena waved her hand. Amidra and Elianna finally entered the Training Room. I wondered what Jada had done to them to keep them away for so long. Dankra enclosed around us and the spiders were back. I didn't know if they ever left. I needed to do something now.

I let go of Lila carefully, while Luke helped balance her. I wasn't letting Sioena get away with any of this. I needed to find a way to capture her which would hopefully send a message to Thomas. I charged at her, not bothering to Flash. I wanted her to see I was coming for her. Luke was in my head screaming at me to stop. Sioena stood there, her arms crossed looking calm while Amidra and Elianna were tense, at the ready. I knew deep down I could take them all out. I just had to tap into the power that was suppressed deep inside of me. I was almost on top of her, when suddenly, someone was in front of my path. I slowed down ready to take whoever it was out, but then I recognized the suit this person wore. Sioena's rattled laugh shook what remained of DEATH, as Harrison stood in between us. The Dankra stopped moving as he sent his power out, freezing the Dankra in their place with ice, killing some of the spiders that surrounded them. Everyone was frozen except for Sioena, Elianna, and Amidra. I stood there shell shocked. I thought I heard Jada take a sharp inhale. I didn't bother to look back at her, as Harrison stepped in front of me.

"It's over Sioena," Harrison said, giving me a shove backwards. I fell back into Frank's arms. He held me in place as I squirmed for Harrison. Sioena only shrugged at him, a slow thin smile stretched across her face.

"We'll see," She said, pushing Amidra and Elianna to the side. The scales popped out as she fully took on her Dankra form. The frightened snake tattoos detached from her jaw and slid right back into place on her arms waiting to attack.

"Hailey, get Jada, Jordan, and Lila out of here. Just like you trained," I heard Harrison say. Lila was suddenly invisible. Luke looked around in shock. Jada stepped forward towards Harrison, but then she was gone too. I noticed then that the ice Harrison had in place on the other Dankra was starting to melt. Amidra stood melting the ice with her power. I looked at Frank. He silently nodded letting me go.

"He's trying to make it right, isn't he?" I said to Luke. He didn't answer, as he just sprang into wolf form as each and every Dankra melted like dominoes. Hunter joined him. Frank gave me a wink and Flashed to one side of the room. He slashed easily through the demons. Sway demons plunged from the sky, as Sioena snapped her fingers. Harrison stood at the ready, as Sioena tackled him to the ground. I wanted to help him, but more and more demons were coming at me from all directions. I picked up the knife Hailey had given me and stabbed my way through them. I caught glimpses of Harrison and Sioena. Harrison and her were stuck in a battle of Flashing. Sioena attacked with precise cobra-like strikes while Harrison calculated her every move with beautiful finesse. I forgot how skilled he was. I had just sliced a wing off a Sway demon when I heard Harrison's voice.

"Why are you doing this? You know he's never going to love you!" Harrison shouted. Sioena shrieked and lunged for him with such ferocity, but Harrison was faster. He caught her and slammed her into the floor. She was pinned down. I smiled with black blood dripping down my face. He only had to squeeze and she was done. Harrison hesitated as he looked at Sioena's scared expression just for a second...

The sound of tearing flesh echoed in my ears. Sioena's snake struck Harrison and bit into his throat, tearing it out. The world slowed as he fell to the floor. I Flashed to Harrison's side. Elianna and Amidra had my arms dragging me back. I fought them off. I heard the snap of Amidra's arm as I broke it and Elianna's grunt as I sent her flying with a push of my power. I made it to Harrison and put my hand on his neck. Sioena watched me, licking her bloody fingers as her snake slid back into her arm.

He wasn't healing. He wasn't healing.

I felt something inside me snap, as I cried out. The world around me stopped.

I was sobbing as I looked around at what I'd done. I was radiating power just like Jada did with King. I held Harrison in my arms. I tried to heal him. I didn't have that power like Hailey.

"You can't leave me! You can't leave me!" I screamed at him. He was fading fast, but he was still conscious. He put a hand on my cheek, brushing away a tear. He was crying too, I went to wipe away the tears streaming down his face and was pulled back in time. It wasn't the same as it usually was. I saw images quickly pass by my eyes. Harrison hugging my mom. Harrison and Jada's first kiss. Jackson carrying Lila and me, as Harrison ran to him. Harrison searching for my mom. I saw all of us. Luke. Hailey. Dan. Frank. All of Harrison's students crossed his mind. I was staring at Harrison again and he tried to smile. His mouth was bloody and his hand fell off my face, as he drew his last breath. I flinched as I felt a hand on my shoulder.

"It's okay, honey. I'll take it from here," I let out another sob, as my mom knelt down beside me.

Chapter 20

DawnBreaker

S he was just as I remembered her. The curl to her hair. The imperfect nose and dazzlingly warm smile. I held on to Harrison tighter. This wasn't right.

"You're not here. I'm hallucinating. You're a trick. They're trying to get in my head," I choked out. My mom smiled and put a hand on the one that laid on Harrison's chest.

"No, my brilliant girl. You're not hallucinating. When you stopped time, it allowed me to reach out. We're in a pocket of time that exists, but doesn't. The Divine realm technically. It's all quite confusing, and I don't have the time to explain it all right now," She looked at Harrison and then at me with sadness in her eyes. I looked at her more closely and there was a natural glow around her, a light that made her almost too perfect to look at. She was right. I could already feel the power within me starting to strain.

"I'm going to help Harrison pass on. He did a good job with you, much better than I ever could. You can say goodbye to him as it happens," She said with a soft smile. I let more tears loose. My mom put a hand on Harrison's chest, a white swirling light wrapped around him. A part of him was standing in front of me while his body was still in my arms. The ghostly figure looked at my mom and then me.

"Darcy," he whispered, with relief on his face that quickly faded as he looked at me, "Dawn."

I sobbed again as I looked at him, "I'm sorry. I'm so so sorry." Harrison knelt to my level.

"You have nothing to be sorry for, Dawn. I will forever be proud of you, no matter what happens," Harrison said, brushing away my tears, as his ghostly figure disappeared. I let go of his body. My mom helped me to my feet. That's when I noticed the wings on her back.

"You're a Gelical," I said in shock. My mom nodded and the glow around her became a little brighter.

"There's a few things I need to talk to you about before your power runs out and this time pocket collapses. I became a gelical after my death. I was killed by your father in front of the Dankra. He made an example out of me. I have watched you all these years grow into a person I'm proud of," She said, grabbing me into a hug and I hugged her back. She pulled away and I looked up at her glowing aura.

"There's something I need to give you," She pulled a short sword out of thin air. I smiled at her and reached for it.

"Ah wait, this isn't just another weapon. This is imbued with gelical magic. It can kill any Dankra for good, including your father," My mom paused then smiled as she said, "I like to call it DawnBreaker." She handed the beautifully crafted hilt to me. I blinked at her. I didn't know what to do. I was very confused by all of this, "it's a cheesy name I know." She let out a windchime laugh. I just stared at her still in shock.

"Dawn, I need you to use this on your father, but only when the time is right. You already have seen what you have to do. Only you can do what I couldn't; you can put a stop to all of this. And I'm not just saying that because I'm your mother, although I admit I'm biased," My mom grabbed my hand and put DawnBreaker in it wrapping my fingers around it.

"How do you know it works?" I whispered, my voice almost failing as I tried to keep time from resetting.

She gave me a look that broke my heart, her eyes welled with tears, her beautiful face twisted with anguish. She turned her gaze down for a second composing herself then sighed.

"It was used on me by your father. I was looking for a way to escape him. A way to get back to Lila, Jackson, and you. I found my way to the gelicals. Michael himself made me this weapon, but everything went wrong. He killed me and the gelicals punished him, erasing his existence from history. It weakened his power because he fears insignificance. He's been hiding...until now," My mom said, the bright light growing around her more as she started to fade away.

"Wait, I can't do this. How did you not become like him?" I said, grabbing at her arm, my hand going through it. She looked at me, her golden eyes softened. The world around us started to move again. My power was waning. I thought for sure I saw a flash of a tall man, clad in battle armor, with gold wings reaching for my mother. The warrior gelical Michael.

"Dankra aren't fully evil. You have to choose to be that way. Remember that, Dawn. I love you," She squeezed my hand. The gelical put his hand on her shoulder and she vanished.

The world around me snapped back into place. I collapsed to my knees, as my power slipped away. Luke Flashed over to me. Hunter and Frank were still fighting.

"*I felt it. I felt you stop time,*" Luke said, trying to help me to my feet. I pushed him off and turned towards an amused Sioena. Harrison's body still laid between us. I was able to push down the tears that threatened to spill again.

"Which one of your friends is next?" She hissed. Luke growled by my side. She had no idea what I had just done. I looked down at my hand. I still held DawnBreaker. As I looked around, I knew we weren't going to win even if I did have DawnBreaker. Hunter and Frank were still fighting off Dankra as Luke supported most of my weight. I pushed him off and stepped forward.

Sioena noticed the sword and hissed taking a step back. Frank Flashed to my left side, ready for what had to be done. Hunter in his wolf form stood next to Luke. I knew they would fight with me, but this was only the beginning. We weren't going to win today. The Dankra had to be destroyed from the inside. I knew what my mother was talking about now. My vision had to come true. Sioena lunged for me and I instantly put a shield around us. She slammed into it and fell backwards onto the ground. The Dankra melted into the shadows as Sioena stood up, her eyes full of rage. Amidra and Elianna joined her looking unamused. There was only one way. Sioena was pacing waiting for my shield to come down.

I grabbed Luke's elbow. He turned to me slowly not wanting to take his eyes off the enemies that surrounded us.

"*I need you to make me a promise,*" I said in his mind. Frank looked at us confused, but then stepped in front of us blocking us from view. Hunter did the same behind us.

Luke paused, then said, "*Anything.*"

"Do not intervene. Do not come find me," I said in his mind and managed not to cry as I showed him the conversation I had with my mother. A tear streamed down his face.

"I can't promise that," He said angrily, his eyes flashing yellow. I sighed.

"I know. You are my stubborn, protective best friend, but I have to try. Thank you for showing me how to love," I pressed up onto my toes and pressed a very light kiss against his lips. He stood there shocked, as I turned to Frank putting a hand on his shoulder and whispered.

"Follow my lead and don't say anything. I'm really sorry," He looked at me with confusion in his eyes. Then realization crossed his face. I started to walk with my head held high. Frank followed, taking up a defensive position. Luke stood there paralyzed. Hunter went to go too, but I waved him off and let my shield fall.

After I do what I was about to do, I know there will be a fight, but as soon as they get what they want they'll disappear as if the Dankra were never here. I'll disappear. I kept my gaze forward as I walked towards a cluster of Dankra who thought I couldn't see them, I ignored Sioena's gaze. I gave them a smile and waved the sword my mom gave me. I understand now what I had to do. Dankra jumped back and hissed like Sioena did before.

"Scared of this are you?" I asked with an evil laugh. They kept backing away.

"You know what this is? Hmmm..." I walked in a circle. Frank shadowed me like a bodyguard.

"This is the one thing that will kill you all. Once a Dankra is stabbed their Dankra sides are killed, but the human Guardian or whatever other half you are survives, but forever suffers. So you die a slow and painful death," I walked back to the center of the room. It killed my mom because she never truly embraced becoming a Dankra.

"So here's my proposal. I know I can't take all of you on with one single solitary sword, but I am half Dankra too. I bet it would kill me too, right? Well I'm guessing you don't want that," I pointed the sword at Sioena. She glared at me, but didn't move or say anything.

"How about I stab myself with this or maybe my friend here will?" I gestured to Frank. He looked at me eyes wide and shook his head slightly. I didn't know why my voice wasn't shaking. I felt completely calm and very serious. Hunter whimpered and I felt his protest. I looked at him very quickly, sending him calming thoughts.

"Dawn don't-," Luke started to say, but I shushed him. He was trying to break through the block I had in my head. I shut him out harder and he audibly winced.

I continued, "Or I can go with you with a little bit of cooperation and you all leave my friends alone. So what's it gonna be?"

No answer from any of the Dankra. Sioena didn't move and her face stood solid and emotionless. Amidra and Elianna shifted uncomfortably looking at Sioena. They didn't know what to do and were waiting for orders.

"Okay then," I said, handing Frank the sword, "Go ahead."

"I'm not going to-," Frank said appalled.

"Go," I gave him a look. I knew he was the only one capable of handling this and what comes next. He most likely was Dankra already, Elianna confirmed it.

"No, what happened to we're in this crap together?" Frank tried to joke, getting teary eyed.

"Sometimes rules can be broken, just follow my lead, remember?" I said and grabbed his hand. He looked down at our conjoined hands. I seemed to have convinced him. He started to bring the sword up to my chest and I closed my eyes. If I was wrong, this could end very badly. Frank grabbed my shoulder, his hand trembling.

Then the Dankra were in motion.

Elianna snatched him up and started to run with him. The Dawnbreaker dropped to the floor, there was no way I was allowing them to get a hold of that. I reached my handout, but I was too far away. C'mon come to me I thought and all of a sudden it was in my hand. I Flashed it over to Luke. He looked at me and knew he had to grab it. I heard in his mind he thought this was the end. He shook his head and came to join me. I let my block fall, as I looked into his hopeless eyes. A Dankra stepped in front of my view of him as they began to retreat.

"You need it more than me now. You might need it to protect the Guardians from me. When I find my way back, I'll need that to finish what my mother started. If I don't-," I couldn't finish as I saw Luke crying. Then of course like I was expecting they took me too. I was right. Luke and Hunter started to fight through Dankra. I fought my attackers too. I wasn't going down without a fight. That didn't help me whatsoever so I just stopped and went numb. Then I saw Hunter kicking and punching, changing in and out of wolf form. He was pushing his way through. I had seen this happen in the Seers Domain with Jada.

"No! You idiot go back!" I screamed at him. I had already sacrificed Frank. I wasn't doing that to Hunter. He was running and screaming my name. He caught up to me and leaped, catching my arm. Hunter's fear overwhelmed my mind. The Dankra dragging me away kept going, not paying attention to Hunter clinging onto my arm.

"Let go of me!" I screamed. I knew what I had to do. I grabbed the knife Hailey had thrown me earlier from my jacket, which was now soaked in demon blood. It would slow down his ability to transform for a while.

"I'm sorry ," I cut his wrist and he winced in pain, finally letting go of me. The betrayal he felt coursed through my body. I let myself cry as he was thrown back rolling away.

"Dawn!" He screamed.

"Take care of them!" I screamed back with tears rolling down my face the farther and farther I was dragged away. Then we suddenly came to an abrupt stop and the Dankra threw me to the ground. I was kicked in the stomach causing me to grunt and roll over.

"On your feet Shadows," Sioena's voice beckoned me. At the sound of her voice, anger flashed before my eyes, white and hot. I jumped to my feet and immediately went for her throat, but I was held back.

"Haha that's right you silly girl let the animal out. Let's get this show on the road shall we? First, we take away the pesky Bound," Sioena's acidic voice hissed. How did she know about that?

"What?" I asked, fighting against the arms that held me, playing dumb.

"Don't you dare play games with me, Shadows. I sensed the Bound as soon as you two showed Talahan your symbols. I admit, it was a clever way to suppress your demon side," Sioena's purple eyes turned to slits again. I spit blood on her face and she simply smiled.

"Hold her still. I don't want any accidents," She ordered the ones around her grabbing my right arm. That's not my arm with my Guardian symbol on it. Spiders materialized around us as she pulled my arm to her. I felt the spiders creep up my other arm, surprisingly strong and pinning them down, along with the Dankra hands on me. She brought it to her mouth and her fangs came out. Then she clenched them down into the crease of my elbow. I controlled myself not to scream as venom seeped into my body. I wasn't giving her that satisfaction. After it was over, something appeared on my arm. It looked like two swirly lines intersecting to make a heart. There it was, the symbol Luke was talking about. The solution Jackson and my mom had gone to great lengths to keep hidden and protect me from the Dankra, now out in the open. I felt woozy. The venom from Sieona was already spreading across my body. I tried to yank my arm away, but it was no use.

"This might hurt just a little," Sioena said with her smile, then without hesitation stuck her claws where the sign intersected and ripped the skin of my arm open. I don't know why, but I didn't expect it to hurt like it did. Jackson had said that breaking the Bound would be painful. I wasn't expecting it to utterly destroy me. I screamed and screamed until the symbol bled away. Sioena was breaking the Bound. Luke had to stay alive at all costs. I tried reaching out to Luke, but he wasn't there. The connection I had my entire life just went dark in an instant. He had to be alive. This wasn't part of my plan. I tried to force myself to stay awake as I felt a part of me slip away.

Hunter

"Dawn!" I screamed trying to change into wolf form. The demon poison stopped me. I winced trying to get to my feet.

"Take care of them!" She screamed back at me. I watched helplessly until she was out of sight.

I let go. I let go of her. She made me do it. Is it really my fault? Yes, yes it is. This is my fault that she's gone. Why does that make me sad? Luke is going to kill me.

I sat there in the dirt my head hung not knowing what to do. I felt like it was my responsibility to go get her. Mine alone. I could no longer see the shape of her being dragged away. When the poison finally wore off, I ripped into my wolf form, painfully, running after her. I ran until I could no longer stand on my paws, until exhaustion consumed me. I would get her back no matter the cost. I reached for our connection, the only thing I could hold onto now. I changed back into human form clutching my chest as I felt her indescribable pain.

***

Luke

I felt unimaginable pain, dropping DawnBreaker. My right arm felt like it was on fire. A scream escaped my throat. Something was gone. It was ripped out of me, the connection was gone. She was gone. I looked at her and I didn't believe this is how it would end. End like her vision said it would. I didn't even kiss her back. The only thing clear to me right now is I had to get her back. I had to find her. I looked down at my arm and saw a swirly heart symbol bleeding away. I grabbed it, needing to stay alive. My knees hit the ground and the world went black.

Jada

The vision I worked so hard to prevent was coming to fruition. No, it happened. I felt it in my bones. I screamed at Hailey as she rushed me out of DEATH. She didn't seem to care because she couldn't see what I saw. I held Jordan in my arms as we ran back to Jackson's camp. Hailey had an almost unconscious Lila slung around her shoulders. Hailey had used some of her healing power on both of them, but it wasn't enough. They both were not strong enough to Flash and I lost that ability as soon as I became a Seer. I felt numb. I felt like it was all happening again and there was still no way I could stop it. When we made it back to camp, Jackson immediately scooped up both of his daughters and brought them to see his healer's, probably Mama G. I felt my power surge through me uncontrollably and I saw everything that was happening. That will happen. I felt all of their pain. The worst feeling was seeing Dawn and Luke's face as their Bound was ripped to shreds. Hailey was at my side saying something. No, she was screaming for my attention. I tried to talk and tell her what I was seeing, but my power silenced me. Jackson came back and was shouting at me. I couldn't move. I couldn't talk. *Jada Moon*, I thought to myself, *The Slave of Time*. My only hope was that they were able to get to Luke in time.

Frank

The moment I looked into her eyes. I knew what she was doing. We were to destroy our enemies from the inside. I realized I was ready to walk into hell with her and do whatever it takes. I would help her do it even if I became the thing I was most afraid of. The needle Dankra, Elianna, dragged me away and I didn't even fight her. At some point, I lost consciousness. I felt a part of me crack open. The part that King had created. King would get what was coming to him. I forced that sinister part of me down, as my eyes fluttered open. It was pitch black, but I knew Dawn was with me and that's all that mattered. I gripped her hand that was coated in blood. There was a pulse. I waited for her to open her eyes and waited for the hell we would no doubt experience together.

***

Dawn

My eyes opened lazily. It was pitch black. I could feel I was surrounded by the hooded figures. Dankra. I was slowly falling deep into the void of nothingness trying to cling to what was left of me, reaching for the connection that gave me comfort for as long as I could remember. I was reaching for him. He was gone. Where was he? Where am I? It seemed to slide down. It buried itself. That dark part of me that was blocked and buried was swallowing me whole. I tried to push it down, but it was too much. It was...me.

Acknowledgements

This has been such an amazing experience. So many people made this possible. This has been a long journey, and I have so many people who I feel indebted to. This includes everyone listed below and so many more.

I want to thank Jessica Cragen and the team at Twisted Words Publishing for making my dreams a reality, for turning a no into a yes.

My family for standing by my side, always telling me to reach for the stars.

To my mom and dad, Beth and Jim, for everything you sacrificed to get me where I am today.

To my sister, Elise, who never ceases to amaze me with her creativity and compassion.

To my brother James, who was not even born when this was first written, but now cares for these characters as much as I do.

To my forever partner, Sean, who read more renditions of this book than I can remember. He kept me going through it all.

To my best friend, Grace, who not only believed in this story but in me.

To my future sister-in-law, Bella, for being there when I needed advice.

To my middle school teacher, Mrs. Grandits, for encouraging my writing and letting me explore that in the classroom.

For my friends, who let me make a book report IMovie with them in sixth grade you'll always be a part of this.

Lastly to you, the reader, thank you from the bottom of my heart.

I can't wait to continue this journey with you.

About the author

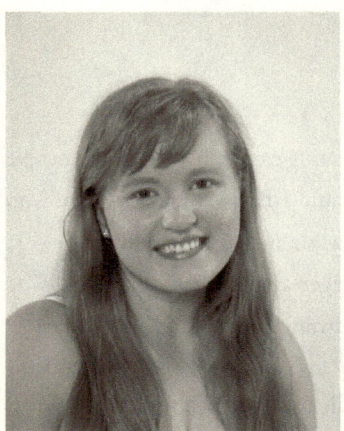

Amelia Waddell

Amelia Waddell is many things in this lovely life. A Buffalo, NY native, a dancer, a reader, a writer, a performer, and a healthcare provider. She has a BFA in dance and Master's of Science in Athletic Training. Amelia aspires to combine both her love of science and art into fantastical creations.

Also by Amelia Waddell

The Guardians:

1. DEATH

Sneak Peak of Book #2

Prologue

Dawn

10, 9, 8, 7, 6, 5, 4, 3, 2, 1.

I counted down the seconds till my imminent death. A lot can happen in ten seconds as I've come to learn. If you think about it, time controls everything and nothing. It is woven into our beings. How much time do you have till Time no longer matters anymore? It didn't matter what I could predict. The future...would not be something I would see. And neither would he.

***

Oh, dear human how I wish I had your life. Would I have said that months ago? Of course not. I was an ungrateful Guardian who should've kept out of things she didn't understand. I shouldn't have gone looking for answers. The Dankra would have never found me. DEATH would still be standing and my friends...wow, it's been a long time since I thought about them. I guess it's the place I'm in now.

This was a dangerous move on my father's part and a calculated one, he must know it could easily backfire in his face. I think that's what he's counting on. I'd sooner die than give him any satisfaction.

The cool rain drops should have provided me some relief, but as they fell on my hot skin I wanted nothing more than to make it stop. I could make it stop if I wanted to, but I was ready to get this over with. The fact I was standing here of all places when I never thought I'd be back here again made me want to throw up whatever was in my stomach. The Cassie Camp didn't look any different from when I last saw it. The shields I tore through without even a thought worried me. It's like Jackson wants to get attacked. The sight of the green grass made my breath catch. The unlit campfire where so much joy occurs made my eyes burn. The bar where Mama G glared at me not that long ago almost made me want to chuckle. When's the last time I laughed? They've changed me so much or maybe I changed myself? I didn't want to look at it knowing what I was about to do, but I couldn't stop myself. I needed to feel something. I couldn't let that dark unyielding part of me take over ...not yet.

I was sent to do a job to complete my Initiation, well just before the final step. The camp was asleep. There were guards posted, but I easily knocked them out. I needed to keep moving but my feet felt like they had been buried with bricks tied to them. I almost Flashed out of here and straight back to endure whatever punishment Sioena wanted to give me. She'd already done her worst, but I'm sure she had more in her. A shiver ran down my spine. Yup. I was gonna throw up. I had to get out of here.

"Dawn, we have to keep moving," Frank Summers materialized next to me.

I'm sure he sensed my hesitation. Urgh, I had gotten him into this. It was my fault he was here. He was Frank, but he wasn't. He wore the same leather jacket, his dark hair had grown a little longer. The thing that worried me the most about him was how dark his chocolate eyes had become and the gaunt look of his cheekbones. He looked...menacing. Although, he still had a toothpick in his mouth. Any Dankra would lose more than just a finger if they tried to take that away from him. I'd seen it.

I just nodded at him. We haven't been on speaking terms since a minor argument. He went to touch my shoulder, but then seemed to think better of it and moved ahead of me. I wanted to reach out to him, but in truth I was frustrated with him too.

"You were supposed to stay outside the Shield," I said, crossing my arms and leaning into my hip, but my voice sounded weak.

This situation messed with my usual fake confidence. Frank simply ignored me and kept walking in the direction of the prison cells. I could have enforced rank, but that would've made things worse. I took a deep breath and trudged after him. My feet still felt weighted down. I kept myself from looking at my surroundings other than what I needed to see. If I looked, it would be harder to leave this place. We made it to the cabin house on the east side of camp where Jordan had led me to when I was staying here. The prison cell where King, my Dankra evil half brother, has been locked up for six months.

"I'll see you when you come to aid in my escape little warrior!" King's last words to me before I was captured had echoed in my mind since that day.

He knew this was going to happen. I gritted my teeth as I followed Frank in. There were of course two guards standing watch, but before they could even move. Frank had them knocked out without his tooth pick even moving an inch. I scoffed and kept going to the stairs. He wouldn't follow. Frank wouldn't be able to resist peeling King's skin off.

I walked down, careful to not touch anything.

As I descended, the stirring power in my chest urged me to be released. I pushed it down inside of me.

It will not control me.

There were four cells like last time and the first one was occupied by none other than King Shadows himself laying on the floor. Sleeping. Damn. If he were dead, I wouldn't have to do this at all. He looked the same. They had been feeding him and if there was any sort of torturing, they were healing him after. Not that he deserved that. Jackson was too moral to do any real damage to him. The power dampening cuffs were still on him which I plan on leaving on till he's out of here. This is ridiculous, but I have to do this. I take a deep breath and put both hands on the iron bars with as much strength as I can muster. I pull them apart giving enough room for me to sneak in. I'm still shocked at how much strength I gained. The Dankra Initiation process is utterly terrifying, but it's giving me unimaginable power.

I lean over King and blow a slow breath into his ear. He groans, turning his head away from me.

"Rise and shine, looks like someone is valuable after all," I say, giving him a quick jab in the ribs. As if recognizing my voice, he abruptly sat up. King's black eyes narrow onto mine. As far as I know, I've made my eyes retain their goldish color for the most part. They were more bronze now. King let out a throaty laugh and plopped back down on the ground turning onto his back.

"Hey lil sis, I missed you," King smiled, his terrible scheming smile. Wrong move. I grabbed him by his shirt with one hand and lifted him to his feet. The smile grew.

"Brother or not I would watch what you do around me," I seethed. My power beckoned me to be unleashed again. My control was starting to slip all because he annoyed me.

"You've gotten stronger. The Transition is almost complete I see, which means you've reached the last step of the Initiation. What other new tricks did you get?" King asked, genuinely curious. I ignored him and let go of his shirt, he stumbled back a little bit, but didn't fall. I took a deep breath steadying myself.

"Let's go," I commanded.

King tilted his head and squeezed through the separated bars. King looked extremely weak, his muscles had deteriorated. I wasn't carrying him up the stairs. I was only asked to bring him back alive. They said nothing about bringing him back unharmed. I placed a hand on him and Flashed him up the stairs. Frank was waiting with his feet propped against the table that sat in the middle of the room. The two wolf guards were still unconscious piled on top of each other. Frank didn't even look at King, his eyes were only on me as King chuckled at the sight of his former right hand.

"Oh little sister, how well you've done that little Frankie is now one of-," King started to choke. Frank was now inches in front of King's face, dark swirls wreathed Frank's hands and a matching set were around King's throat. I wanted to let Frank punish the man who had forced him to become someone he wasn't, but I couldn't.

"Enough," I said pretending to be bored.

Frank stepped back and found my eyes again nothing but rage shined in them. I wanted to comfort him but instead I said, "We're done here."

I shoved a still cuffed King out of the building. We couldn't Flash out of the camp because it would sound off alarms. Jackson's security was unimpressive, but that much was smart. Frank followed close behind. When he stilled I felt it, my senses became clearer as we were being watched. Well, if they knew we were here, I guess there was no point in not Flashing.

I was attacked from the side. King was sent flying. Sea green eyes bore into mine. Frank was already making his way towards King. A calming feeling was trying to break into my mind. The wolf pinning me to the ground was none other than my former protecti, Hunter Loves.

He didn't know I could no longer feel. I pushed him off with a hard shove. A soft whine escaped him. I whipped my head around and my breath caught as I saw him.

"Dawn," The most familiar voice called to me with restrained sadness. The hole in my soul felt heavier as my body habitually tried to find our connection.

Luke. Luke. Luke.

My power erupted and everything froze.

www.ingramcontent.com/pod-product-compliance
Lightning Source LLC
Chambersburg PA
CBHW030647110726
47901CB00002B/608